A

Butler

Christmas

A Butler Christmas

Rahiem Brooks

PRODIGY GOLD BOOKS

PHILADELPHIA * LOS ANGELES

A BUTLER CHRISTMAS

A Prodigy Gold Book

Prodigy Gold E-book edition/December 2017

Prodigy Gold Paperback edition/December 2017

Copyright (c) 2018 by Rahiem Brooks

Library of Congress Catalog Card Number: 2017944617

Website: http://www.prodigygoldbooks.com

Author's e-mail: rahiembthewriter@gmail.com

ISBN 978-1-939665-22-5

Published simultaneously in the US and Canada

PRINTED IN THE UNITED STATES OF AMERICA

For

Lkia Nicole Brooks

(1979 - 1999)

ACKNOWLEDGEMENTS

If I were an island this page would be irrelevant, but as you (my esteemed readers) see, it's here, so let the praise commence.

My wonderful family, you came through for me in my darkest moment and blessed me with the mental wherewithal to get back to the light.

My editor, Locksie Locks, I call you "Mum" for your English heritage, but your support on a professional and personal level is infinitely nurturing. My literary siblings (Envy Red, Kristofer Clarke, Leonard Anderson, English Ruler), you all dragged me into your lives and never let me go professionally or personally; you loved me in ways only family can and taught me the definition of friendship, proving I am not the wordsmith that I like to think I am considering I've been defining friend wrong my whole life. Tanisha Grant, you never let me down.

It's odd to thank a barber, but I must thank Vergil Austin, as he has supported every novel that I've written; and, every time that I sit in his chair I always get up a tad wiser. Thanks for the words of wisdom.

Devone "Reds" Johnson, thanks for the inside job, bro. One day we'll laugh about allowing me to use your...well, it wouldn't be an inside job if I exposed it here. Frankie "ChukTizzy" Taylor you read these words when they were chicken scratch in a notebook and want to play, Naim Butler, in the movie adaptation. Thanks for dragging me to the gym to work out to clear my head. I'm down thirty pounds and feeling good because of your help, persistence, and dedication to my physique goals. Jermaine Coleman, Perry Williams, Kaseem Clark, Lamont Fleming, Tye Davis, Juma Sampson, Aree Toulson, and Basheer Mumin thanks for helping to shape my main character into the man that he is.

Kisha Green, what a way to pick me up by answering all of my questions along the way to completing this project; thank you, again.

As I wrote this novel, I taught a literary workshop to some men in prison, The Fort Dix Six: Sage, Craig P, Six Pack, Rob, Woo, and H. Helping you, helped me, as every class that I prepared for you, I learned a lesson of my own while researching. You will all be grand authors one day soon.

Lastly, I must thank my initial critique squad and reviewers. I needed your fierce feedback. I laughed, I kicked, I screamed, I grew, and now the readers are blessed.

A

Butler

Christmas

$\mathscr{PROLOGUE}$

Five Months Earlier

With just under two years left in his second term as president of the United States, Jackson Radcliffe was entertaining a request to chat from the senior New York Senator, James MacDonald. Both men sipped neat Johnnie Blue doubles from glasses specially commissioned for the president from Swarovski, engraved with the American flag.

"So, Mr. President, how's your Latin?" MacDonald asked and shook Evian ice cubes which rattled against the crystal glass. *Clank-Clankity-Clank.*

"Awful," Radcliffe said, taking a seat on the sofa across from MacDonald in the Oval Office.

"Certainly, you know *quid pro quo*, though?"

"Funny," the president said through a weak smile. "I do know that one."

Good, thought the senator, *then I don't need to remind you of my efforts that helped get your legacy-making Affordable Care Act passed in a bi-partisan senate.* "You're the first president to visit a federal prison and talk to inmates. Just last week you gave a glowing and flowery speech on Crime Justice at the NAACP Convention in Philadelphia. A speech that later had Bill admit that while he was in office he signed into law a legislation that caused an overwhelmingly obvious racial disparity with respect to prison terms and continues to cripple the Black community."

"Is there a compliment in there somewhere, Senator?" the president asked as he leaned back on the sofa, and crossed his legs. "I doubt you've come this far for that."

"Funny," Senator MacDonald said through the same weak smile that the president had just offered him. "I'll get to the point."

"Great." The president looke2d at his watch.

"I'm announcing my run to replace you, and I'll need your help to win the nomination."

"I see," Radcliffe said flatly. *Clank-Clankity-Clank.*

"Republicans will focus on immigration; thank God for Donna Lincoln. On our side, Chang and Johnson will have to focus on explaining their history and records during the primaries. And, then, there's me, the liberal-conservative Democrat concentrating on day one in office criminal justice reform which work in tandem with reducing the prison population and the money saved will be diverted to improve education and keep your beloved Radcliffe-Care around. I have vetted," he paused and handed the commander a file, "a New Yorker that I'd like you to expunge and seal his criminal record using your pardon authority."

"And why would I do that?"

"So that he can take the bar exam and become a criminal defense lawyer, and potentially a politician if he desires such a place in our government."

"Why would I be involved in that? That's not my job, and doesn't seem to be high up on the list of *quid pro quo* I'd expect from you."

Caution. The president had a reputation of being prone to it. He wasn't a risk taker. No gray area with the Blue Dog Democrat from Illinois. It was black and white; a bona fide reflection of his bi-racial heritage.

"Precisely why you're going to do it. It's low on the pole. The action, though, carefully reported in the major newspapers and news networks will carry favor with Black and other minority voters. They'll see me as a champion of the underdog and second chances."

"Interesting. Why this Naim Butler guy?"

"He'll go on and fight injustice. He wants to do it now, but he can't because he can't argue in court because he's not a lawyer. His mentor and confidante, Max Devers, will see to it that Butler works with me to get the job done. He'll be my Martin Luther King to Lyndon Johnson. We will get the job done."

"What job?" The president wasn't convinced.

"As you know with Hilary being a former New York senator, she's undoubtedly banking on winning the state in the primary. I need to make a strong statement to thwart that and in a blue state like New York, I'll have to make an appeal to minorities through action. Not lip service. That's a tough job."

"I could be wrong, but this could back fire, as your work could actually work. Pun intended. What am I missing?"

MacDonald, the senior member of the Senate Judiciary Committee was an expert at staying off the radar. His sudden desire to be thrust into the spotlight of a presidential campaign forced Radcliffe to proceed with uncertainty. MacDonald was a country club, white boy, with a Cuban housekeeper, and his sudden interest in minority affairs would be loved if he netted real results. Radcliffe knew MacDonald figured that he was in charge of this conversation, but he knew otherwise. If the senator went down this path, Radcliffe would see to it that he played along for the long haul. Radcliffe was Monte Hall and MacDonald could not ignore doors number two and three, once he opened door number one. Of course, this because MacDonald was fully aware of the impact of *quid pro quo*. It never ended.

"To be frank." *Clank-Clankity-Clank.* "You're not missing anything. I just want help getting into the White House."

"News flash. Look around," Radcliffe said sarcastically, "you're in the White House."

"Cute, for the president," MacDonald said and dug into his briefcase for another folder. He slid it across the table. "Therein lies legislation to reduce the eighty-five percent that federal prisoners must serve of their sentences to sixty-five percent. We need to make this effective immediately. It's been talked about for fifteen or more years, and it's time to enact it. I have the two-thirds majority to do it. We're prepared to vote on it Monday. After your speech at the NAACP and prison trip, this will send a very loud message to everyone that you meant every word spoken at these events."

"Why not..." The president stood and walked over to the window. "...fifty-percent like California state prisoners." He looked out beyond the White House lawn at visitors behind the gate taking selfies using the Executive Mansion as a backdrop.

"Tougher to sell." The senator chuckled. "So, can we get these two done before I announce so that I can add them to my record and platform?"

"The reduction in percentage of time off you can have a bill on my desk Monday afternoon and I'd sign it. I need time with this Butler expungement."

"One out of two. Fifty percent. I'll take that, but I assure you that Butler's the guy for this. He's an open book, and one thoroughly scrutinized." The senator winked.

"Perfect."

MacDonald stood, shook the president's hand, and thanked God for Latin.

CHAPTER 1

The Present

It was the New York Giants' flag atop the beat-up pick-up truck that immediately caught Naim's attention as he jogged in place at a light. He had been running for two miles and headed for the last few blocks of his three-mile jog along Central Park when he saw a truck speeding up in a failing attempt to catch the light. At the speed the truck was going it was in danger of flipping over if the driver suddenly stopped, or worse hitting a car coming down Fifth Avenue.

Naim glanced at the other pedestrians at the light and it seemed that they were aware of the aggressive New York driver. Everyone except the woman whose back faced the street as she peered into the park; allured by the Christmas holiday decor set up by the Metropolitan Museum of Art. She was captivated and had no idea that the pick-up was destined to take her out despite the engine roaring at full throttle.

Tires screeched as the idiot behind the wheel of the truck swerved around a taxi, and jumped over the curb right where Naim and the woman had been waiting for the light to change. He gripped up the woman's upper arm and pulled her away just as the front bumper missed her. The truck penetrated the park and slammed into a tree.

When Naim's eyes zeroed in on the accident, he saw a maniacal looking man with a long beard and disheveled hair matted to his pale scalp. The man had a closed right eye that forced him to look sinister when the door violently swung open.

Naim's adrenaline pumped and he choreographed moves in his head to respond to any sort of physical gesture from the man. Calm fury enveloped him as he prepared for the worse scenario. The man kicked the door and stepped out. He was burly with arms bulging through an oil stained sweatshirt, forcing Naim's heart rate to quicken and his own muscles tightened, ready to fight.

Just as the man walked towards Naim, flashing lights and the cry of a siren from an unmarked cop car, which was technically a New York taxi stopped at Fifth Avenue and Seventy-Ninth Street. After the Nine-Eleven terrorist attack, policemen posed as many ordinary professionals to blend in with the public to quickly solve crimes or stop potential ones. The man stopped in his tracks, and thought about fighting or running when an undercover NYPD officer came out of the shadows. "Freeze."

Naim's world refocused. The tension rushed out of his muscles, and he became calm. He loosened his grip on the woman's arm but didn't let her go. Turning his attention from the man being arrested he found the woman staring at him. Her eyes were a luscious shade of brown. She appeared un-bothered by the driver, glancing down at his large hands that saved her, and tried to figure out why his hand remained on her.

She looked up at him further commanding his attention.

"My apologies," he said, letting go of her arm. "I imagined you about to be run over by Santa." He smiled lightheartedly, looking at the driver whose beard was long, white, and a lengthy mess.

She replied with silence.

His chivalrous attempt to make her smile failed. Her demeanor indicated that she had no desire to joke. Perhaps, he had grabbed her harshly. He did have a firm grip on her and knew his strength, but saving her was significant.

Naim cleared his throat and then smiled in an attempt to shift the mood. A mood that was interrupted by a police officer.

"Are you two all right?" the cop asked approaching them, his voice being carried through heavy breathing. "You weren't clipped by that imbecile were you?"

"No," Naim said. "I'm fine."

"And thanks to him, I am as well," the woman said. Both men analyzed her curves from top to bottom, all covered in high fashion and a mink jacket. Her luxuriant, reddish-brown hair-obviously dyed-rested on the collar of the jacket.

"OK, may I collect your names and contact information. Apparently, the man's been drinking and has not had a valid license in over four years. He'll be sobering up at the Tombs this morning."

"Sure, I'm Naim Butler..." Naim said and rattled off his telephone number and home address.

"And, I'm Brandy Scott." She dug into an expensive purse and took out her business card holder. It was gold with her name engraved on it.

Naim noticed the New York Times logo on the business card and wondered what her role was at the newspaper empire.

"I'm sure detectives and an insurance adjuster will be in touch. If you two are OK, you're free to continue your morning."

"Thanks, officer," Naim said. "What a Monday morning."

Brandy nodded.

"Brandy Scott, can I buy you a hot chocolate to make up for this episode? It could warm you up."

"Perhaps, or it couldn't."

Feisty. Unreadable. He couldn't guess her position and was unsure of how to reply.

Was she attempting to be lighthearted as he had? She was looking at him. Scrutinizing him. Sizing him up. He had the kind of perfect white commercial-quality teeth, deep waves in his hair, and double chocolate complexion that usually got him to first base. His charm, wit, and funny-bone carried him around the bases to home plate. Brandy's standoffishness didn't want him up to bat. His heart rate was pounding all over again. His fear of rejection surfaced.

"I assure you that I know a woman as attractive as you deal with men constantly trying clever lines to get you. I was, and still am, being a gentleman by treating you to cocoa considering our awkward meeting."

Finally, she smiled. Not a big grin or any sign of gallantry, but a simple curve of her lips to acknowledge the approval of his line.

He smiled back.

"Really." She looked at him and tucked hair behind her ear.

"Yes, I live nearby and was out for a jog with plans on stopping at Starbucks anyway."

"Is that right?" She looked dubious.

"I'm not kidding," he said and chuckled. "There are a few black folks that live on the Upper East Side, and I happen to be one. I jog twice a week, swim three, and weight train the other two. On any given day, I could have saved you." He smiled and lit up the corner.

"Nervy, confident and disciplined. That's original," she said and winked. "Thanks, by the way, for that."

"No problemmo," he said, and then asked, "so..."

She pulled out her cell phone. "I'm late for a meeting, but I'd like to have cocoa with you another day."

"Oh, so now, you're asking me out on a date? I guess you want my number?"

"Your sense of humor is attractive. Actually smart. For technical purposes, you asked me out, I declined, and now I am offering you a rain check."

He admired her manicured hand that held a cell phone taking notice that her ring finger was one solid bronzed complexion. He gave her his number and then offered to hail her a taxi for the remainder of her journey, which she accepted. When she left, he watched the taxi for three blocks, and thoughts of his next encounter with her were heavy on his mind.

CHAPTER 2

Naim Butler and Derrick Adams were at a Brazilian steak house for lunch and drinks. They stared at the menu before they were joined by Hector.

"How nice of you to join us. Perhaps, since you own this joint, you can suggest something to eat," Naim said, and then waved his hand in the air, "in this fine establishment."

"You're such a wise ass." Hector laughed. "Let's try this again. Welcome to Hector's Brazilian Bistro; this grand ol' steak joint."

"Slow down, playboy," Derrick said, "we knew you before winning Top Chef. That's the only reason this place is hot, and don't forget that."

"Spoken like a true federal prosecutor," Hector said. "You find the bad in everything."

The three men chuckled. It had been a while since the three of them had the opportunity to laugh and joke like they had in college.

"Listen, *Bon Appetite Magazine* is here, so I have to get into the kitchen and actually cook today. I'm going to send over our recently added lump crab. It's the Tuesday special and pure perfection."

"Now, you're talking," Naim said, "don't burn down the kitchen, you have company."

A fancy kitchen that was encased in glass in the middle of the restaurant and slowly spun three-hundred-sixty degrees, affording every customer a gaze at their food being prepared. There was an elevator in the middle of the kitchen that led to the basement where food was stored and dishes washed; certainly, those acts were done off screen. The ambiance drew in hordes of wealthy clients and was the anchor restaurant of the grand St. Helena Hotel on Manhattan's Upper East Side at Eighty-fourth and Madison Avenues.

"We should order a bottle of Veuve Cliquot, too," Naim said.

"Yeah, we can do that," Derrick replied.

They sat quietly for a moment, Naim sipping on straight vodka, Derrick sipping his jack and coke.

"When does Stefon get home for the holidays?" Naim asked. Stefon was Derrick's teenaged son that attended a private prep school in Alexandria, Virginia.

"He arrives on an Amtrak train at eleven a.m. tomorrow," Derrick replied. "I can't wait for my boy to get home. After Chanel's death, the house feels eerily empty without either of them there all of the time."

"I can dig it. Nothing like the noise of family. How about dinner with him tomorrow night?"

Derrick furrowed his eyebrows. "I suppose we can if he doesn't have plans. You know he thinks that he's grown. What's this all about?"

"It's about Sinia concluding that she'd finally like me to meet Marco, my son. What a Christmas gift?"

"You didn't tell me this. Does Hector know?"

"He does. I didn't know until we confirmed paternity. We've actually been chatting more."

"Oh, boy. Rekindling an old flame?"

"Hell no. Not my intent at all. Especially, the way that she left me, and all. They're due in tomorrow afternoon." Naim pulled out his cell phone, called up his Instagram app, and found Marco's profile: Marcotheprodigalson. He showed it to Derrick.

Derrick scrolled through the page. "Your twin." Both men chortled. "Dark complexion, bushy eyebrows, waves and tall just like ya. His posts and style seem awfully mature. How old is he?"

"Seventeen in the twelfth grade."

"Does he know that he's coming to meet you, his father?"

"Yes, I've talked to him and we've chatted via Facetime. Apparently, Sinia and Kyle Love had an argument about paternity when he was about thirteen. Unbeknownst to them, Marco had heard the whole argument but never said anything. When he turned fifteen, he asked them about it and they confessed that Kyle wasn't his father. Kyle divorced her a month later."

"Must've been tough for Kyle to look you in the face every day. He's light skin and has that good Puerto Rican hair, and you're black as midnight with nappy hair posing as waves."

Both men laughed.

"I'm sure, but he contributed to her leaving me for dead so to hell with him. I've never gotten over the way that she left me. Because I was arrested wasn't a good enough reason with all that we had shared. She had never even given me a real shot, although she pretended that she had."

"Academy Award acting, huh?"

"Man, she was done as soon as agents handcuffed me at the airport." Naim's shoulders sagged. "And to think I had a ring in my luggage to propose to her during our nine day trip."

"You never told me that. Were you really ready to marry her?"

"Hell, yeah. The Friday that we were set to leave for a swing through three cities she had to work, and our flight wasn't until seven p.m. I spent the day looking for a ring to propose at dinner on my birthday, which was day four of the trip."

"Wow."

"I knew she'd do something simple like dinner because she was an aloof woman, dull on the creative side and very predictable."

"That damn warrant caught up to you and ruined it all. Too bad that case didn't come before you met her."

"Right. Who knew I'd change my life and then get busted years later," Naim said and frowned. He showed a sinister smile, and then said, "I was emotionally killed when I got the Dear Naim Letter via the prison E-mail system."

"Well you did leave her with a gas bill, too," Derrick said and burst into laughter. "As a prosecutor, I know that spouses are left stuck with debt often and some people can deal with the pain and others can't. It's funny because the good guys in relationships most times get left to rot in jail alone. But I'll have surveillance of some nut cheating repeatedly and when that comes to light at trial they'll have a woman fighting for their release. It's sad. I mean he may be beating her ass, and I'll have proof of it, yet, she'll be crying to a judge to give him leniency during sentencing."

"Man, that's bullshit. I remain convinced that her friends contributed to her leaving me. If not directly, she just feared what they would say had she stuck around. She was mad that I didn't tell her my whole rap sheet."

"It's a fine line there, bro. One may never know what to tell and not tell while getting to know someone. I guess if she was a hood rat your rap sheet would have been something to brag about."

"Well, she wished me luck with her Dear Naim Letter. Some chutzpah. I needed her and not luck. I replied to the rejection letter with a simple 'OK, thanks,' as if nothing had happened, manned up, and dealt with it."

"She probably had Kyle by then."

"She had been flirting with him. Other dudes, too. I had caught her several times, but did I leave her? She always made these empty promises to do better."

"By the looks of your life now, bud, it looks like she should have made a much better decision."

A server slid lavish plates in front of them, and then Naim said, "Yup, let's eat, because my blood is percolating just thinking about it all over again, especially learning that she's kept a son from me for seventeen-damn-years." He smiled again. "It's time that I find a new love and stop rejecting most of the woman that I date or that pursue me. Success and non-committal sex has consumed me." Naim thought of Brandy Scott; could she change that?

"I'll eat and drink to that. This is going to be an interesting holiday. Boy, what I would pay to be a fly on the wall at your place this week."

"You're crazy," Naim said and jammed a bite of lump crab into his mouth.

"I'm not. See, perhaps she knows that she made a mistake all of those years ago. You're a New Yorker now, extremely successful and wealthy, and no criminal proceedings pending, so what stood in your way before is all gone."

"So." Naim wasn't persuaded.

"You're the perfect bachelor, and maybe all of the love that you two shared hasn't really died."

"It has. Now, how about you eat, Dr. Phil." Naim smirked. He knew that Derrick was off base, as he didn't take rejection with a grain of salt.

CHAPTER 3

Wednesday morning, Sinia Ferguson-Love, awoke in her expansive manse in Raleigh, North Carolina and immediately smelled the odor of a man. It was pleasant but quite different than when her bed was empty.

She slowly lifted her head from his chest, she didn't want to awake him yet. She brushed the long black hair from her face and the soft curls extended past her shoulders. She was in her diaphanous white night gown, the lacy bodice barely covering her large breasts. Today, she had to give him the bad news, and she wanted to send rejection his way without giving him time to change her decision. Austin Mills was a divorced man accused of assaulting his ex-wife, very jealous, and over-bearing. She managed to deal with him because, after all, a woman had needs. He doubled as her oncologist. He was an elitist amongst North Carolina doctors and a professor of medicine at the University of North Carolina in nearby Chapel Hill.

Discreetly, she crept out of the bed without disturbing him and walked across the hardwood floor to her large walk-in closet where her luggage was packed and stored waiting for her departure. In the *ensuite* bathroom, she pulled the door shut to drown out the sound of the shower. She shivered when the first few drops hit her skin. She adjusted the temperature and then flung her head back, letting the water flow over her.

Austin's deep brown eyes swept across her from head to feet as he watched her from the bathroom door. Sinia was modelesque, perfectly proportioned, with high, supple breasts, a slim waist, narrow hips and smooth legs that never stopped. She was thirty-six with an old soul, and as a flawless lover—she fulfilled his wildest dreams, and then some.

The shower door opened and his six-feet-plus of pure masculine perfection towered over her. He was strikingly handsome with strong dark skin and big hands that pulled her into his arms forcing her back to rest against his broad chest. She elbowed him in the stomach and demanded that he get out of the shower pushing him into the frosted glass.

"You're not a morning person." He grinned and then stepped out of the shower.

"I'm trying to shower in solitude. Please just get yourself together and ready to go," she said roughly.

"I see that your bags are packed. Where are you headed? And without me?"

"Please, Austin. Just get ready to go." She pulled the shower door shut as if he wasn't there.

Sinia shampooed and conditioned her hair and then using cucumber shower gel she scrubbed Austin off of her body in an angry attempt to get rid of him. Finished her shower, she stepped out, collected a large towel and rubbed herself dry. She dropped the towel and studied her reflection in the mirror. She looked fresh, and radiant, after fully washing her night of passion away. It was a pity that she could not wash away her memories of the last year of fooling around with Austin, nonetheless, she was moving on. In due time, she would forget him and their intimacy; that was how she operated. Her mind was made up and none of his cleverness would be used to weaken her position. Their fling was over; end of discussion.

After blow drying her hair, she put lotion on her body and then walked into the bedroom finding her visitor on the edge of her California-king bed. He was fully dressed in his shirt unbuttoned and his tie in his hand.

There was a knock at the bedroom door.

"Mom," Marco said, turning the door knob.

Sinia rushed to the door and motioned for Austin to hide in the closet. She cracked the door, peeked her head out. "Good morning, Hun. I just showered and not dressed. What's up?"

"Nothing much. I am making a light, very light, breakfast, and I've put coffee on for you. See you when you come down."

"You're a tad chipper this morning," she said to his back as he traipsed down the hall. She expected him to be nervous, but he showed no signs of anxiety.

"I'm going to New York City for the first time to meet my real dad for the first time. I'm anxious and ready."

"OK, I'll be down in a sec," she replied and shut the door. She locked it and then headed to her closet.

"New York, huh?"

"Yes, and at this point, we can no longer see each other intimately again. Only in your official capacity as my doctor. With this breast cancer seeming to come back, it's best that I continue to see you for that only."

He looked deflated.

"I wish you the best, Austin."

"What's this about? That ex-con that you had a baby with nearly twenty years ago?"

She ignored his comment. "Don't text or call me on any personal level at all. I mean it," she said fully dressed, and then zipped up her suitcase. "And now we have to get you out of here before my bastard child sees you, Dr. Mills," she said with sarcasm. "He's in the kitchen, so you need to head out the side door."

"There has to be..."

"Please, Austin, just go. I have a plane to catch."

——— ———

A BUTLER CHRISTMAS

With Austin out of her hair, Sinia glided into the kitchen and joined her son at the table. He wore jeans with a cardigan over a button-up. That was him; her sophisticated son.

"What's for breakfast?" she asked and glanced at CNN on the TV mounted on the wall.

"Spinach and cheese omelets," he said, sliding a perfectly folded egg from a square pan onto a plate. He had been preparing recipes from a book in an effort to groom himself to be self-reliant and to cater to his future wife. Sinia had been guiding him to becoming the faultless man for years, and as it turned out she had done a good job.

He placed the plate in front of her, poured her a glass of orange juice and a mug of coffee, and then, she asked, "What do you want?"

They laughed.

"Nothing, mom. Just treating you to a nice breakfast. I'm excited and ready to go."

"Perfect, will you be ready in an hour?"

"Yes, I'm packed and ready to go now."

She finished a bite of egg, and said, "Marco, I'm sending you alone. I have an emergency doctor's appointment that can't be postponed. I have you in front of the plane in first-class, so that you can get on and off the plane quickly. There will be a driver at JFK to scoop you up at the luggage carousel."

Marco shrugged. Disappointment spread across his face. "I see," he said. He was no fool but would pretend to be to keep her from worrying about him.

Sinia finished her egg and then headed back to her room to retrieve her luggage. She returned and loaded the cases and her son into a Range Rover for the trip to the Raleigh-Durham airport.

Marco couldn't understand why she had put her luggage into the car if she had no intentions of flying out with him. He didn't even ask because he didn't want to make his mother uncomfortable.

Besides, nothing was stopping him from getting to the City That Never Sleeps.

CHAPTER 4

Naim had spent the morning working on a sentencing memorandum for a federal defendant. He was the only person ever elevated to full partnership at Baker & Keefe without a license to practice law. Not only did he work in their criminal division, since his appointment to the boards of Broadway Music Group (BMG) and Families Against Mandatory Minimums (FAMM), he had been required to stay abreast of all things relevant to maintain success at both of them. Today, he and Henry Winthrop, Chairman and CEO of BMG meet Jacqueline Beard, the CEO of FAMM.

Naim, after a thirty-six-month prison term was served, had finished a combined bachelor and master Criminal Justice program at Tulane University in New Orleans in 2003. He received those degrees in five years summa cum laude, where he was named a College Scholar and was elected valedictorian of his class. He was recruited by B & K right out of Tulane and relocated to New York. Ironically, the firm forgave him for his past crimes, but not Sinia Ferguson-Love. After a three year break from school, he graduated from the University of Pennsylvania Law School in 2008 with honors, where he served as an editor of the Law Review, and received the Benjamin Jones Award for Public Interest Service.

He had a slice of pizza at his home desk, anticipating the arrival of Sinia and their son, Marco. He buzzed his secretary, Ginger Robertson.

"Yes, my friend."

"I'm going to have this grown man, posing as my teenage son for about two weeks," Naim said. "What on earth am I to do with him?"

"How old is he?"

"Seventeen. Very mature."

"Well, that's easy. Girls are in, so let's assume that he's a ladies man like dear ol' dad. How about prime seats at the Giants or Knicks?"

"Good one," Naim said, jotting down her suggestion. "Tell me more."

"A stroll through Times Square for you to bond would be nice, too."

"Perfect. More."

"Broadway. Go see last year's Best Play, *All the Way*. That'll be great and could be included in the Times Square trip."

"Yes, I need to see that, just in case it comes up in conversation with a colleague or client."

"It's exciting and you'll love it. Those things will get you through a few days. I'll look up other things to do, like the nearby museums and TMZ tour. Once you get to know him for a few days you can make better decisions with respect to what will excite him. Definitely a nice dinner tonight, and not Hector's for Christ's sake."

"Why not Hector's? He may spot a celebrity. Derrick is bringing Stefon who'll be in for Christmas break."

"Don't worry, you'll have Sinia here to be his parent. She knows what he likes."

"Don't say, parent, Ginger," he replied and smiled. "To become one overnight is scary."

"Get over it, sir," she said and then hung up.

Naim wolfed down his pizza and kept glancing at his watch. Sinia's flight was due in a half-hour earlier, and he had expected a call to inform him that she had landed safely, but he knew that she wouldn't give him the impression that she was obligated to report to him. So, he surmised, they should be here about...his front doorbell buzzed...now. He took a deep breath, got into his cardigan, and ran from his office to the front door.

A handsome young man stood there holding boxing gloves, wearing a tweed jacket over his cardigan, and holding an alligator-skin briefcase; the driver behind him with a set of Louis Vuitton luggage.

"Naim?" the young man said.

"Marco? You look like a grown man. Come in. Where's your mother?"

Marco stepped into the home and peeled off his jacket. "Not here, sir," he said.

"Sat the cases on the elevator," Naim said to his driver. "Then put the car in the garage, and you're done." He pressed a hundred into the man's hand and closed the front door.

"Now," Naim said to Marco. "Where's Sinia?"

Marco pulled out his iPad and handed it to Naim. He pulled up a video. "Press Play. She left you a video message. I can tell you that she does that when she wants all of your attention, and to catch all of her facial expressions so that you know how serious she is. It's ridiculous."

Naim smiled and liked that his son had a woman, albeit his mother, all figured out. He took a seat in the family room by the fire place and played the twenty-one-second video.

Naim, I'm sorry for my last minute change of plans, but I had an emergency medical appointment with an oncologist that I could not reschedule. They have to run tests that may require me to stay a few days leading to more tests. I hope that this is over soon and I can fly to New York City. In the interim, take good care of our boy, he needs a father. I'll be in touch.

The screen went black and Naim was concerned about her. She actually had a smooth almond complexion, but it was dull in the video. Her beauty, which he loved, was evident, but not as radiant and he detected pain. Absolutely, he'd take great care of his son. He waited a long time for this moment.

"She's sick, Naim, but won't tell me everything about it. She seems to think that I am not old enough to deal with it. I am more than she'll ever know."

Naim was lost for a reply. As he recalled it, she was very obstinate and could be downright mean beyond description. She was an expert at the silent treatment. He told Marco, "She'll be fine. I guess it's just you and I then, Marco."

Marco grinned. "Let's do it."

"OK, what's with the gloves, champ?"

"I box and found a gym in Manhattan where I could train, so I plan to hit the bag a few times while I am here."

"Oh," Naim said and smiled. "So when is your birthday again?"

"Next month, same as Martin Luther King's Day. I'll be grown."

"You look grown now. How tall are you?"

"Six-feet-one inches, sir."

"Quite tall for seventeen. And don't call me sir. I'm not a stranger."

"OK, cool. Docs say I'll be about six-three by the time I am twenty."

"I agree. And your voice is deep."

"Just like yours."

"No doubt."

"So, what exactly do you do for a living? This house has to be worth millions. I have checked out the Lenox Hill section of the Upper East Side during the plane ride here, and it's the richest zip code in Manhattan," he said, looking around the family room. "And how many floors is this place to need an elevator?" he asked, walking over to the fireplace.

Naim chuckled. "There are four floors. Five including the underground garage area."

"Wow."

"Yes, I am a mitigation and sentencing specialist mostly for federal courts, but sometimes for the state, too. After defendants plead guilty or found guilty after trial, I assist lawyers with garnering leniency from judges at sentencing hearings."

"Even for a murderer?" Marco says puzzled.

"Well, yes, there's always deeply rooted mental and emotional dysfunction with murderers and I piece those problems together into a story for judges to understand that those dysfunctions contributed to the crime. Simply put, poverty stricken, uneducated men and women will do anything to survive and I help judges understand what each person has experienced."

"Sounds very interesting and makes me thankful to be a Black kid with a pretty good life thus far, attending private school, learning piano and to box, and I've never experienced poverty."

"Yes, you're very fortunate. More than me. Have you had lunch?"

"Just the cheap food on the plane," Marco replied.

"OK, I have to go to a meeting with the head of BMG in a few. Why don't you get unpacked and familiarize yourself with the place."

"Naim, you're seeing, Henry J. Winthrop? I'd like to meet him. I have a full album completed. I'm a music genius according to the music director at my school."

Naim was taken aback. He couldn't even believe that Marco knew the name of the BMG head, much less his middle initial. *Music genius* was also a new attribute, and, perhaps, explained Marco's maturity. "Of course, you may tag along. I'm headed into my office to prep. Be ready in twenty minutes."

"All right, cool," Marco said, and then added, "Thanks."

CHAPTER 5

Naim and Marco arrived at BMG's Park Avenue offices on time. Marco carried a black attaché, and Naim wondered what was inside, but didn't ask. He wouldn't want anyone asking what was in his own briefcase, so he respected Marco's privacy. They were asked to wait for Henry Winthrop who was on a call with a pop star's agent brokering a deal.

"So, you're a music genius?" Naim asked Marco. "In high school?"

"Not exactly, but I play the piano very well. It's just one music class at my school, but I've been studying music at home since I was four."

"Oh, of course," Naim said. He was amazed but withheld his awe. "What genre of music interests you most?"

"Jazz and classical. And before you judge, yes, I like rap, hip hop, and R & B, also, but I enjoy live instruments. I'd be a great producer."

I'm sure you would, Naim thought. "Good," he said.

"Mr. Winthrop will see you now, Mr. Butler," the receptionist said as Henry walked out of his office.

"Sorry to keep you waiting," he said, shaking hands with Naim.

"No worries, we were getting acquainted," Naim replied. "Henry, this is Marco, my son."

"Of course. The resemblance is apparent," Henry said, shaking the boy's hand.

Henry escorted them into a large conference room, which was decorated with paintings from the Renaissance Era. Jacqueline Beard rose from her chair and shook the men's hands. She was tall, attractive, and brunette. She waved an unlit cigar when she talked.

"And this is my son, Marco," Naim said.

For some odd reason, Naim didn't use Marco's last name. Deep down, he was pissed that it wasn't Butler.

"Good to see you Naim, Henry. And Marco, how nice to meet such a debonair young man."

Marco smiled, and said, "The pleasures all mine." And as Ginger had expected, he was a ladies man just like his father.

"Marco is a student of music," Naim said, "and wanted to meet you."

"Yes, Mr. Winthrop, I've been living vicariously through your work with Lydia and the Spanish sensation, Carmen." Marco couldn't contain his excitement.

Winthrop raised an eye. "You keep that up and you'll develop the same eye for successful acts. But know that they aren't my highest earners."

"Oh, I like the chart-toppers, too, but there's a difference between commercial success and pure genius."

Winthrop looked surprised. "Good observation. Let's take seats." He waved them to sit anywhere and after a few pleasantries, Winthrop dug into the point of the meeting. He wanted to help the FAMM organization expand by raising capital and awareness. This, after his son, a first-time offender, was sentenced to a mandatory ten-year sentence for buying drugs from a dealer who happened to be under investigation for running a drug organization. When the conspiracy became public, his son was arrested and tied to a crime that he had little to do with. "Any questions?" he asked after he was done stating his purpose.

"None from me," Naim said. "I can see how huge pop stars could be with bringing awareness to this pressing issue. If many issues were brought to the public regarding the flawed criminal justice system things would change rather quickly."

"I have a question," Marco said, "and pardon the interruption."

The three adults in the room heads whipped in his direction.

"Of course, Marco," Winthrop said.

"Can someone explain what FAMM is?"

Winthrop removed his sunglasses and blinked. He looked over at Jacqueline Beard.

"Thanks for showing interest," Jacqueline said, waving her cigar. "Like Henry, I had a family member that fell victim to the mandatory minimum federal sentencing guideline. It was my brother, convicted for growing marijuana in Washington State. He was given five years hard federal time for his first non-violent offense, so I sprang into action and created FAMM in 1991. Although my brother is free, I continue to fight for punishments that fit the crime and the offender, not just the offense itself."

"Yes," Naim said, "and she does a fine job of it. More than two-hundred-thousand people have benefited from sentencing reforms championed by FAMM."

"I have countless awards for the work we've done while working with the Supreme Court and Congress. Specifically, in 2005 we filed a 'friend of the court' amicus brief in a case for a defendant named *Booker*, which prompted the high court to rule that the guidelines were advisory and not mandatory."

Naim said, "It was that case that helped make the relevance of my job as a mitigating specialist very trendy. See, because the guideline ranges are advisory, I can present facts for the judge to sentence below them."

"Except when it's a mandatory minimum involved," Jacqueline said, "and we're steadily getting Congress to see why that area needs reform."

"I'm amazed that Congress needs an outside group of civilians to rally about this to see that it's wrong," Marco said, attempting to understand the intricacies of criminal law. He shook his head.

"If that is all, I will gather a team of students and legal-eagles to conjure up strategies to create a benefit concert and marketing/PR campaigns starring athletes and celebrities to help the public understand that we need their help to put pressure on Congress to act. The money saved in prison population reduction could be dedicated to something better like education."

"Very well," Winthrop said, and then clasped his hands together.

Jacqueline was the first to stand and throw on her coat. She shook the men hands and bid them farewells. Naim was next out of the door, but Marco stayed behind and spoke up again. "Mr. Winthrop, I am not looking to infringe, but I wonder if I could ask your opine about a project that I've completed."

"Sure, Marco. Why not?"

Marco opened his attaché, retrieved a CD and handed it to Winthrop. "I've finished an album and I'd like you to lend me some expert advice."

Winthrop took the disc. "How can I reach you?"

"Contact Naim. That will be best," Marco replied, nodding assuredly towards Naim.

"I'll let you know as soon as I'm done."

The three of them boarded an elevator and were silent. When they reached the bottom floor, Marco exited the elevator and walked towards the exit.

Winthrop whispered to Naim, "Um, how old is he?"

"Seventeen."

After a chuckle, Winthrop said, "You mean thirty-seven..." He pressed the button to be taken back to his floor. Before the door closed, he said, "Take care, Naim," and Naim gave him a thumbs up.

Out on Park Avenue, Marco had his iPad in his hand surveying a map of the vicinity.

"How about a trip through the Fifth Avenue boutiques? That is if there are no other plans."

"Let's do it. I am working on a memo for a client caught in a reverse sting operation by the ATF, but I can shop with you and mentally prepare for what I am going to write."

"Reverse sting?" Marco said as Naim hailed a taxi.

"It's when the ATF tries to get bad guys off the streets by presenting them with the opportunity to commit a fictional robbery of a drug stash house. Only they arrest the guys in possession of the guns set to be used for the faux robbery before it's carried out. Their only real objective is to get the guns that the men bring."

"I see. Sounds like a movie," Marco said, entering the taxi. "Let's discuss that in detail later. All of this criminal law sounds interesting. Much better than all of the flavors of crime shows on TV."

"What are you thinking about college? What school? What major?"

"I'm undecided on all of that. Music would be ideal. In fact, I've been accepted to Boston College and NYU to study music. But I have acceptance letters to ten other schools, even your alma mater Tulane, and four Ivy League schools."

Naim was relieved. Most seventeen-year-old Black boys were planning which state prison they'd do their first prison terms as opposed to college. He was in a deep reverie about how he was going to keep Marco's intrigued for two weeks.

CHAPTER 6

When father and son arrived back at their East Seventy-Fourth Street abode, Naim took Marco through the office entrance to meet Ginger. He explained that he was a partner at the second largest firm in New York City, but maintained a home office and an office at the firm's HQ.

"I'm very glad to finally meet you, Marco," she said, and then added, "Naim, the *United States v. Carter* sentencing has been bumped up, so your schedule has been rearranged to complete the memorandum. It's due in a week, not the month that we thought. I'm prepared to help get it done timely."

Naim sighed. "This is going to ruin my plans with Marco and Sinia."

"No worries, Naim," Marco said and smiled. "Like, Ms. Ginger, I'm ready to help, too."

"I couldn't impose on your Christmas break like that, but thanks for the kind offer."

"Sure you can. I'll go up and change and you can tell me what needs to be done." Before Naim could resist further, Marco had left the office with his shopping bags.

"How much did you spend on the spree? You're about to find out how much kids cost."

"No, I'm not. He has an Amex and insisted that he buy his own things."

"Why in the hell wasn't I that lucky to be his parent?" she asked, rolling her eyes. "My kids are always begging."

"Stop it. Get out the Carter file, please." He was laughing. "I want to fully prep what needs to be done."

"Right on top of that, boss," she said and smiled.

———— ————

An hour later, Naim introduced Marco to his profession with a crash course. They both had tea in front of them at a table in the corner of Naim's office.

"Marco, I force prosecutors to work hard to give defendants the sentences that they often ask for. Congress, many of whom are rich and privileged, have little experience with determining what sentences are best for their poor counterparts. But certainly they relate to the white collar crimes; hence, their low sentencing ranges. I write memorandums for judges highlighting facts about my clients that warrant special attention for leniency."

Marco listened intently and managed to nod his head on cue. He had his iPad in hand and Naim glanced at it observing his son's notes.

Naim continued, "Let's take Mason Carter for example," he said and opened the file in front of them. "He's the urban prototype. Drug addicted parents. Lived in a homeless shelter as a child. Uneducated. He attended the tenth grade but admitted that he can't read beyond a fourth-grade level. In sum, he's one ball of dysfunction."

"So how do you get all of that across to judges?"

"Get him an IQ test and psyche evaluation by a psychologist. The psyche's report will suggest that Carter has deficiencies that diminished his capacity and with his life experiences, he's unable to make rational decisions. For that, he needs therapy and less incarceration. Over ninety-percent of defendants that present mental defects are granted a departure or variance that lowers their actual sentencing guideline range. No judge could defy the findings of a trained expert. Now the bigger question becomes how many months does the judge take off for this. Next, I have family and friends lined up to testify about his horrible upbringing, and that testimony is live or through coached letters directed to the judge. And kids, I video tape them and play the video during sentencing. They make the strongest impact."

"I'm assuming that prosecutors make this out to be a bunch of bologna and the judge throws the book at 'em?"

"Nope, this method works, but it costs big bucks because of the time and money needed to do it right."

"I am so glad that I do not have to go through this. I know a lot about life despite not knowing you were my dad. I don't feel abandoned by you. Thanks for having me with a great woman, although she lied to me and Kyle. And thanks for welcoming me into your life despite that lie. She did a good job raising me, even after Kyle left her."

"No problem, son," Naim said, and it seemed awkward having such an intimate conversation with a teenager. "The proof of this is in your maturity and goals."

"I see that you're mature, too." Marco laughed. "I want to call you dad, and I want to be a Butler. I've thought long and hard about this."

Marco had said a mouthful. Naim was never lost for words, but in the instant situation, he was dumbfounded.

"I am OK with you calling me dad. But Sinia has to have some say-so in the name change, as she named you."

"That's fine. I want to be a Butler, though, so I can carry on your name and legacy."

"Wow. Thanks. We will be the only Butlers if that happened."

Naim didn't add that he was estranged from his family and old friends because they also abandoned him; some because of his arrest, and others because of his new outlook on life. He refused to reach out to reconcile any differences and had adjusted to his new friends. Besides, he now had Marco to start a whole new family.

"Let's postpone this crap," Naim said and closed the folder. "I better take my run, which I missed earlier this morning, anticipating your arrival, but since things are so good, I need it."

"I have a lot on my mind, too."

"I can imagine, so make yourself at home, and tour the place. There's a lot of amenities. The guest room on the second floor is all yours. Remember dinner at Hector's tonight at seven. I'll only be out an hour."

"OK...Dad."

————— —————

That evening, Naim and Marco arrived at Hector's earlier than Derrick and Stefon, so they observed them as they entered. Derrick was dressed in a blazer over jeans with a V-neck T-shirt. He looked nothing like an assistant United States attorney. Like his father, Stefon was expertly dressed in all black and an Oakland Raiders fitted cap. Everyone was introduced, and they shook hands solemnly, if not warily. They all had seats.

Stefon stared awkwardly across the table at Marco's tweed jacket and necktie. "You dress like that all the time?" he asked. "Or just when you're looking to impress people you've never met?"

"It's a part of my style, so I'd say all the time," Marco replied, reading the menu. Without looking up, he added, "Women like it."

Naim and Derrick glared at each other and shrugged.

"I'm not getting into that," Naim said.

"Neither am I," Derrick replied.

Marco nodded at Stefon's Oakland Raiders cap. "Isn't that the worse team in the NFL right now?"

"Shots fired," Derrick said.

Stefon laughed in spite of himself. "What do you know? He can talk sports," he said to Naim.

Naim and Derrick stopped laughing long enough to order their drinks and appetizers. The boys settled their battle and began comparing schools and how many young ladies they had dated.

"I'm graduating in June," Stefon said.

"As am I," Marco replied.

"Where at for college?"

"Not sure. That's in the works. I have a plan, though."

"Oh, you don't want them to know," Stefon said and nodded at their fathers.

"Something like that."

"Let's roll," Stefon said. He got up, grabbed his milk shake, and Marco followed. They took seats at the bar and jumped into the deep conversation.

"I think this was a good idea," Derrick said.

"It was. I can see this foursome going places. Damn, bro, we can now take our sons on trips and mold them to be great men and avoid poverty and prison. This is just awesome, man," Naim replied. He then told Derrick about their afternoon and the meeting with BMG and FAMM.

"That's going to be huge, but it's going to take a lot to accomplish this goal of having Congress confess to being wrong about the mandatory sentences. I mean, as a prosecutor, I may not agree with every instance I've seen someone get a mandatory sentence, but they are necessary and I follow the law. I wish you luck with this endeavor."

"OK, thanks," Naim said and then dropped a bomb. "So will you join a task force to effectively tackle this, since, after all, you have reservations about mandatory sentences?"

"I said some," Derrick said and sipped his cocktail. "I'm not drunk. Come on, Nai, you know that I cannot get into that without asking the US Attorney for permission, and he'll tell me no. You may get help from our office, but maybe someone from the appeals division, not a trial lawyer."

"Suit yourself," Naim replied. "Quite awesome both of our sons will be graduating this year and selecting colleges. Can't wait, since, I missed out on the baby steps."

"Dammit, that was cruel of her, man. Sinia will pay for that. But, yes, picking college will be a big deal for them, after all, they have fathers with Ivy League degrees," Derrick replied but didn't indicate how he felt about Naim switching the subject so abruptly. "I don't know if Stef is ready for college where he'll be responsible for attending classes all on his own."

"Guess he'll be home, so you can keep an eye on him. I don't know what Marco is planning for college, but we've gotten quite fond after a day. He decided to call me dad and asked to change his last name to Butler. I said he had to ask Sinia about that?"

"Where is Sinia?"

"I'm not sure. She left me a video message indicating she had some medical tests."

"I hope that she's good."

"She doesn't seem to be; they're running tests. I'm looking forward to a call, though. I didn't let on to him, but I was pissed that she didn't call to personally tell me that she wasn't coming."

"After what you told me about her yesterday, I'm not surprised, man. Guess she hasn't changed."

"Right," Naim said and sipped his drink. "Besides I met a woman yesterday that I like beyond a noncommittal fuck."

"Whaaaaaat?" Derrick said through laughter. "Let me see, she's an art curator that's traveled Europe thrice, lives a block from you, and her parents are on the *Forbes* List?"

"I'm not that bourgeois, or am I?" Naim said and smirked. "But, no, I have no answers to any of that. I just know that she works at the *Times*."

"We will see if you're talking about her in a month. Maybe she will be the one to take you down the aisle."

"You're going too far. I'm thirty-eight, bro..."

"Yes, and time to raise a family, get married, and prep for retirement."

"Yeah, Yeah."

The two boys returned to the table and looked at the menu again. "What's chicken cordon bleu?" Marco asked.

"Try it. You'll like it."

"Is that right, Dad?"

Stefon spoke up. "It's chicken breast, layered with cheese, and wrapped in ham. I'm going to have it also, Pop."

"Stef, you'll starve and walk home if you call me Pop again," Derrick said.

"You don't like, Pop?" Naim asked.

"Hell no. I'm thirty-six, not sixty. How can I snag a pretty young thing, emphasis on pretty and young, with my about to be grown son calling me Pop?"

The entire table laughed.

"Dad, speaking of walking, I need your car for a double date next week," Stefon said to Derrick. "Don't worry Uncle Naim, his date lives in a great zip code and attends NYU on a soccer scholarship."

"Um...OK," Naim said, "I'm sure, at least, I hope I am sure, Marco can handle dating decisions."

Marco simply nodded. Undoubtedly, he did.

Derrick spoke up as their food appeared. "I know how to make great decisions, too. You'll be taking the Subway on this date."

"OK, Pater."

"Keep it up, and you'll be hit upside your head. Pater? Unbelievable."

Stefon laughed. "OK, Dad."

———— ————

On the way home in a taxi, Marco talked quickly and seemed excited about his new friend, Stefon. "He seems like he'll be a lot of fun, Dad."

"He is, and I am glad that you two hit it off. Derrick and I went to Tulane together and have been friends since. Stefon's a lot like his Pater."

They laughed.

"Well, I guess he would be since he was raised by him. I wish you were more involved with me for my upbringing. I mean, I'm not mad or anything, I just know that we missed out on a lot."

Naim blinked. "But, we're going to make it all up. It's never too late to get it right."

They arrived at Naim's jumbo brownstone and Marco realized that his father had two homes joined to make one because they entered the door next to the one that the driver used earlier. That was what made Naim's place a colossal masterpiece. There were six bedrooms, but two of the former bedrooms served as a home theater and card room, leaving four.

Entering the home, they hung their coats in the closet and walked into the two-story foyer and ascended one of the dual floating staircases that lead to the grand salon. The men stood there a second, chit-chatting before retiring for the night.

"Dad, I think that I know what I want to do."

"And what might that be?" Naim asked. *Where the hell is your mother*, he thought. Just when he thought that he was over her, he really wanted her there.

"Well, remember, I told you that four Ivy-League schools accepted me. Columbia U is one of them, right here in New York. I'd like to come here and stay with you and attend Columbia. I just may study law and pursue music, too. I could be an entertainment lawyer. Stefon helped me plot this. Coincidentally, he also has a Columbia acceptance."

"That's very interesting," Naim replied and thought about his earlier advice to Derrick about Stefon staying in New York City for college. "Don't you want to be a performer, though? I'm cool either way you go."

"I will perform, dad. Trust me, *we* just need to figure this all out."

"We, huh?" Naim smiled. "That includes your mom. I like all of your suggestions, and they seem very thought out. But I can't say yes, and usurp her role as your mother."

"I understand."

Too grown, Naim thought. *He understands*. "But if you were to do that, there's a studio apartment on the top level with a private entrance and has a kitchen. It was set aside for me to hire a live-in house staff, but that never happened. It'll be all yours if you were to stay."

"Now, that's what I like to hear," Marco said.

Naim walked Marco to the guest room door. They shook hands and hugged briefly before parting ways for the night.

Naim lay in bed, undoubtedly, feeling like a new man.

A father.

CHAPTER 7

LED lighting at the bottom of the fourteen-meter-long pool in the basement of Naim's lair had been programmed to light up and control his lap speed and swim duration. He had to pass each light along the pool before it lit up, or he was not swimming fast enough. He completed his last lap and the lights flashed uncontrollably applauding his efforts. He climbed out of the pool and walked across the stone floor taking a seat in front of a fireplace. His housekeeper, June, a nice grandmotherly Black woman, had a pitcher of lemonade and glasses filled with ice waiting for him.

After his heart rate became normal, he changed out of his wet clothing and returned to his bedroom. He took a quick shower, and then relaxed in his bed having breakfast, also complements of June. He checked his E-mail and then visited the *New York Times* site for reports by the woman he saved. Naim smiled at the sight of her. There she was, Brandy Scott, Executive Editor. *Sounds important,* he thought.

"Good morning, Dad," Marco said, opening the bedroom door interrupting Naim's admiration of Brandy's smile in her bio head shot. He was reading the bio, as his son said, "I thought you'd still be asleep at eight."

"Nope, I am an early riser," Naim said. "I've already done my laps in the pool and as you can see I am already at work. It's convenient to do it from my bed watching Sports Center." He chuckled.

"You left to swim? I would've joined you in the gym."

"The pool and gym are in the basement, so you still can. The cars are parked behind glass separating them. It's a unique sight. You have to tour the home to learn the amenities and how you can take advantage of them."

"Oh, I see, there's a lot for me to learn. Why do you have such a big house?"

"In its most basic form, as a devout single man, I needed to do something to spend my time and money on something that looked like an investment. This was a simple project, but my neighbor moved and I set out to invest in property so I copped the neighbor's house. Then the real estate crash hit and I couldn't sell. So, I combined the two houses and now I pay taxes on one property."

"That was smart. I can learn a lot from you."

"I reckon you can, and I'd like to teach you, too."

They lightheartedly laughed.

"I can dig it," Marco said, as Naim hopped out of bed.

He threw on his robe, and said, "I have to go into my office and start my day. Have you had breakfast?"

"Yes. I missed the pool, but I did manage to find the kitchen, and June made my egg whites, English muffin, and fresh orange juice. She demanded that I not add Miss to her name."

"OK, what would you like to do today?" Naim asked, taking a seat behind his office desk.

"I was texting Stefon. Michael Moore has been accused of tweeting some foul comments about snipers that seem to throw jabs at the film, *Sniper*. We were going to see it this afternoon at the theater on Forty-Second Street, and then he was going to show me around Times Square."

"Do you need a car?"

"Dad, I don't need an S-600 with a driver shadowing me like a private detective. I want to learn the train and taxi system."

"You're a funny boy," Naim said, laughing. "You just be sure to think for you and Stefon." He wasn't sure about letting him wander in the Big Apple. Where was his mother?

"Trust me, I'm on it, Dad."

"OK, 'cause, you know the last movie for him was probably Saturday morning cartoons with Derrick's supervision." They both laughed. "He has book smarts, but his common and street smarts are lacking."

"I'm good in all three, so have no worries."

"Out, I have work to do." They chuckled and Marco headed for the door. "Be sure you have the address and my number stored in your phone. Let me know before you head out."

"OK, cool," Marco said, and left his father there sounding like an overprotective mother.

Naim picked up the phone and buzzed Ginger.

"Yes, boss."

"Will you please go to the Faust Harrison Piano shop on West Fifty-Eighth and buy a white Stien Brothers grand piano."

"Oh, Naim, that's great. You're planning to learn to play?"

"No. No, not at all. It's Marco's Christmas gift," he said.

"Sure. That's nice. A hundred-thousand-dollar piano," she said.

"Buy it under my name with the Amex, so they will have no problem. Use this house for the address of delivery and tell them you'll pay extra for delivery as late as possible on X-mas Eve."

"Will do. Any bows or wrapping?"

"All of the bells and whistles, too. Get any fancy accessories and add-ons, if any, too."

"I'm on it. Hang on the phone is ringing." She put him on hold and then came back. "It's Trevor Milan. Carter's attorney."

"Got it," Naim said. (He picked up the other line.) "Hey, Milan, how are you?"

"Great, bud."

"Oh, good," Naim said. "Where are we?"

"Well, sentencing has been mysteriously bumped up. According to the Pre-Sentence Report, Carter's guideline range is calling for 188-235 months. He's been deemed a career offender, but without that designation, he'd face only 70-87 months. So, I need you to dig up the goods that prove his poor upbringing, lack of guidance, abandonment, and anything else the judge should know to give meaningful consideration of the sixty months that I will ask for. I've just e-mailed you the outline for the Psychosocial Assessment as we speak. I've completed the Identifying Data and Sentencing Recommendation sections. Where are you with the other parts?"

"Quite frankly, I haven't started it, but I have reviewed the case yesterday. I will get to the prison to interview Carter today to get the Personal History section done. Perhaps, I can reach a family member so that I can interview someone today for the Family Background and Development History section. I'll get this puppy done and have it ready in four days for filing with the Court."

"Perfect. Please message me daily updates."

Naim turned to his computer and retrieved Milan's draft of the report. As he read it, Ginger buzzed him again.

"Sinia Love on line one."

"OK, thanks. And Ginger could you send two dozen roses—twelve red, six white, six pink—to Brandy Scott, an executive editor at the *Times*. In the card have written 'Enjoy your day, and watch traffic. Naim.' Add my cellular number, too."

"Got it, boss."

Naim picked up the phone. "Good morning. How are you feeling?"

"I could be better, but I'm not complaining. I'll be in this afternoon," she said.

"And what about the test results?"

"They're not back, yet. They will be next week. Gives me all week to stress about them," she replied and sighed.

"Perhaps being in the Big Apple could get your mind off of that. A little anyway."

"Yes, it can. How are you and Marco getting along?"

"Swimmingly. He's such a cool kid. Practically an adult."

"Yes, he's quite mature and smart, but still a kid. Taught himself to read by three and was saying complete sentences by four. They wanted to let him out of high school two-years ago, but we objected."

"I can see that. At least he's got smarts from me." He chuckled.

"He's quite the charmer with the ladies, too. Guess that's from you, also?"

"No doubt."

"Naim, take care of him. He's determined to have a bond with you. He's emotional about it and can be quite his age emotionally. Remember that."

"I hear you, but I see no emotional weakness. Maybe he's hiding it. Either way, I'm in this for the rest of his life, so I'll get to know him inside and out. We've had dinner with Derrick and Stefon, too. They're going to Times Square for a movie and sight-seeing later."

"Oh, good. You all went to Hector's?"

"Yes."

"OK, let's do dinner tonight. Us three, some place different."

"We can do that."

"Then it's settled. I'll be in about three."

"I have to meet a client at MDC and maybe I'll have to visit his parents, but I should be back by then. If not, my driver will bring you here and you can make yourself at home."

"Well, see you soon."

They hung up and Naim buzzed Ginger so that she could make him reservations for three guests at Aquagrill in SoHo for seven p.m. He then headed to the Metropolitan Detention Center in Brooklyn.

CHAPTER 8

Naim was at his desk at mid-afternoon when Ginger buzzed.

"Trevor Milan on one."

Naim picked up. "Yes, Milan."

"Just got your e-mail with the rough notes of your interview of Carter and his mother. Surprised, you were able to squeeze in his grandmother, too."

"Well, mom lives with grand mom, so that was easy. Mom was hesitant to confess things about her parenting, or lack thereof, but when I told her the worse that Carter grew up, the more likely he was to have his sentence reduced, she confessed to things that he had told me. That, despite how embarrassing and regretful."

"Good stuff. When can I expect the draft for review?"

"Hammering it out as we speak. This time tomorrow I'll e-mail you a draft."

"Thanks, Butler. You're the best when the game is on the line. Will mom be willing to testify?"

"Of course. I offered to get her a ride and something to wear. She'll do whatever it takes to get her son's sentence cut."

"OK, good. The good ol' U.S. Attorney for the Southern District of New York won't like this. They hate this approach."

"To hell will with of them over there." Naim chuckled.

Milan did, also. "This coming from a man whose best friend is an assistant to said U.S. Attorney."

"Yup, to hell with him, too, when in the courthouse. He knows we're like the Manning brothers. Off the court, it's all love; but, on it, we're mortal enemies. May the best man win."

"That simple. I'll look for the draft tomorrow."

"I'm on it," Naim replied and hung up. He buzzed Ginger and dictated the memorandum. Fifteen minutes into it the doorbell rang. Naim hung up and went to the mirror. He checked his face, popped in a mint, and then ran to the front door. Sinia stood there looking beautiful in a full-length chinchilla fur coat with perfectly pressed hair parted down the middle resting on her shoulder. They embraced tightly and Naim had her luggage sent to the master suite.

"I'm glad you're smiling," he said, taking her coat and hanging it in the closet inside the vestibule. "You really look as beautiful as I expected."

"Oh, Nai, don't charm me. You've been in my pants, and I am fully aware of your magnetic masculinity which I am sure gets many women into that master bedroom you had my bags taken to."

He leaned his head to the side, and then blinked uncontrollably; his signature move indicating caution. "Sinia, for the record I absolutely do not bring any women to my home."

"Of course not," she said sarcastically. "You can afford any hotel in this city. I'm not sure I wanna sleep there."

"That's ludicrous. You're not a guest, and I am not sleeping in another room away from you. You could afford any hotel room here, too, but you're here and you're in the master suite with me."

"Excuse me." Shockingly, she liked his masculine tone. After a moment of silence, she said, "What the hell. It's not like Marco doesn't know about us."

"Exactly. He knows how he came to be," he said and laughed. "Well maybe not the exact positions," he said and pressed his body against hers and rested his hands on her ass. "Despite our differences, I'm sure that you recall that much."

"I do," she said and wrapped her hands around his biceps. "I'm sorry, Nai. I really am. I have to make better decisions."

"About what?" he asked after she delivered her classic default line. She began to talk, and he added, "Let's not talk about the past. So you're in the master suite with me, right?"

"Well..." she said, stammering.

"Come on," he said, pulling her toward her sleeping quarters.

When they reached the room, she marveled at how everything was pure white, except for a fire-engine-red chair in the corner and his collection of cologne bottles atop a white leather dresser.

"I guess the bed is big enough for us," she said looking around the expansive room. Not a trace of a woman was there.

"The bed was custom made. It's a yard wider than the California-king." He hugged her from behind, and said, "Somehow, I don't think that you want to sleep that far from me." He kissed her neck, and then said, "Get unpacked and relax. I have work to do that's urgent." He gave her another kiss and left her there.

Ginger was buzzing him as he got back to his office. "Mr. Winthrop on line one."

Naim picked up. "Hello, Henry. Are you in traffic? I'm getting feedback."

"Not traffic. Flying to Miami," Henry replied. "I have a question: Are you sure Marco is only seventeen?"

Naim paused and pondered for a second. "Um...I'm pretty certain he is." Was there a scandal about to be revealed?

"Dammit," Henry said.

"Why?"

"He needs to be eighteen to enter into a contract."

"Contract? What contract?"

"I want to buy his album. He's beyond genius."

Naim had forgotten Marco's elevator pitch for the music mogul to listen to his album. "OK, buy it for him to perform or someone else?"

"Him or someone else. Doesn't matter," Henry said, sighed and paused. "Naim your son is what music royalty is made of. I'm talking Michael, Whitney, Elvis great."

Hmmm...They're all dead, too, buddy, Naim thought. "Henry, send the CD back, please. Overnight express from Miami. And do not mention it to anyone until I give you the green light."

"But, Naim, it's great. Someone else may say perfect—especially when it's revealed a seventeen-year-old produced it."

"That's the issue, Henry. The sudden exposure could shift his childhood and I'm asking that you help me preserve what little youth he has. He's already a fully grown man. And he has his parent's money, so he doesn't have to make any quick decisions to get money."

"I get it. Done. I understand, too. Great game time decision, by the way. That's what our youth need. Guidance," Henry said. "But I want exclusive rights to this baby, Nai, so I am sending a check for three million with the CD."

"That's fine," Naim said and hung up.

A bead of sweat traced his brow as he stared at the Carter sentencing memorandum. There was no way, he wanted his son thrust into a national spotlight without exploring college. He looked at the effects of Carter's upbringing on the screen, and thought perhaps because Carter's family needed the money, he could use the break. Marco, however, had two parents with at least seven-figures in the bank, and he didn't want for anything. According to Naim, it would stay that way. Ergo, there was no rush for him to enter into any contract. Justin Beiber and Chris Brown crossed his mind. *Oh, hell to the no.*

CHAPTER 9

Naim tugged at Sinia's foot, before giving her a light kiss to wake her.

"Oh-my-Gosh. I over slept. What time is it?"

"You're fine. We have two hours until dinner," Naim said. "Marco just got in from his trip around Times Square and is freshening up."

Sinia threw the covers over her face. "I am going to shower. That'll wake me up."

"Are you all right? We don't have to go out for dinner. I can send for an on-call gourmet chef to prepare us a meal."

"I'm fine. Just needed a nap after traveling." Sinia pulled the cover from her body. She was naked.

She stood, and he said, "You've lost some weight in the right places." He squeezed her ass and her breasts. "I see all of your pertinent parts are still voluptuous, though."

"You're still silly, I see." She kissed him on the cheek. "Maybe you can explore later."

"No doubt, I can. I knew you couldn't resist all of this chocolate," he said, watching her walk to the bathroom.

She laced her toothbrush with toothpaste, and then asked, "What have you and Marco been up to? Anything I need to know?"

"Not really, but I've bought him a grand piano for X-mas, which I'm hopeful he'll enjoy when he's visiting New York with me."

"Yes, that's the best gift. I see that you still have your knack for gifts and surprises. I remember you went through my phone and got all of my friend's numbers to throw me a surprise party."

That wasn't all I did to your phone, Naim thought. "Yes, I did and you were speechless and surprised." *I also went above and beyond for a Valentine's Day and I hardly remember your excitement.* "Marco has some ideas about the next few years of his life that I expect him to express at dinner."

"Um, anything that'll make me choke?"

Naim laughed hard. "Nope, but listen to him without reservations."

"I'll try," she said, turning on the bath water.

———— ————

Ten minutes before seven p.m., they walked into Aquagrill and checked in with the hostess.

"Now this is the kind of place to take a special lady. Thanks for showing me this place, Dad," Marco said, beaming with happiness.

"Dad?" Sinia's eyebrows had risen to her hairline. "He never called Kyle that."

"He asked me not to because it made him seem old, Mom. Besides, he knew something that I didn't all along. I mean he's light skin with curly hair. He knew he wasn't my dad," Marco replied as they were ushered to their table.

"Filter, my dear. Remember to edit your words before they leave your mouth," Sinia said, and then added, "Don't be like your dad."

"Excuse me," was Naim's only reply. Sure, he said what he wanted, and when; but, he stayed out of the match between mother and son. It was good to witness how they interacted. At the table, Naim ordered white wine for Sinia and himself. Marco asked for Sprite.

When the wine arrived, Naim raised his glass. "Happy birthday, Son." He nodded to the waiter, who brought over two gifts wrapped boxes. "The tiny one is from your mother."

"But my birthday is a month away."

"Yes, and since we gave birth to you we wanted to celebrate together, before your mother and you head back to Raleigh," Naim said.

"OK, that makes sense. Thanks," Marco said and opened the big box first. Inside was a fruit stand: Apple Mac Book Pro, latest edition iPad, and wireless Beats by Dr. Dre earphones. "Now, I can make even better music with Garage Band and earphones to listen to while on the train. Thanks, Dad."

Naim nodded.

"On the train?" Sinia asked puzzled. "Not that dangerous thing."

"Let me open your gift, Mom, and I'll explain the train thing in a second," Marco said, tearing the box open. "You're so predictable, I bet it's jewelry." He found a key to an Audi A6, and Sinia pointed out of the window. There it was, a shiny navy-blue luxury automobile. "Thanks, Mom. You really over did it. They're going to recognize me at Davis Hall when I pull up in this."

"Davis Hall?" Sinia asked.

"Yes, Davis Hall. As in Clive Davis, music legend that spawned the careers of Whitney and Alicia Keys. The school is here in New York and I want to attend. It'll make for an easier transition into Columbia U if I decide to go there."

Sinia looked at him with confusion spread across her face. Was he going to leave her in North Carolina alone? "Is that what you really want to do?"

"No doubt. And I want to study law."

"Law? Naim, what have you done to my child?"

"Our child."

"He's going to be a famous Black composer. Write scores for Oscar movies. Not be anybody's lawyer."

Naim chuckled. "Like father, like son," he said and smiled. "On a serious note, I have zero to do with his choice, other than being pleased about it," he said, and then replayed for her how his decision was born.

"So, you like it since you can't be a lawyer. You just want to live vicariously through him," Sinia said to Naim with venom.

"That's nonsense," he said and then dug into his wallet. He pulled out a Yale University ID. "Look at the date. I am about to have my doctorate degree in Law, and upon completion, I'm combining that along with my nearly twenty years of crime free living, nineteen to be exact, and twelve years experience as a sentencing specialist to have a judge rule me capable of carrying out the oath of attorneys. So, I have a strong chance of becoming a lawyer. Nice to know that you still think so low of me."

"Now you two should just get married after that," Marco said and laughed. "Mom, I assure you that Dad was just as shocked as you when I announced my plan."

"I guess I like it if that's what *you* want," she said flatly. "But, again, get a filter. Because that better be the last time that you make such a crazy marital suggestion, even if joking."

"Fine, but I'd like that." He was still smiling.

"OK, no more about that," Naim said sternly. His cell phone vibrated and he looked at a text message: *Thanks for the roses. I blushed. I would call, but I'm very busy, so I decided it only fair to thank you, even if, informally. Please call me tomorrow at your convenience for chocolate. Brandy.* He looked up and Sinia was staring angrily.

"No phones during dinner. I'm certain you know that."

"It was work related."

"See, that's why I think I'll be a good lawyer. Dad helps people get lenient sentences if they've had poor upbringings and a lack of adult guidance. How does society expect the disenfranchised to stay away from crime if no one teaches them the ropes like you've done for me? See, you just bought me a new car for my birthday, but a lot of Black kids never have their parents buy them a car; not even a cheap one. It's sad."

Sinia just shook her head. "It is, so I support whatever career direction that you go in."

"Glad to hear it. Oh, and, by the way, I want to change my last name."

"What's wrong with Love?" Sinia couldn't believe her ears.

"Well, one, that's my former step-father's last name, but once you have a final divorce you will drop that name. Two, Marco Butler will be more catchy on a business card and a college degree. Marco Love makes me sound like a singer from Latin America."

"Your updates are getting more and more outrageous like my Facebook feed, but I can't disagree. If that's what you want I'm all for it." She looked at Naim, and then said, "I assume you knew this, too?"

"I did. And again, it was his idea, not mine, ma'am," he said. To his son, he added, "Marco Butler, welcome to the family. Right now it is just you and I."

"So there we have it. I am now Marco Butler, student at Davis Hall in New York City, more than likely headed to Columbia U, and on to practice law. I'm going to make you proud."

"I reckon you will," Naim said. "Now let's eat. *Coq au vin* doesn't taste good cold. And, Marco, you're driving home, as I've sent my driver home."

"I have my junior license, so I can do that," he said confidently.

They ate dinner, and then shared a birthday cake, specially made for Marco, and then retired for the night.

CHAPTER 10

Naim woke the next morning with a warm hand fondling his morning wood. "I guess he's happy to see you," he said and grinned.

"I would hope so," Sinia said. "After all these years, I see it still works."

"And without pills."

She rolled on top of him, straddled him, and then slid him inside her.

"I see the faucet still works, too," he said. "That thing is soaked."

"Part of me finds that a little offensive, but this morning I'm all for it." She moved up and down on him slowly, before she sat with him pressed deep inside of her. She looked at him. "I liked how things went last night."

"I'm glad you approve. Things are going even better this morning."

She laughed forcing her walls to contract and tightly squeeze on his piece. He liked that feeling. "Laugh some more," he said.

She complied.

———— ————

Ginger barged into Naim's office. "I reserved Sinia and Marco for the ferry to Ellis Island and the Statue of Liberty tours. It should be fun for them, and occupy them while you work," she said.

"Um, why am I not going. I'd like to visit Lady Liberty, too."

"That's too bad. You have work to do, and your three law students that plan to help you with the FAMM project are outside waiting."

"Is that so?"

"I'll usher them in."

CHAPTER 11

Baker and Keefe were like New York's version of the firm featured in John Grisham's novel, *The Partner*. Naim didn't know of any deaths occurring at the direction of any B & K partners; but, he wouldn't be surprised to learn of any. The firm was full of high-end pedigree, power, with persuasive men and women that made it a force in New York courtrooms and boardrooms. It was also Max Devers firm, a man that reminded Naim of Atticus Finch in *To Kill a Mockingbird*. He was the brain behind all of the firm's brawn.

Naim attended a partners' meeting at B & K around one p.m. after meeting with the students. When the partners' meeting ended, he huddled into the office of Max Devers, a confidant and former college professor of his at U of Penn Law School.

"How can I help you, Butler? You look stressed."

Max was a tall man who was filling out and showing his age. Hidden beneath his slight bulge remained some evidence that he was athletic in his past; a fact, as he was a college wide receiver. He had a strong demeanor and enjoyed steaming hot coffee that fogged his expensive glasses whenever he took his first sip.

"I'm not, quite honestly. I'm rather happy," Naim replied. "Just a few things I need to be settled. Or help with. You know, things on my mind."

"Let's see what we can come up with. Take a seat."

Naim sat. "So, I've finally met Marco Love. He's been in a few days."

"Ohhhh, Sinia finally consented to that paternity test? I'm telling you, when I saw Sinia, Kyle, and Marco in LA, he looked like their adopted son."

Naim chuckled. "Well, we have hit it off quite amazingly. It's awesome and he's very, extraordinarily, bright and mature."

"Naim, every father thinks that, trust me."

"You're right, but my son was prompted to leave high school two years early, and smartly, he declined the offer. He has already composed an album that the top BMG exec offered him three million dollars for exclusive rights to. I'd liken the boy to both MJs."

Max raised his eyebrows. "Oh, that sort of bright."

"Yes. Genius. He's huge for his age, very thoughtful, and speaks like he's forty. He could stand in for me at court and no one would question his authenticity as a lawyer."

"Um...bruh, you're not a lawyer," he replied laughing.

"That's fine," Naim replied stone-faced. "I'm making five-hundred an hour, so I may as well be one."

"Shaking-my-damn-head," Max said. "I need to meet him."

"Of course," Naim said. "But we have to make some adjustments."

"Well, we can all use some fine tuning."

"He's a senior at a prep school in North Carolina, and he hates the last name, Love. I would, also."

They both chuckled.

"So you want to adjust his last name?"

"No, he does."

"OK, what else?"

"Marco wants to attend a performing arts academy on the Upper East Side called, Davis Hall, doing college level course work and attending their music school."

"That's grand. And I guess that's his bright idea?"

"How'd you guess? And he wants to be a Butler before he starts in January. As in next month."

Max blinked and became wide-eyed. "And has he figured out how to do that?"

"That's why I am here," Naim said and laughed.

"I never knew," Max said, chuckling. "I'll have a sister firm in North Carolina change his last name and notify the school to request that all of his records there be changed to Butler."

"OK, can it be done quietly? I think he hates the reason that his name has to change and doesn't want to be embarrassed by it."

"It has to be advertised locally, Nai. You know that."

"OK, we will do that."

Max slouched in his chair, pressed his elbows into the desk and clasped his hands together. "How about this?" He was in deep thought. "Let's just change his birth certificate name and have it reissued. We'll get a judge to seal the old one."

"That should require bribery. Certainly, a crime and I'm no longer a con man," Naim said and laughed. "No judge will see a reason to seal it."

"Please, you con for judges to lower sentences all of the time with your charm. But, remember, Casey Bailey. She was our executive partner until she was appointed to the United States District Court in North Carolina, her home state. I'm sure if you make a ten-thousand-dollar donation to her charity before I call her, the certificate will be sealed immediately."

"I'll make the donation today."

"OK, now Davis Hall. Have Henry Winthrop write Marco a recommendation and be sure that he mentions the album and the rights that he paid for. I can get him thirty letters to compliment Henry's. Just be sure he maintains an A average at Davis, join some clubs, and do charity work. That's all that I ask that he do for these favors."

"He'll do that happily."

"Great. I have to get to a class. I'm teaching two a week this semester at Columbia Law," Max said. They shook hands solidifying their deal and Naim headed home a short eight-minute brisk walk.

———— ————

Naim walked into his office and Ginger called out, "Max from HQ is on line one. You're in trouble."

"Not hardly, Hun," Naim said and went to his desk phone. "What I do?"

Max laughed. "Nothing. Kasey called informing me that you made a donation to her charity. You work fast."

"I called my banker during the walk home and had him wire it."

"Well, she gets a text alert after every donation and when your name came up, she was surprised and called you here. You weren't in so she talked to me. Her order will be issued tomorrow, and she's having a dozen certified copies of the new birth certificate sent by FedEx on the next day."

"Damn, man. Speechless."

You should be," Max thought. *This was a little down payment on you working with New York Senator MacDonald's plan to get the senator into the White House. Can you say bribery of a judge?* He said, "Marco has an appointment with the headmaster at Davis Hall on Tuesday afternoon at four o'clock. Have Marco take a grand sample of his work. As luck would have it our firm represented Nancy Slomsky, the headmaster, with her estate matter a few years ago." Max gave Naim Nancy's address.

"Max, how the hell can I thank you?"

"Listen, you're the partner of a powerful firm for a reason. You worked your way in, and it's about time this relationship works for you." *Or, against; depending on who's keeping score.*

"No doubt."

"I do have a small request, which you can decline, but I have to ask."

"Let's hear it."

"I know that you do speaking engagements at local colleges, but what about a professorship at Columbia. One Criminal Law class with an emphasis on defensive sentencing strategies a week. Fifteen students tops."

Naim paused. "Are you asking me to be a professor, Max?"

"Yes, I am. You can prepare the course during the winter. Submit an outline to me for fine tuning as I know what the department head likes. You can be in your finest tweed jacket and bow tie in front of a classroom by the fall. I can hear it now: Professor Naim Butler."

"How about Professor Doctor Naim Butler?"

"I didn't know that you had a doctorate?"

"I don't, but I will in May when I graduate."

"From where?"

"Yale."

"Holy fuck," Max said with elevated surprise in his voice. He already knew, though.

Naim burst into laughter. "Yes, I take an Amtrak train up twice a week for classes. I have been for two years now. Just keeping it quiet." Max knew that, too. He knew everything about his staff.

"So what do you say? Can you say, Dr. Butler, professor of Criminal Law at Columbia U?"

"Yes, let's do it."

Naim hung up. Ginger waltzed into his office and pressed a FedEx package from Henry Winthrop into his hands. "Just for you," she said.

"Thanks, and I have news for you."

"This I have to hear," she said and he told her about his conversation with Max Devers.

CHAPTER 12

Later that afternoon, Naim called Brandy Scott.

"Yes, Naim," she said, picking up her line. He loved the way that she sang his whole name.

"Just looking to touch base and perhaps set up a date and time to have a face to face chat over chocolate, of course."

"I see. I'm sure you expect me to give in to your request easily, huh?" she asked with a sneer.

"I do, and you will. You're curious as am I."

"About what?"

"Naim Butler, of course."

She laughed. "You're too much for TV."

"I'm better than TV, Brandy. Let's just explore that before you even come back with a comment slicker than mine."

"Funny, but I don't know much about you. You could be a serial killer."

"Hold on a sec," Naim told her and placed her on hold. He came back on the line, and said, "Check your e-mail."

She did. "Clever. You are thee, absolute first guy, to send me his resume via e-mail. We haven't even had a first date. Usually, I gotta dig with the help of the *Times* researchers, who can find anything, by the way."

"Oh, just be very sure that you know when you dig, you will find something. The true question is: how will you use that information?" He had a flashback of his set back with Sinia.

"True. So college in New Orleans, is that where you're from?" she asked after viewing his resume.

"No, Chicago. I just wanted to get away from there and ended up in New Orleans. I was recruited to Baker and Keefe forcing me to move to New York. I've been here since."

"Nets or Knicks?"

"Knicks."

"Jets or Giants?"

"Jets."

"Oh, no. This call is over," she replied, laughing.

"What? They're a good team."

"Yeah...yeah. Single, divorced, engaged, or it's complicated?"

"What is this a Facebook survey?" he replied, laughing. "I'm very single."

"And mingling apparently."

"That's what we are both doing, right? Mingling with each other."

"Yes, we are," she replied, and added, "but I am also single."

"Tell me more."

"I'd like to chat more in person."

"Just give me a time and place."

"Now. Starbucks between Forty-second and Forty-third on Eighth Avenue."

"Will a half hour do it. I know you have to apply makeup and get your hair done, et cetera before you meet me."

She ignored his point, but said, "I'll see you there in a half, Mr. Naim Butler."

———— ————

Twenty-five minutes later, Naim was a block from the Starbucks and had the taxi leave him there. He preferred to walk up to the coffee shop. Despite his wealth, he tried to mask it as best that he could. He wasn't looking for a gold-digger, nor was he looking to run a woman away by flaunting.

As he walked past an electronics store run by foreigners, two women, one Black and one White, both wearing en vogue business suits, were toe-to-toe on the sidewalk. No one had thrown a punch, but two police officers had separated them, and one of them said to the other, "You're blessed the po-po arrived or I would've shoved that laptop right up your boney ass."

The White woman replied, "Bitch-face, let me fuckin' tell you..." What she said included most of the seven words deemed prohibited for television.

The Black woman was ready to go, and replied, "Fuck the police. Let's go crack whore."

The officer grabbed her, and said, "If we have to take you in, they will definitely find that laptop during a body cavity search."

That line restored order, and they both went their own ways. So did Naim.

When he reached Starbucks, Brandy was approaching, and he opened the door for her.

"A scholar and gentleman," she said. "You held the door and are on time."

"Always."

"We will see. You all start off like this."

"For me, it's what you see is what you get," Naim said. "How about we sit over here by the window, it's a nice day. What're you drinking?"

"What I need is a vodka double with this stressful boss of mine, but I'll take a frappuccino. Mocha."

"Coming right up," he said and disappeared.

He returned with their drinks, straws, and napkins.

"It's awfully cold for fraps, but I am drinking what you're drinking."

"Copycat."

"So you're an editor at the big paper situated at Forty-first and Eighth?"

"Yes, and it's draining. And before you ask, I'm a Boston gal. I have a Masters in English, and I've been editing or writing since my high school paper."

"Wow, you must be a great writer?"

"I guess so." She smiled.

"Awe, you're modest. What college did you study at?"

"U Conn."

"There it is."

"And Boston College."

"Yes, not so modest now."

She giggled. It was a feminine gesture that caused her boobs to bounce around in her blouse, seemingly purposeful.

"Are you admiring my breasts?"

"Not just that. You as a whole. I've been thinking about you since the moment I saved you. You're attractive and smart. My favorite two qualities in a woman. Smart being number one."

"God forbid, she's attractive and remedial," she said and laughed. "I will say that I enjoy your light hearted sense of humor. It doesn't seem like a partner at B & K would be enjoyable to be around unless they were representing you."

"Whatever do you mean?" he asked, making a comical face.

"Stop it." She was giggling again, and the ta-ta's were doing their mandatory bounce again. "But it's like this. A lot of Black men in corporate America become stuffy, boring, workaholics when in your position. And they run to White woman because strong Black woman offends them."

He sipped his drink. "I literally started from the bottom of a Chicago ghetto and clawed my way out. My fun, free-spirited, but smart approach has gotten me to where I am now, and it hasn't changed my character or nature. Deep down, I'm still the kid from the Cabrini Green projects that attended Cooley High on the South Side of Chicago."

"That's interesting and amazing. Knowing that helps me put your coolness into perspective."

"What you thought it was fake? A *facade?*"

"No, not at all, but some men in your shoes will pretend, especially to get into a woman's pants. I'm not a fan of that."

"Is that a warning?" He squinted his eyes and looked at her deeply.

She laughed. "No, boy."

"Man." Matter-of-factly.

She smiled.

"Are you on the clock?"

"Why? Are you done here?"

"Not at all. We can camp out here, but I was just wondering how much time did I have to enjoy you without making you late back to work."

"Awe, you're considerate, too. I'm scared."

"Of?"

"Your attributes in the plus column."

"Don't be. They're all real as this first date and they will only get better and not worse. I assure you that."

"OK." She blushed. "For the record, I set my schedule. I'm fairly independent at work as an executive editor. But I have deadlines to meet and a bitchy boss. So I want to get back and hammer out this edit on a piece about the quietness in Ferguson, Missouri since the two cops were killed here in cold blood."

"Fine by me. I'll walk you back if that's all right with you."

"Yes, I'd like that, Naim."

"Let's do it."

A BUTLER CHRISTMAS

———— ————

Sinia and Marco slipped in from the Statute of Liberty, shaking a light dose of snow off of their coats and rubbing their hands together. "I need to warm up."

"Let's have hot tea," Naim replied and led them into the kitchen. They all sat down at the island on bar stools and sipped hot tea with lemon or creamer.

"How was the trip?" Naim asked.

"Very interesting and informative. Plus, I was able to add it to my list of historical sites that I've been to," Marco said.

"Yes, and we walked to the top of the statue. The view was spectacular," Sinia added.

"There's a lot more that I want to do. I am a fan of exploring and I want to travel more too, guys."

"We can do that," Naim said. "As luck would have it, I travel out of New York City once a month for a weekend of relaxation and fun. Earlier this month it was Cleveland. I went to a Cavaliers game and the Rock and Roll Hall of Fame."

"OK, that's cool, Dad. I would've loved that."

"Where to next month, perhaps we can do a family outing?" Sinia said with enthusiasm.

Family? Naim thought. *Them days are long gone, Sweetheart.* "Anything is possible," he said.

"Yes, it is," she said and winked over her tea cup.

"Can we go to Hector's tonight? That's my spot," Marco said.

"Listen to him," Sinia said, laughing. "He's going to have great taste and high expectations."

"Perfect," Naim said. "Let's do it about seven. I have to finalize a report for Milan and then I can play. But I have some news."

Both of their eyes darted to him.

"An associate of mine at Baker and Keefe arranged for a petition to be signed for Marco's name to be changed in North Carolina court, and also—this was totally unexpected—a North Carolina federal judge is having Marco's original birth certificate reissued with his new name, and the old one sealed."

Marco was fist pumping the air like his favorite NBA team was up forty points.

"If you agree," Naim said, "you'll be named after me: Naim Marco Butler, Junior."

"I love it, Pops," Marco said and laughed. He put his arm around Naim's shoulder, and said, "Hi, I'm the junior and he's the senior. How may we help you?"

"Sounds catchy," Sinia said. "I like it."

"There's more," Naim said.

Marco was rubbing his hands together.

"You have a meeting with the headmaster of the music program at Davis Hall at her home," Naim said and then dug into his wallet and pulled out the address written on a business card. "You're to take a sample of your work, and be prepared for a drilling of questions."

Marco grabbed his heart. "I'm having a heart attack. Elizabeth, I'm coming to join ya."

They all laughed.

"All I can say is thanks," Marco said. "And, Dad, call up the driver. I think this calls for bringing out the 600. I need the HM to know that I come from an educated pedigree with money in the bank."

"For Christ's sake," Sinia said, "we've created a monster."

CHAPTER 13

Sinia stood in the bedroom admiring herself in the mirror when she heard the shower water turn off. Moments later, Naim walked out of the bathroom and went to the dresser to get underclothes. He put lotion on his body, splashed on cologne—Three AM—and deodorant. Out of his periphery, he saw Sinia watching his every move.

"You think I got a big dick? Don't you?" he asked and flexed his chest muscles in a full-length mirror.

Sinia fell back on the bed and covered her face. She said, "You're too damn much. I don't know what big is per se."

"Oh, pah-lease. But that's what you're thinking."

"Man, you please. You've seen about a thousand more penises than me, since you spent your entire adult life in somebody's prison showering with men," she said. "I've seen about six."

"Six?" He was doubtful "Liar."

"OK, ten. Or twelve. More like eight, maybe."

"Sad," he said, "and for the record, I've never been to a jail where showers were in an open room and if they were my eyes would've been above the chin."

"I'd say you're on the big side, now get dressed," she said.

He pulled a tank top over his head, and she said, "Now, I confess that your body gets me going."

Naim walked over to her and rubbed her nipples. "I'm feeling the same about yours." He kissed her.

As he continued to get dressed, Sinia said, "I have another confession."

"Here we go. What?"

"I was seeing someone back in Raleigh for the past few months."

Naim thought about all of the women that he had beneath him in that time frame. "Cool," he replied.

"You're not mad or even jealous?"

"Not really. You're single. Is he a problem?"

"A little. He's my oncologist."

He raised his eyebrows. "Oh."

"During my last hospital visit for the testing, he showed up at my room cursing me out and seemed violent. A nurse escorted him out."

"Why is he becoming a problem?"

"I broke it off and told him that I was coming to New York to see you and he flipped out."

"He knows me?"

"Just as Marco's dad. He's a professor at UNC and very well respected, so I just hope that he leaves me alone."

Was she trying to brag about this man's background, he thought. *So what he's a professor, I will be one soon, too, but since you're not my woman that's not your business right now.* He told her, "I can help him, but I'm curious why'd you break it off?"

"Come on, Nai, don't make me say the obvious."

"You have to."

"I have no idea about you and I. What our future holds. Especially for Marco's sake."

"Sinia...Sinia...Sinia. There's not much here, but fun and raising our son. Our Titanic sank many years ago?"

She looked sour. "So you're still mad about seventeen-years ago?"

"No, but you left me high and dry at a time that I really needed you to be there. I mean, despite all of this house and career, I'm still the same ex-convict that you rejected. I assured you that this would be the outcome and begged you to understand and rather than you believe me and love me the way I loved you, you sent me a Dear John rejection letter and that was that."

She sat on the bed dumbfounded. Naim walked in front of her and pulled her into his arms.

"I don't want to seem cold because I love you very much. In fact, by the way, we broke up, I've never really stopped. But that's my heart's position. My brain is screaming for me to be careful here."

"I can't be upset with you. I'm going to pack my things and go to a hotel for the rest of my stay."

He let go of her. "There you go trying to run again. You can't leave here, Sinia. That would be very selfish and we don't know how an argument with us would affect Marco, so you're not going anywhere. We will be our loving selves for his sake. It won't be an act on my part because I do love you very much."

"What's that supposed to mean?"

"It means nothing, Sinia. I'm dressed and ready to do dinner. This hasn't ever consumed us, and maybe I've been bottling it up, but I want to leave this in the past. I'm over it."

"I can't do that. I love you too much, and don't know why I just left you."

He sighed and closed his eyes, before staring at her, "I don't either, but please respect my position."

CHAPTER 14

Naim text Derrick and invited him and Stefon to join them for dinner, to distract Sinia from their failed reconciliation, and by eight they were waiting to be seated at Hector's.

Marco tapped Naim's shoulder. "Dad, can Stef and I sit at the bar again?"

Naim sought Sinia's approval, and she nodded.

Derrick said, "No liquor either."

"Who would do that?' Sinia asked with faux grave concern.

"Stefon was brought home last night by NYPD for being past curfew and causing a disturbance. They claim, but he denied drinking."

"Oh, God." Sinia looked at Naim. "You have my son around a delinquent?"

"Huh?" That was Stefon.

"Sinia," Derrick said. "My son is hardly a delinquent."

"Marco and Stefon, you two head to the bar," Naim said.

They walked off, and Derrick said, "Hello to you also, Sinia."

"Sorry, Derrick. That came out all wrong."

"I bet."

They sat at the table and ordered drinks.

After catching up, Sinia asked, "So where's Stefon headed for college?" Her settled way to confirm his delinquency.

"He had early-acceptance letters to Yale and Columbia, thanks to his granddad who donates to both. But I'm certain his perfect SAT score and high honors got him the green light." *Her nerve,* Derrick thought.

"Congrats, I see you raised a bright boy."

"Yup, an Ivy-Leaguer like me and Uncle Naim." Not like you, he didn't add.

Naim kept fairly quiet as he was through with her disrespect.

"So, Sinia, how are you making your money?" Derrick asked.

"Twenty FedEx routes that I own. After working for them as a driver I saved my money and used some of Kyle's military pension to buy one route, and the rest is history."

"Sounds nice. Glad you made it. Most of us from the ghetto don't. And Marco is on a path to the White House."

She chuckled.

"Yes, my boy could be president," Naim said.

"That's probably what they're discussing now," Sinia said.

Later when they had all dined and were leaving, Naim retreated to the men's room and Derrick followed him.

"She has to go. Still the same shit-don't-stink-bitch she was twenty years earlier. I don't know what I was in love with."

"She's a miserable lady, man."

"That's fine," he said and thought of Brandy Scott. "This time she's temporary."

———— ————

When they arrived home, the parents said good night to their creation and retired to the master suite. Sinia got into bed nude next to Naim.

"I think Marco needs some New York clothes for his interview at Davis Hall. He hates when I buy him things to wear, so how about you take him to get a few things tomorrow."

"I can do that."

———— ————

The next morning as promised, Naim took Marco down to the Prada boutique on Fifth Avenue between Fifty-eighth and Fifty-ninth Streets. They went to the basement men's department and bought Marco a blue suit, a gray suit, over coat, three blazers, a few tweed jackets, and some funky ski pants. Marco also picked out jeans made from Japanese denim, some shirts, shoes, and sneakers. Everything was custom fit on the premises and would be sent over by courier in two days.

They then had breakfast at the Plaza Hotel before heading home with Naim feeling like a father, a condition he respected and welcomed with an open heart.

CHAPTER 15

Early afternoon Tuesday, FedEx delivered two packages to Naim Butler, the father. One contained a dozen certified copies of Marco's reissued birth certificate, and the other held a letter from his school which deemed Marco as a true scholar and perfect gentleman who deserved to receive his diploma early for historical purposes. Attached was a Raleigh, North Carolina high school diploma in the name of Naim Marco Butler, Jr.

Naim buzzed Marco in his room and asked him to join him in the office for a chit chat. Envelopes in hand, Naim moved to the family room and sat on a mohair, smoke-gray sofa. He handed the documents to Marco.

"It's all official now," Naim said. "Ginger is making a copy of your transcript. All A's. She wants to show her children. But it appears that the school has issued your diploma." He was excited.

"Dad, between you and I, of course, I knew this was going to happen. Two weeks before the X-mas break they gave me a battery of standardized tests. I didn't tell my mom because I knew she'd object. I should be a college sophomore right now."

"That's awesome, son, and your secret is safe with me. We have to get you a safe in the suite upstairs for all of your important papers."

"OK, cool."

Naim pulled out a check. "Also put this in there."

"Huh? What's this about?" Marco asked, holding the check for three-million-dollars from Henry Winthrop.

"It's from BMG. They offered this check to give them exclusive rights to be your first option to sell the material."

"They wanted to buy it?"

"Yes, very much so. Winthrop sent a recommendation to Davis Hall as soon as he got word that you wanted to attend."

"Dad, you sure do have a lot of connections. I have to send Winthrop a thank you note with a fruit basket."

"See that's what I'm talking about. You have respect and charm. You can't lose with them two traits."

"Right. I'm learning from you. I have to tell Stefon about this. He wants to do some work in music on the business side."

"That sounds nice. I'm excited about you being friends, but I want you to be on point around him. You two are the same age, but he has a lot of city experience and impulsiveness that can cause him to nearly get into trouble. His dad's name won't keep him out of BS if he crosses the wrong officer."

"OK, but I won't aid and abet any criminal or embarrassing act. I'm a firm believer of keeping my image."

"Good, but since you're going to be living here in this fast paced city, I have some rules."

"Yes, sir."

"Number one, you do not under any circumstance drink alcohol or try drugs. I don't give a damn what kind of situation you're in. Until you reach twenty-one, no drinking, and never drugs. Period."

"OK, but I know about the effects of both on the brain. While I'm smart, my brain is not fully developed yet."

"You're under no circumstance to commit a criminal act. None. No matter how innocent. Here's your warning that bars and clubs are out of the question until you're twenty-one. If you go into one or get a fake ID to go into one, you would have broken the law. Do not do it."

"I know better, Dad, and I won't do that. And if you're wondering, Stefon can't convince me to."

"Good. You're a handsome kid with money, so there will be girls, young and old, after you. Act with restraint and always use protection, that is, condoms, always."

"I know the ropes about diseases and unwanted pregnancy, OK."

"Just making sure. Other than that, once your mom leaves, this is a man's world."

"Sounds about right," Marco said and shook his dad's hand.

"One last thing, before I have to get to work, I implore you to talk to me about any problems. And I mean anything. I give advice for a living and trust me, I'm very good at it. As your dad, you can have all of my attention for free."

Marco grinned. "Believe me, after what you've made happen for me the last few days, I'm convinced. If a problem comes up, I'll talk to you, Dad."

"Very well. Now that we've created the perfect son, you have to go so that I can go on working on being the perfect dad."

Marco left, and Ginger walked in.

"Nice words, Boss."

"You have permission from a judge to wiretap me?"

"No, but you should take your own advice about women."

"Funny," he said and handed her an envelope with three-thousand-dollars cash. "Merry Christmas. And it's tax free."

"Thanks, Mr. Butler."

CHAPTER 16

Naim buzzed Ginger. "Could you please find me the number and connect me to a professor Austin Mills at the University of North Carolina at Chapel Hill."

"Coming right up, Boss," Ginger said. Seconds later she buzzed him. "Pick up on line one, Butler."

He picked up, and said, "Mr. Mills."

"I prefer Dr. Mills, thanks. Who is this?"

"Naim Butler, certainly, you know me."

"I don't."

"Sinia Love is with me in New York. Ring a bell?"

"Not exactly."

"I am an attorney and I represent, Mrs. Love."

"Your point?"

"Mrs. Love asked me to see that you no longer attempt to contact her, except for medical business."

"I'm sure she can tell me that herself."

"And I'm sure that she already tried that, hence my call. You showed up to her room unannounced with anger," Naim said, ratcheting up the stakes.

"What is this really about?"

"Perhaps, I can show you in writing by way of a restraining order that would make it illegal for you to contact or be near her except as I've already stated. Maybe call into question your position at that fine university."

Doctor Mills was silent.

Naim asked, "Is there anything else needed to convince you?"

"Man, I don't even understand why she's doing this."

"Listen, bruh, a restraining order is a public record and I assure you that it'll be made public. Can't work for your practice, as women have to trust you. Do you understand that?"

"You know, fuck you. You're nothing but a two-bit, cleaned up criminal."

"Pardon me, did I inform you that I was recording this conversation, Dr. Mills?"

The doctor hung up.

Naim was chuckling when he looked up and saw Sinia standing there.

"You were very professional," she said. "Did you really record him?"

"I record all conversations in these circumstances to have Ginger transcribe."

"He must've been pissed."

So am I. "He was, but I am, too. He called me a two-bit, cleaned up criminal. Know anything about that?"

"Yes, I told him why we broke up."

"You left me, that's why. Does Marco know him?"

"No."

"And how much of my past does my son know, since you're telling strangers."

"I don't know. Perhaps you should tell him everything so that if he ever finds out he won't be blind like I was."

"I know all that there is to know," Marco said, entering the office with his new Prada overcoat on. Wrapping his scarf around his throat, he said, "By twenty you had ten arrests, four actual convictions, completed three years in federal prison during which time you left him alone and married Kyle Love. After his release at twenty-three, he worked to get where he is now, and frankly, I don't care about any of that. Right now, I am headed to one of the most prestigious prep schools in the country thanks to my dad, the ex-con who is about to have a doctorate degree, living in a multi-million-dollar home, and partner at New York's second largest firm. Yes, I checked. Now can we all just get along."

The parents were speechless. Sinia's mouth was covered with a hand. Naim's brows raised. Marco gave his mom a hug, and then shook his dad's hand. "I'm off to my Davis interview, wish me luck," he said and walked out of the office.

From the window, they watched him hop into the back of the S-600 before being whisked away.

CHAPTER 17

The driver pulled in front of One Riverside Park and then opened the door for Marco to exit. The doorman of the humongous, glass encased, condominiums held the building's door open and Marco walked inside. A concierge asked if he could help him.

"Yes, I have an appointment with Miss Nancy Slomsky."

"Of course, but know that it's Mrs. Slomsky, and she requires that married designation."

"OK, got it. Thanks."

"Your name?" the man asked, picking up his desk phone.

"Marco Lo—Butler," he said quickly, remembering his new name.

The man announced him and then directed him to the headmaster's condo.

Marco entered the elevator, the door closed and the numbered floor he was headed to lit up. As the elevator ascended to the seventeenth floor, he checks his Windsor knot and his teeth in the mirror, before popping a Cert mint into his mouth. When the elevator opened, he entered a hallway and heard a door opening. A butler that seemed to be on stilts welcomed him to her place.

"I'm Marco Butler," he said, and the man took his coat. He led him into a curtain-less living room with an amazing view of the river. A coifed, chic woman sat in a wooden rocking chair.

"Marco? I'm Nancy Slomsky," she said and offered him a seat in a matching rocking chair.

"Thank you, and nice to meet you," he said, offering his hand, as he sat down.

"Would you like iced tea?"

"Yes, ma'am. Unsweetened."

"Just how I take mine," she said, pouring them glasses.

"Thank you."

She waved at a tray of cheese and crackers. "Help yourself."

"Thanks, ma'am," he said, using a toothpick to pick up a piece of sharp-cheddar.

"Now that that's over, let's get to the nitty-gritty," she said. "I'm told you have a sincere interest in Davis Hall."

"Yes, that's correct."

"Well, now, tell me why?"

"My goal is to be a contract attorney for musicians, but I can also play the piano and flute, so I'd like to learn about the business of producing music before law school."

"Interesting. Records indicate you graduated high school this December. Tell me about that."

"I completed over twelve Advance Placement courses in high school and school officials deemed me prepared for college coursework. They gave me a series of written and oral examines before five faculty members all of whom unanimously decided to graduate me. Apparently, they had nothing else to offer me."

"You must be very intelligent, Marco."

"So I've been told. I'm just little ol' Marco Butler, though. Not too special."

She chuckled. "Have you ever been given an IQ test?"

"Yes."

"And how'd you score."

He looked at the floor. "I...perhaps it was one-hundred-fifty-eight," he said.

She giggled and then sipped her tea. "You shouldn't be embarrassed by that. Our young ladies are fine with brilliant young men."

"Yes, ma'am."

"Why do you want to be an entertainment contract lawyer?"

"Well, my dad works in criminal law and I'd like to follow in his footsteps. I was captain of my debate team and am a convincing debater. I'll be great in the courtroom."

"Ah ha. Did you bring a sample of your work? BMG's Winthrop wrote me indicating it contained advanced compositions for your age."

He pulled a CD from his attaché. He passed it to her, and then told her, "You can judge it and let me know, ma'am."

She had the butler put the CD into the player and then he handed her a remote. She cruised through the openings of each song and smiled delightfully as the surround sound delivered the song snippets around the room. She was in Marco's musical fantasy.

"Brilliant," she said when the sample was done.

"Assuming you were let into Davis Hall, where would you go next?"

"I've been accepted to Columbia right here in New York."

"Perfect," she said, "as we like to hand deliver them our best." She handed him a folder with an application inside. "Fill out the application and place your credentials inside."

While he did that, Nancy Slomsky called the music director of Davis Hall at home. She confirmed his availability to meet with Marco and hung up.

"OK, Marco, I'd like you to come to the school tomorrow with your parents for a tour and to meet the music director."

"Yes, ma'am. What time?"

"Do you have plans?"

"Well, no, but on Tuesday's my dad has a class at Yale. He's pursuing a doctorate degree. The earlier in the a.m. will be best."

"No, problem. Let's meet at seven-thirty in the morning. The school will be in session, so Marco don't come with your driver or the tie, OK. Don't want to scare away potential friends."

"How'd you know about the driver?"

"I'm all knowing," she said. "Remember that if you're admitted into my school. With Christmas on Friday, it'll be the perfect gift for your parents having you admitted into Clive Davis Hall."

CHAPTER 18

Marco returned to Naim's home office and strolled in as if nothing had happened.

"So?" Naim asked unable to read his son's face.

"It went...Brilliant," Marco replied, smiling. "I think I am going to be let in."

"OK, that's great. Things are coming along. Tell me what we need to do next."

"You, mom and I have to be at the school at seven-thirty tomorrow morning for a tour and to meet with the music director."

"So early."

"Yes, you have class tomorrow evening."

"I'm off for the break like you, but that time is good."

"For what?" Sinia said, entering the office.

"Our school interview in the morning," Naim said.

"I'm available," Sinia said and smiled. "We will be one family tomorrow."

That evening they attended *All The Way*, a Broadway production, which Naim liked more than he imagined he could. Afterward, they dined at The View inside the Marriot Marquis with a panoramic view of Times Square and beyond.

Fresh out of the shower, Naim climbed into bed, his black hair damp, the clean, boyish scent of him filled Sinia's sense of smell and, to her amazement she could feel her nipples hardening. He took a moment and looked her over, a glimmer of enjoyment in his eyes. He was fully aware of how he affected her. A sly grin crept across his face, making her aware of his sexuality emanating from his hard body. "Tomorrow we get to be a couple for the day or naw?" His lips feathered across hers, and she shivered as their kiss intensified. The heat of his mouth burning hers.

Sinia panted, caught in a trap of lust much stronger than she was. *How could this be happening?* she thought helplessly, while every part of her burned in need of him. Jerking back to her sad reality, she said, "We don't have to be a couple tomorrow. Let's not lie to them to accept our child."

He absorbed her angry face. "You're right." He didn't want to talk about this. He curved his large hand around her chin and tilted her face up. "Try to forgive me for my misgivings when you return to North Carolina. I really wish this would've been different."

Sinia tensed, her bodacious frame was attached to his. She didn't like his dismissive undertone, but what could she do. "Just like that."

"It's as simple to do now as it was...Never mind, Sinia." He chuckled, lying back with his lips curving back over bright-white teeth in a broad grin. "Forget the foolishness of yester-years, sweetheart; I have. You were not thinking logically; it is perfectly understandable."

She was instantly absorbed by his heavy-handed arrogance and forced to lay speechless.

He pulled her into his chest and then kissed her. They kissed for a long time, allowing nature took its course.

CHAPTER 19

Naim went down to his office in his PJs and robe, the top benefit of working from home. It was five a.m. and he had an early morning telephone conference in ten minutes. Besides that, he wanted to get some work done before heading over to Davis Hall. Ginger wasn't in and he heard the telephone and answered it something that he typically didn't do. He was a lawyer and dodged calls with perfection. It was Dominick Suarez, Carmelo Anthony's and Brooke Lopez's sports representative. He'd been tracked down for Naim's FAMM media blitz and the rep wanted to chat at such an odd hour, which was not disputed by Naim. He knew when not to argue.

"Good morning, Suarez," Naim said.

"Morning, Butler. Sorry for the early call, but I'm headed to Brazil for the holidays and figured this needed to be handled considering the Nets and Knicks play at the Nets' Barclay Center in late January."

"Yes, thanks for reading the proposal. We'd like to have the team wear black T-shirts with the FAMM website printed on them. Of course, we'd provide the shirts. And we'd pay Anthony to briefly discuss FAMM during a half-time or game ending interview because we're sure the media will ask once they see the web site."

"OK, I think that can happen, but Anthony doesn't need your money. His foundation does, though."

"Certainly. Quiet or public donation, Suarez?"

"Quiet, of course. It's much better to have the public awareness come from the players genuine motive."

"And your fee?" Naim knew there was one.

"Seventy-five-thousand," he replied. "A steal considering what national ads costs. They play on a Saturday, so the game will be on ABC and syndicated. You can't pay for better attention."

"I agree. Let's get this all settled. Send over the contracts."

"No contracts. I'm sending bank wire account numbers for my payment and the foundation. I'll have the teams contact you for T-shirt distribution, and Carmelo will be briefed on FAMM."

"*Gracias*, Suarez," Naim said and thought highly of his recording devices.

"Talk to you later, my friend."

Naim hung up and smiled broadly. His dedication to working to restore a semblance of fairness into the judicial system was coming to fruition on a grand scale.

He joined Marco and Sinia in the kitchen for breakfast at seven.

Sinia said, "Good morning."

"Good morning," he replied, pouring a glass of orange juice. "I've been thinking. We should style ourselves as divorcees this morning at Davis Hall."

"Yes, Dad. That way I won't be a bastard child. Pardon my language." He winked.

Naim laughed.

"I'm not thrilled about that, but I guess," said Sinia.

———— ————

Davis Hall occupied an entire corner at Seventy-ninth Street and Fifth Avenue.

"It looks like a cathedral's been gutted, and modernized," Sinia said, exiting a taxi.

"The endowment must be the size of Russia," Naim replied. "I can imagine we will hear about that inside." They continued climbing the front steps, making their way to the administrative offices.

A receptionist took their coats. Then, Lance Kraft, the music director met them and introduced himself. "Marco, I'm very glad to meet you and your parents. Let's get our tour started while class is in session. Today is the last day before the break. We set our own demanding schedule that has very little reliance on what the public schools do; ergo, our academic and program specific success."

They walked by an auditorium and peeked inside. "We can fit the entire student body of about two-hundred-thirty in there," Kraft said, and then continued down the main corridor.

Passing two classrooms, Sinia said, "The classes are small. That's nice."

"That's our gift. No more than eighteen students per class, but we like to keep it close to fifteen."

They stepped into a music class and Kraft pressed his finger to his lips. Students were crowded around a piano being lectured by an instructor; a fussy, red-haired woman.

"There's only one piano?" Marco whispered.

"We have three more, but they're being repaired. I'm begging for brand new ones."

Naim nodded.

They completed the tour and convened in Kraft's office, where they were offered coffee.

"We'd like to have Marco here at Clive Davis Hall," the director said. "After speaking with another faculty we're persuaded that his classes should be divided between music classes and courses from the university curriculum for the freshman year. They're completed on-campus at Columbia and NYU. His choice, but we prefer our music students to select Columbia. Simply put, NYU has Julliard and they're not starving for musical talent."

Marco said, "I have freshman credits completed already."

"You do, we've seen that, but we think that you need more history and social sciences to complement pursuing a law degree, and a foreign language." He passed along an envelope with the fees.

"Marco," Naim said, slipping the envelope into the inside pocket of his blazer, "is that what you want to do?"

"Yes, I can handle that. I think I'd do well with French."

"What about Latin?" Naim asked. "That's important in law. I know quite a bit."

"I know, but French will allow me to do some international business in France, perhaps."

"Then you can start this January session," Kraft said.

Everyone shook hands and Marco Butler was an official student at Davis Hall.

They left the school and had lunch at Hector's.

CHAPTER 20

The following day, Naim was at his desk chatting with Brandy Scott when she asked him to join her for breakfast. He agreed and had met her at the Tick Tock Diner across the street from Madison Square Garden. They had ordered their French toast and shredded potatoes and were having coffee while talking.

"It was good that you met me," Brandy said. "Proves you have a spontaneous side."

"Oh, is that it?" Naim replied. "I assure you that I am spontaneous. But I'm envisioning you were testing more than that."

"Like what," she said, "smart guy."

"Perhaps you were looking to see if I had a lady friend that would have prevented me from meeting you on short notice."

"Come on, Naim. I'm woman enough to ask that. Besides, I have an eye for missing wedding bands causing light skin, too. Surely, I sized you up already."

Naim leaned in close to her and put his lips to her ear. "Have you really sized me up, Brandy Scott?" His lips brushed her ear and she quivered.

She pulled back and sipped her coffee.

"No reply, huh?" Naim asked and watched the waiter put food in front of them.

"Don't need one. You got that, though." She thought about her reply and realized she hadn't made any sense. As proficient as she was with the English language, she was speechless. His charm had consumed her.

They nibbled their breakfast in silence for a bit and watched other patrons ebb and flow through the diner.

"We're both single and never married in our thirties," Naim said. "I confess that you look twenty-five easily."

"Why thank you, but I'm forty-two, and I have had a divorce," she replied frankly. "Just like an attorney to ask a leading question."

He smiled. "My apologies. You're gorgeous for the early forties. I'm thirty-eight."

"OK, you're my young buck," she said and laughed.

"That's doubtful," he said. "I'm always the man of the house regardless to age factors." She smirked, and he added, "Tell me the quick version of why you divorced?"

"Well, he was a high school sweetheart, headed for a minimum wage job, while I was headed to a six-figure career. He hated my college and career drive and cheated resulting in a child being born and left me alone. I was becoming stuck-up and acting White, were his words in a letter because he wasn't man enough to leave me in person."

"Wow, a Dear Jane Letter."

"No, a Dear Brandy Letter," she said, laughing.

"That's funny," he said, smiling. "I've had a Dear Naim Butler letter myself. Rejection is rejection, I see. And I've been accused of acting White which is absurd. I've learned that people that have more than me and that I look up to see me as ambitious and driven, but never acting uppity. Our people can be sad. As if we're supposed to stay poverty-stricken and illiterate."

"I couldn't agree more," she said and sipped her coffee. "But do tell about the rejection letter."

"Well, I was raised poor on the South Side of Chicago and committed a crime to get by, but eventually, I was caught and my girlfriend at the time left me while I was serving a three-year sentence in a federal prison. I got the rejection letter and months later my best friend sent me a picture of her and her new husband."

"Oh, no."

"What? My prison trip is too much for you?"

"Not that." She chuckled. "The fact that she left you while there is disturbing. As for you being there, that was then, apparently, you cleaned all that up. I want to know how?"

"OK, after I was released, I joined my best friend, Derrick, in New Orleans who was a law student at Tulane. He convinced the school to let me in and I maintained a four-point-oh GPA the entire time. Baker and Keefe recruited me and created a job for me. I'm their first mitigation specialist. Now, I head the department and am the only partner without a license to actually practice law."

"That's very interesting, Naim. Quite shocking. I was going to ask how you practiced law with a record."

"I'm actually working on that. My criminal stain won't ever be invincible, but I have worked towards becoming a lawyer despite that blemish."

"I believe that you can, and should be able to. Your past doesn't determine how effective you'll advocate for clients."

"Right," he said, laughing. He rested his hand on hers and then squeezed affectionately. "Wish you were a judge that could expunge my record, and let me get on with my life."

"It's going to happen for you, Naim," she said seriously. "It'll be a historical moment, although I am sure it's been done. I think that you'll serve for the bigger picture and not just the financial reward and that will make all the difference."

Something magnetic had consumed them, and she smiled.

"It's Christmas Eve and we have to get to our prep," she said.

"Yes, we do."

"Any children?" she asked him.

"No," he said with a straight face.

"Thirty-eight, single, and no kids," she smiled again. "It's a miracle."

He laughed. "Not quite. I have a grown man. He'll be eighteen in January. He attends Davis Hall." It felt good to say that.

Her eyebrows raised.

"Don't fret," he said. "I'm a single father and his mom lives in North Carolina." Felt good saying that, too.

"Seems you have it all figured out."

"I do," he said, smiling.

"Such a confident little poodle. Let's get out of here."

"Yes, and for the record, I'm more like a pit bull," he replied, stood, and winked.

CHAPTER 21

Marco walked into his father's office fully dressed, pulling on his coat. He didn't find Naim there, but his mother was at his father's desk scrolling through his cell phone.

"Where's my dad? And what are you doing on his phone?"

"I'm not sure where he is," she replied, lying to her son. She knew exactly where he was, and that he was with Brandy Scott. Her only question was how deep was Naim and Brandy's relationship? She sat the phone down, and then said, "And I never had his phone, right?" She winked, stood up and walked over to tie her son's scarf.

"Hello, you two," Naim said, entering his office. "I see someone is headed out," he said as he pats his son on the back.

"Right," Marco said to his dad and then winked back at his mother. He had effectively replied to both of them. "Stefon and I are headed out to do some last minute Christmas shopping. I'm picking him up in my car. I should be home late afternoon."

"Sounds good," Naim said, and then added, "Drive safely."

"Of course," Marco replied and walked out.

"So where were you this marvelous morning?" Sinia said and ran her hand down his chest to his crotch.

He backed up before, he said, "Well after my circuit weight training, I had a breakfast meeting with a client." He had no reason to lie to her, but he did.

"You happen to bring me a bite back?"

"No, I'm sure you found food or had it prepared," he said, and then took a seat. He was scrolling through his phone when, he asked, "What's on your agenda today?"

"Not too much. Just a little shopping. Are you and I exchanging?"

"We can. I have the piano being delivered for Marco tonight, so we need to take him out. June will have it all set up before we return. I am also getting him a home office for when he moves into the suite next week. He needs to get used to working in an office for the future."

"It's amazing how he's going from Raleigh to a studio and an office," she said and paced to the window. "I don't really like you trying to live through him."

"You're out of your mind. I haven't persuaded him to do anything, but I don't mind him following in my footsteps."

"But you're not a lawyer."

"Are you kidding me? Look around you. Does it matter one iota if I am a lawyer or not? I'm doing what I love and making one helluva living doing it. He's on his own making a career choice. You're starting to aggravate me with this bullshit. My Mr. Nice Guy performance is about to hit the road."

"I bet. You're the same guy from the past. You've not really changed. It's all an act."

"Listen, why don't you go take a bath and clear your head. How about a spa day?"

"Look at you. Always have advice."

"What's your problem? Why do you keep antagonizing me?"

"I'm stating facts."

He chuckled. "You are something else. A piece of work."

"No, you are," she said and pointed in his face.

He moved his head back and looked at her strangely. "OK, now you're going overboard. How about this: gather your bags and get the hell out."

"Oh, you're going to put me out in the cold?"

"With pleasure. You didn't even want to stay here, remember?" he said, walking to his office door. "Ginger," he called out. "Can you make Mrs. Love a reservation at the nearby Marriott Courtyard for checking in now," he said with a heavy emphasis on *Mrs. Love*.

"Don't bother, Ginger. I know my way around town."

"I'm sure you do," he said, heading for his bedroom.

"Fuck you, asshole."

"The only person been getting fucked around here is you," he said, pointing a finger in her direction.

"We will see who gets the last fuck, though," she said, pulling out her luggage. "Yes, we certainly will, 'cause I have a trick for you."

Naim hopped into his bed, rested his head against the headboard and grabbed the remote. He commanded the TV to emerge from the foot of the bed and tuned into Sports Center as if she wasn't there.

———— ————

By three-thirty that afternoon, Marco and Stefon shuffled into the house and hung their jackets in a hall closet. Naim made his way out of his study and greeted them with handshakes.

"How was your day out without parental guidance?" Naim asked and genuinely wanted to know. He needed to be certain that Marco adjusted to the New York life without any hardships.

"It was just like any other day *with* guidance," Marco replied and chuckled. "We're going to go to the theater and watch a movie, so please pardon us."

"Of course, go on up. I'll have some snacks brought up."

The boys raced up the stairs to the guest room where Marco was temporarily staying, and he found the disc for *The God Father*.

"I'm glad you moved here and we hit it off as friends," Stefon said. "My dad seems to think that I need to be out of this city purlieu, and tries to control all of my friend selections."

"I know," Marco said, walking through the house. "You're a smart man, Stefon. And a good guy. But my dad asked me to keep you out of bull-crap."

Stefon laughed. "It's bullshit. But your dad has been talking to my lame ass dad. He's a prosecutor, bro, everything is bad too him. He never sees the bright side. He needs sex, that's his problem. He's probably backed up from the moment my mom died."

They laughed heartily.

"That's funny," Marco said, "but in all seriousness, I have too much to lose, so I can't do anything dumb, Stef."

"What's that?" Stefon asked, walking into the theater.

"I'm Black with a lot to lose, and you're White so you don't face the same stakes as I."

"Put that way, I totally understand."

"You'd make a wonderful producer, Stef. Think about that. We could do some things as a team working towards a common goal. Fame."

"I'd like fame. We already have money. Now we got to do the right things to flip it over."

"I understand."

"You should study music with me."

"Study music? Me?"

"Of course. You'll learn how to produce music for movies, plays, and radio. And you'll meet all of your future connects right there. Take music with a business minor."

"I may do that. Let me ponder on it."

———— ————

Around eight o'clock, Marco found Naim in the kitchen having soup and tea.

"Trying to warm up, Dad? Or you're sick?"

"Both. Where's Stefon?"

"He just took the train home. He is supposed to text when he's there," he replied, fixing himself a bowl of cereal. "Where's mom?"

"Good question," Naim said and hung his head low.

"Did she leave?" Marco asked nonchalantly. "Did you two have an argument?"

"Yes, we did." Puzzled. *How'd he know?*

"About her going through your phone?"

"No, but now that you say that, I am sure that's a part of the argument. How'd you know that she's been in it?"

"I saw her with it in her hand, but I don't know what she found."

"I see," Naim said and grinned. "Well, she decided to go to a hotel for the evening." He let that sink in and then said, "Look, Marco, I know that you were hoping for your mother and me to kiss and make up after all these years to raise you in a two parent home, but I don't think there's any way to ameliorate our current status. Was I bitter and angry that she left me when I was down, yes? But it was her quick marriage and hiding the fact that I had a son that kind of ruined any ideas I had about chasing her upon my release. Despite that, she made me a better man."

"How so?"

"Well, her rejection letter forced me to work hard to get to where I am now. I focused on the pursuit of perfection and ignored the idea of love. This especially while I was on probation because the last thing I needed to do was fall in love again and get a probation violation to be returned to jail for a frivolous infraction. I put all of my efforts into loving my career, which has always loved me back. My career never lets me down or rejected me. But before I was crushed by your mom, I put my all into her like I do my career and that's why it hurt so badly."

"But do you realize you hurt her, too? She's told me as much."

"Of course, I do. But I would've never left her. Man to man, a part of me always felt that she didn't love me as much as I loved her. I guess at that time I didn't care because she was the best thing that happened to be mine. She was a breath of fresh air from my prior bad relationships and from my dysfunctional family. We were from two different worlds, so I should've been better prepared for her to leave me if my ghetto attributes encroached on her cookie-cutter, goodie-two-shoe upbringing. Your mom had a two parent working class home, and didn't know a soul in prison or had been to one. I had a broken home full of alcohol and verbal abuse and knew several people in jail growing up starting with my dad. We were just from two different planets."

"So what now, Dad?"

"I don't know. I would have thought your mom would have at least text you by now. I had Ginger make her a reservation at the Marriott. I think stubbornness will force her to stay somewhere else, but you should text her to find out. We can ask her what she wants to do tomorrow. I know you were hoping for one big happy family Christmas, and I'm sorry about this."

"No worries. I'm all right with this. I've gone this long without you two being an item so..."

"OK, cool...How about ice cream and then we can put the tree up. I usually have a decorator do it, but I thought we could do it as a family."

"I'm down," Marco said and shook his dad's hand.

"Afterward, we can hit the town for a bit."

"Oh, yeah," Marco said excitedly.

"Whoa," Naim said, laughing. "We're not going clubbing or anything crazy. Maybe take a pic in front of the Rockefeller Center tree, take in the fun New York City Christmas Eve sights, and grab a late night bite to eat."

"OK, that'll work, too."

CHAPTER 22

Naim was awakened by an incessant banging on the front door like it came from New York's finest: NYPD. He hoped for the best as he went to his bedroom closet, and retrieved a nine-millimeter Rueger. He loaded it and then padded to the front door in boxers and slippers. What if it was robbers looking for a house to break into? Perhaps someone was drunk and had the wrong address. Hell, maybe it was Santa. Either way in New York City, even in the ritzy Upper East Side neighborhood, loud banging on the front door at three a.m. had to be addressed with a gun at one's side.

Naim placed the nozzle of the gun at the approximate point of the potential victim's center mass and then looked through the peephole. When he saw who it was, he hid the gun in the top of the vestibule closet and then unlocked the door. He opened it, and said, "Sinia, what are you doing out this time of morning."

"Boy, please. I can be out at any time," she replied, pushing past him into the home. Her speech was slurred. "I'm a grown damn woman."

"How much have you had to drink? Where are you coming from?" he asked and locked the door behind her.

"Look, get my bags from the curb. Get them..." she said, staring at him. She then sarcastically added, "or get your maid to do it."

Naim's eyes grew wide at her contemptuous tone.

"And, yes. I've been drinking. I had two bottles of the fanciest *Moet* on your dime at the hotel bar. You know, I sat at that hotel bar drinking my pain away and it didn't work. Now, please, get my bags and come give me a good fuck so that I can go back to North Carolina happy. I'll be outta your hair."

Naim's ears had just exploded from the bombs she dropped in them. He headed out of the door and then brought her luggage into the home. He locked the front door and noticed that Sinia wasn't in sight. She had left a trail of her clothing up the stairs and into the master suite. When he arrived there, she laid on the bed spread eagle and naked.

He admired her radiant glow as the light from the bathroom illuminated her beauty. Her nude form was perfect. She watched him slip out of his boxers and smiled.

"Yes, you're big like a porn star. Is that what you wanted to hear the other day?"

He replied by planting kisses from her left foot up her leg while pushing it back until her knee was pressed into her shoulder. His tongue explored her with intimate precision. Her back arched invitingly, and he looked up at her. She was smiling. Paying close attention to her, Sinia felt herself climax making her extremely wet, and then he flipped her over onto her stomach. Naim tucked a pillow under her midsection before working himself inside her inch-by-inch. When he had sunk all the way inside, he let it sit deep inside before he stroked with aggressiveness. He wasn't an ogre about it, but he used the right speed and force to hit her with pleasurable pain. His strokes went from light to heavy pounding causing her to try to scoot away, but he wrapped his arm around her waist and held her in place.

CHAPTER 23

On Christmas morning, Naim and Sinia were dressing for a morning breakfast held at Hector's home in the South Hamptons.

"Is this dress formal enough to dine at Hector's home? There may be a film crew knowing him," Sinia said.

"You're beautiful," Naim said, "don't over think it."

"OK, fine," she said, twirling in the mirror.

"Look at you all happy this morning," he said, smiling.

"I'm great and sorry about yesterday. I overreacted."

"No problem. Let's let that go. We can do this without any problems, Sinia," he said and kissed her.

"Yes, we can. And I have to live with the past."

"Don't be like that." He hugged her. "I wonder all the time how life would've been had I not been arrested."

"Me, too," she said, looking over his shoulder at a shadow nearing the bedroom door.

Marco knocked on the door and then came into the room.

"Mom, what are you doing here," he asked, smiling. "Oh, never mind that. I'm glad that you're here and you look good."

"You're not so bad looking yourself," she said. "Are we all ready to go?"

"We are," Naim said. He asked Marco, "What's in the bag?"

"A gift for Stef."

"Let's get out of here then." They took the elevator to the garage. Naim got them into a Cadillac Escalade and then headed into the street.

"I loved the piano, by the way, mom."

"I bet."

"You never seem to amaze me," Marco replied.

Naim gave Sinia a stern stare and she understood that Naim must've told Marco that she had helped buy it.

Marco let the window down a little. "Um...is this glass bullet proof, Dad?" The glass was two-inches thick.

"Yes, this is an armored SUV."

"And why do you need a bullet proof truck," Sinia asked.

"Don't panic," Naim replied, smiling. "The firm has a client that armors vehicles and they were nice enough to sell me this one for cheap. Sometimes I have to go into areas that let off stray bullets and I wanted to be a step ahead. Or maybe some punk throws something— or himself—over an overpass and hit my windshield. I'd be protected." He neglected to mention the time some woman's husband threw bullets at him after being caught in their bed as the actual reason he had bought the truck three years ago.

——————— ———————

The drive to the Hamptons took three hours for them to pull into Hector's driveway. Carson, Hector's butler, and today his valet, stepped out of the home and opened their doors. He took Naim's keys and then ushered them into the manse. He led them into a large living room where several people were gathered having mimosas and took their coats.

Hector greeted them and introduced them to his family in town from Brazil. Derrick and Stefon were there, as were Max and Dorothy Devers, and then they were surprised to be introduced to the senior senator from New York, James MacDonald.

After everyone had been introduced and conversations grew, Carson opened the doors to the dining room. Everyone found their place cards and were seated. The senator was sandwiched between Naim and Max. After everyone settled, and the senator said a prayer, there was enough food placed on the table to feed the entire New York Jets football team. Nothing was spared to satisfy their appetites.

After Christmas breakfast, they adjourned to Hector's labyrinth library for coffee and tea. Max came over to Naim and whispered something to him. Naim excused himself from Sinia and joined the senator in the hall, who was in his hat and coat waiting for his car.

"Good afternoon, Senator MacDonald."

"James, you can call me, James," the senator said. "It seems that you're in a bit of a quagmire that I may be able to help you out of." Naim looked plainly. "You have a desire to be an attorney, but there's a criminal record in your way?"

"It is, sir," Naim said. He was puzzled.

"I'd like to have a chat with the president about a presidential expungement of your record, allowing you to practice." *I already have done so*, the senator thought. *Just need you to confirm here, buddy.*

"That's awfully grand, sir. But I've never heard of that."

"Neither have I, because I just created it upon Max telling me your story, which I want to hear more of. President Radcliffe and I worked closely together while he was the Illinois senator. I'm sure it's within his power to grant you special leave to practice law."

"Wow. How would I ever thank you?" Naim asked. It was the magic question.

"You already have by redeeming yourself. And your son, he's a remarkable kid. I'm sure you'll work with me to reform criminal justice. I'm running for president."

"Thanks, Sena...James. And, I certainly would work with you."

"I can imagine where your son got his smarts. And your lady granted him the looks. My people will be in touch to have you in

Albany and perhaps my DC office to get you a membership to the BAR Association."

"Well, thank you, again," Naim said and shook the senator's hand.

When he walked back up to Sinia, she asked, "What was that about?"

"A proposal."

"What kind and I hope not an indecent proposal," she said, laughing.

"No, he offered to help me with something."

"Oh, OK, must be private?"

"For now it is," he replied, and smiled. "Just know it's a dream realized. A game changer."

"Although, I don't know, congrats anyway," she said, and then added, "Now, we have to get going, I have a plane to catch."

"What do you mean?" He was taken aback.

"I'm going home. Time for me to get back to my world and out of yours."

He frowned.

"You're not happy that I'm leaving?" she asked.

"No, I'm not. While I should be, I also know that I loved you and you crushed me, but so many parts of me want you."

"And for that reason, I have to go to allow you to heal and for me to heal also. We can do this back at your place, but let's go before we make up here the same way we did last night."

CHAPTER 24

On Monday, December 28th, Brandy Scott was at her colossal desk in a corner office of the Times' New York City headquarters when she got an e-mail from an unknown recipient. Typically, she disregarded what seemed like SPAM, but the subject line NAIM BUTLER IS A FRAUD had her attention. She opened the e-mail and found two attached files. The following message was within the body:

Ms. Scott,

I thought it quite urgent to inform you that the man you've been dating, and I don't know how long that has been, but he has an extensive criminal record. The same has been attached for your review. I'm unsure of any of his misrepresentations, but he has an eighteen-year-old child with a woman that he wasn't married to. Again, a photo of the child's birth certificate has also been attached. I assure you that Mr. Butler is out to take you for your money by way of marrying you and then quickly divorcing you, as he has done in Chicago, New Orleans, and North Carolina, where he left his child's mother. Err on the side of caution and dump this loser before you lose your life savings to him like the other woman. How else do you think that he has made his money? I bet he told you real estate. That's a lie. Take care,

A Concerned Times Subscriber

Upon reading the text she smiled. She knew that there was something exceptionally charming and impeccable about Naim Butler. She couldn't fathom that she had fallen for his chicanery. She printed the two documents and then snatched them up from the printer beside her desk. She gave the birth certificate a cursory glance before setting it aside. She knew that he had a son, as he had told her that much. The criminal history was lengthier than he had let on, but that didn't alarm her. The ferocious gut punch came from the idea that he was a barbaric, womanizing, ex-con lining her up for a quickie divorce and depleting her accounts. Naim was towering, desirable, and always well-dressed with pleasing manners, like the men of the sixties that associated with the likes of Martin Luther King, Jr. She phoned her pal Quinn, who worked in crimes.

"Ms. Quinn," the woman said, "talk to me."

"It's Brandy. Remember when I told you that I met a guy last week?"

"Of course. It's been two weeks and about damn time you called with some details." Quinn Berkeley was the water cooler of the entire *Times*.

"Perhaps you have some details for me. He's a hot shot over at Baker and Keefe, Naim Butler, you know 'em?"

"Honey," she said quietly, "I screwed him. You hit the jackpot. Are you busy, we should have lunch and chat."

"Let's do it," Brandy replied, powering off her desktop.

"OK, let's head over to Hector's that new, happening spot. I'll pencil you in as a lunch date, and bill the *Times*. Meet me in the lobby in five." She hung up.

Brandy boarded an elevator, fuming, and headed for the lobby. Amazingly, Quinn was outside waving to get Brandy's attention. They both threw themselves inside of a taxi. "Eighty-fourth and Madison," Quinn said to the driver.

During the entire ride uptown, Brandy diligently attempted to block the idea of being conned by Naim. By the time they reached

Hector's she was also determined to get to the bottom of Quinn and Naim having sexual relations.

They walked into the packed eatery and was greeted by Donatello, the head host. They ordered drinks at the bar, then Brandy grabbed Quinn's hand, and said, "Quinn, I need to know everything about Naim Butler."

"Well, we could ask him, or the woman and big kid he's with," Quinn replied, looking at Naim, Sinia, and Marco at the restaurant's entrance. They looked pristine and made of money.

Brandy froze when she locked eyes with Naim.

Quinn grabbed Donatello's sleeve when he passed by. She whispered, "Who is the woman and kid with Naim Butler?"

"I wouldn't tell you if I knew."

Quinn started to probe further, but she watched Jonathan, the maitre'd approach the door and smile.

"And, I assure you that asking Hector will get you eighty-sixed, my dear. Hec and Naim go back to Tulane. I'd let it go here. It's like investigating him at his own home," Donatello said to the infamous crime reporter.

"I need a real drink," Brandy said to the bartender. She was captivated, and she didn't captivate easily. *Who is that woman?*

From the looks of things, she was about to find out.

———— ————

From behind the hostess, Naim was flabbergasted that Brandy and Quinn were perched at the bar, but he did what any gentleman and scholar would do since he possessed both peculiarities.

"Good afternoon, Brandy and Quinn. Meet my son and his mother," Naim said and then used his son to shift the reckless encounter by saying to him, they're editors at the *Times*. Perhaps, they may feature you in an article one day."

"Nice to meet you," Brandy said and smiled.

"Same here," Quinn added.

"Like wise," Marco said and shook their hands.

Sinia nodded.

"Well, I'll leave you to your lunch date," Naim said.

"Back at ya," Brandy replied, and then sipped her Tokyo Tea.

"What's that supposed to mean?" Sinia asked. She had the where's-my-Vaseline face on.

"We offered him to be left alone for his date, is there a problem?" Quinn asked. Her Brooklyn accent was apparent.

"I'm not a date, Hun," Sinia said.

"There's no problem," Naim said. "Sinia and Marco let's get to our table and leave these ladies to their lunch date." He could not believe Sinia.

They walked away and had a seat at the table. The waiter left them alone, and then Sinia asked Marco, "Can you leave your dad and I alone a sec?"

Marco looked perplexed. "Yes, ma'am," he said and went over to his spot at the bar where Stefon and he had sat twice.

"What's this about?" Naim asked just as baffled as his son.

"Let me explain something to you," she said and pointed an index finger at him. "You don't ever introduce me to some bitch that you're fooling around with as your son's mother. You have some nerve."

He furrowed his brows, trapped in a state of solid confusion. "You are his mother. What the hell are you talking about?"

Sinia pressed her lips together, and then through clenched teeth, she said, "Brandy Scott. You're not screwing her?"

"Hell no, but if I was what business of yours would that be?"

"You didn't have sex with that bitch?"

"Where are you getting this from? No."

"Your face."

Blank stare. "What? You didn't read that I had sex with that woman from my damn face."

"I didn't. I read it from your phone."

"You're high. There's nothing in my phone suggesting that I had sex with her and if I did her every day in Times Square that would be my prerogative. You should stay out of my phone."

"So you think you can play with my emotions?" she asked with venom in her eyes. "Layup with me and have sex with me, and still be the typical New York bachelor. You're a real piece of work."

"Am I? Wow. You're something else. I think it's high time you get through your head that we are done. Finished. Right about now, I'm thinking you should go back to North Carolina sooner than after New Years. Like on the next flight out."

"First you kicked me out of your house, now this," she said, raising her voice. She grabbed a glass of water from the table and tossed it into Naim's face.

"Mom," Marco said. He walked back over to the table. "What are you doing?"

It took all of Naim's might not to back hand her with thunderous force.

"What?" she yelled at Marco. "You're going to turn on me?"

"Let's go now," Naim said. "Marco outside," he added, pointing towards the door, and Marco complied.

Not Sinia.

"You can't tell me what to do. I know from you being in jail and all you're used to orders, but I give them. You're nothing but a two-bit criminal. You think because you've made it out the ghetto, live in Lenox Hill, and work for some fancy law firm you're some damn body."

"News flash," Naim said, wiping his face. "I am somebody."

"You are. Yes. Trash from the slums of Chicago that got lucky."

"It's not about luck," Naim said, opening his wallet. He handed a fifty to the waiter who refused it. "I am sorry about this, but you know me."

"Yes, Mr. Butler, we all do. Have a good afternoon." He then whispered, "Hector will never hear of this from us."

Sinia was fuming. "You know what. To hell with you, this restaurant, and this entire city," she said, heading towards the door. She flipped a middle finger at Brandy on the way out.

Outside, Naim saw Marco waving down a cab, and his visions of parental guidance were fading. Naim had gone from a dad to nothing in two weeks and was heartbroken about it. Being a father outweighed every other accomplishment he'd ever achieved.

Sinia, while looking back at Naim angrily, slid into the back of the cab. Marco closed the door behind her. He then tapped the front passenger window, and the driver rolled it down.

"Take her to JFK airport, please. Thank you."

"Marco, you better get into this cab," Sinia said, elbowing open the back door and stepping out. "Now."

"I'm afraid, I'm staying in New York, Mom. I'm not going to be in the middle of this. You and Dad need to cool down and resolve this rationally. But while you do, I'm staying here."

"You're choosing him over your own mother?" she asked and looked at him sternly. "Un-freakin'-believable."

Marco didn't reply. He stood there in silence because he saw the pain splashed on the woman's face that gave him life. Traffic began to clog and horns blared.

"Sinia," Naim said to her walking towards the taxi. "Let's cool down and reconvene on this topic tomorrow over the phone, but before this matter gets worse it's really best for you and I that you head to Raleigh tonight. Marco get in the cab and fly back to Raleigh with your mother. I'll send both of your things to you tomorrow."

"You've gotta be kidding me," Marco said. "I'm not going to be in the middle of some battle between you two. Respectfully, I'm going to go sit over there," he said, pointing to a set of tables outside of a small coffee shop, "while you two pull it together." He then turned and walked away before either of them could protest.

"Come on, lady. I have to go," the cab driver said. Good thing Madison Avenue was three-lanes and her antic only blocked one of them.

"This is unbelievable," Naim said. Hector's patrons were watching the show out of the windows and his good-boy image was being taxed. He handed the cabbie a twenty and said, "Run the meter and pull over, please."

Naim looked at Sinia and smirked. He then looked over at Marco and the reality of what the life of a baby mother entailed for a man having children out of wed lock became clear. *Never again*, he thought. At that point, he had to make the crucial decision of handling Sinia or

Marco. Quickly, he chose the lesser of the two evils and walked over to Marco.

"Dad," Marco said. "I'm not sure what's gotten into my mom, but I am going to Davis Hall, man."

"Firstly, let's get this straight. I am not 'man' save that for your friends. Secondly, if I've ever needed you, I can't say that I needed you more ever in life than right now. You have to go with your mother. There's no way you can make such a blatant decision that inadvertently picked me over her. You would irreparably destroy her, Marco. Now, I know how you feel about living here and Davis Hall, but right now despite how pissed I am, I'm not so half-witted or callous to have your mother heartbroken by you unintentionally. So, please just go with her and let her decide what she wants to do, and if that lands you in Raleigh tonight, I'll have the Baker and Keefe jet revved up to bring you back tomorrow. Do you understand?"

Marco curled his lip to one corner, and said, "No." He pushed back in the chair forcefully and it flipped over. "I'll do as you say because I get your point about hurting her. Just know that I'm not happy, Dad."

"That's fine. This'll be repaired," Naim said uncertainly, as they both walked back over to Sinia who held the cab driver hostage.

Marco opened the cab door and hopped in. "Mom, let's go," he said. Despite a cold glare at Naim, she complied.

Naim watched the cab pull away and thought about his walk home, as he ambled back into Hector's. He apologized to the wait staff, maitre'd, and then headed over to Brandy Scott.

"Pardon me, I can't be any more sincere as I say this: I'm very sorry and am deeply apologetic for what occurred here this afternoon. You may never want to chat with me again, but this was as new to me as it was to you. Have a good day, if you can after this show."

"I'm fine," she said. "I'll be in touch."

"I'll be waiting," he said and walked away. He stopped and turned back around. He looked at Quinn, and said, "Now, you have a story," before taking his walk home.

———— ————

"What did he mean by that?" Brandy asked Quinn.

"Well, when I said that I screwed him earlier, I didn't mean in the bedroom. I meant in the media. I had gotten a tip about his criminal past and questions arose about if he was falsely claiming to be an attorney over at B & K. After I wrote up a scathing report slamming the law firm for being so reckless and blatantly crass for falling for a Chicago conman, it was revealed that Naim never presented as an attorney and that they actually recruited him out of law school as a mitigation specialist. He only testified on client's behalf, never represented any. Then, I learned about his road to redemption and couldn't forgive myself for blasting him. We never figured out who e-mailed me the information about him."

"Did you say, e-mail?"

"Yes."

Brandy was stunned and simply sipped her drink again. "Why'd you say you screwed him?"

"Because I did. I messed up his livelihood and screwed up his image all because I didn't fact check. I put him on prosecutor's radar when he was doing good work, which they hated, but had nothing to refute his factual findings. But after my report, almost every one of them would submit motions to block him from testifying on clients behalf until the Second Circuit Court of Appeals ruled against them and they stopped. He has never looked back. I tried to write a new piece on him, but he has always declined any requests from me or any other media as far as I can tell."

CHAPTER 25

Sinia and Marco were in Naim's master bedroom. She packed her belongings. Marco had a seat on the bed and watched her.

"Why is this happening?" Marco asked her. "We didn't come to New York for this. This was supposed to be a fun trip. I mean, what happened at that restaurant, Mom?" He stared at her desperately looking for an answer.

She threw a blouse into her suitcase and then said, "You know, Marco, I messed up. I dropped the ball on this one. And on behalf of both of us, I apologize." She stopped and walked over to him. "Are you really happy here, Son? I mean, aside from all of what happened this afternoon?"

"Mom, I have not been happier. You have no idea what it's like to live life knowing you're nothing like a man who's supposed to be your dad, but then you meet your actual dad and it all becomes very clear."

"I see." She hopped onto the bed and sat next to him. "Are you mad at me about that?"

"Mom, no. Of course, not. You made a bad call. It's OK. I'm moving on from that, and you should, too. Would you believe when he came over to me that he asked me to go with you for one reason? Take a guess at why?"

"That bastard. I know he didn't tell you to get out and to go back with me." She was rolling her neck and waving her hands.

Marco shook his head. "No." He looked at her stiffly. "He asked me to go so that you wouldn't hurt. So that you wouldn't feel like I chose him over you. Now, that's the kind of man that I want to become. That took the kind of rare audacity that one has to gain through regular practice. I want to go to school here, and I want to be bonded with my mother and father." He put his arm around her shoulders and pulled her close to him. "You have had me seventeen years. Let him get a shot."

She couldn't believe how he was as charming as his dad and so young. "I love you, Marco."

"I love you, too, Mom."

"I tell you what," she said and stood up. "I'm happy for you Marco, and I'm actually glad Naim's your dad. He's a great man. A great man that I blew my shot with and I have to live with that. I just feel so rejected by him."

"Trust me, I like you two being together and happy, and wish he'd come around, but he has to do that."

"Are you my son or counselor?" she asked, closing her suitcase. "Help me take this downstairs."

"So, you're leaving?" he asked, and then shot her a deadpan look. "I'll pack," he said with thoughts of a private jet picking him up the next day from Raleigh.

"No...no," she said. "You stay here. I'm going to go," she said, calling up her US Airways app to search for flights.

"Mom." He didn't know what to think.

"Marco, I'm fine. Your dad and I will work out our drama. You're staying here. I'll be setting up a special account for you and redrafting my will."

"Why? Are you sick again, Mom?" Finally, he had the right moment to ask her.

"Nope, I just want things in order regardless. I'll even have your dad's firm handle it. Now grab those bags and take your mom to the airport."

He laughed. "Is that why you bought me a car?"

"Maybe," she said, walking out of the bedroom with him in tow. "And drive like a New Yorker, too. My flight departs in three hours."

———— ————

An hour later, Naim found himself surrounded by his pals, Hector and Derrick. He had apprised them of the afternoon's happenings. They were at Ariana Restaurant and Bar, plowing through a five-hundred-dollar per person brunch including caviar and a bottle of Dom Perignon, which was already empty.

"I'm surprised no one on your staff text you about this, Hector," Derrick said and furrowed his brows.

"I'm not," Hector replied. "They like Naim, you too, of course, they'd try to brush this under the rug," Hector replied. "What's the move now?"

Both men's head whipped in Naim's direction.

"You two gotta be kidding." Naim laughed. "I called you two for this emergency tete-a-tete to tell me the move. I'm lost."

"Me, too," Derrick said. "All of a sudden she's jealous of you having a love interest, but she was married for fifteen years. You're shitten me."

"And Brandy Scott is a looker, not taking anything from Sinia. The crazy ones are usually beautiful."

"Show me to the nearest river to jump in, since you two can't help me," Naim said, and then told the waiter, "Jack shots. And keep them coming." He pressed his American Express in the man's hand, and said, "Run a tab."

"More caviar, too. And keep it coming," Derrick said, and then added, "On his tab, too." They all chuckled.

"I'm glad that you have found time for laughter," Naim said.

"Nai," Hector said, tapping him. "So, you don't want her, right?"

"Nah, bro. I can't bring myself to get around the past. It's just principle. Personally, I think she'd cross me like that again. How can I ever believe that she has my best interest?"

"I can dig it," Derrick said. "This is New York City and an arrest for being Black is very possible. You could even fall victim to a mistaken identity arrest, and she'd leave you all over again."

"Right," Naim said, and thought, *this coming from a damn prosecutor*, before taking back a shot. He looked at his phone after receiving a text alert.

My Boy: Dad. Dropping mom at JFK. Will be home when u get there. Where are u

Naim: Are you texting and driving? :(

My Boy: No. In the garage at your house

Naim: OK why aren't you leaving, 2?

My Boy: 2 much to text. But we talked. I'm staying with her blessing

Naim: Let me know when you're heading from the port

My Boy: OK

Naim: Tell her that I love her and will call her later

My Boy: OK

"That was Marco. He's dropping her at the airport, but he's staying. He said with her blessing and he'd explain later."

"Sounds promising," Derrick said. "Get out your gun and sleep with it under your pillow." They laughed.

Hector said, "She's leaving and you get your boy. Two for two, Nai."

"I hear you, but I was fouled behind the three-point-line. For the three points, I need to get one, Brandy Scott, back into my clutches."

"Yeah, you'd really be winning," Hector replied.

"Game buzzer beater," Derrick added.

CHAPTER 26

Brandy Scott exited the elevator on her floor at the *Times* and stopped at the desk of her good pal, Jenny, en route to her office. "Do we have someone who can track down the physical address of an IP address without a FOIA request?"

"We're the *New York Times*, one of the grandest papers in the world, what do you think?" Jenny replied, looking at Brandy puzzled.

"Who?"

"You," Jenny said. "Your *Times* creds can get you into the White House, so certainly you can get what you need from law enforcement with your smile and wit at the precinct."

Brandy went to her office, powered on her computer, and got the number for the Nineteenth Precinct, then phoned her acquaintance.

"Yes?"

"It's Brandy."

"Well, hello there. You must miss me. Haven't seen you since the day that you stormed out of my apartment."

How could she forget that day? It was the day that she had met Naim Butler.

"I wouldn't bet on that, but I need your help."

"Interesting. You dumped me."

"At least three weeks ago. Get over it. Can you help me?"

"Maybe. Depends."

"Are you still in the forensics department? I need to track down who sent me an e-mail."

"Send over the e-mail."

"Can't do that. It's from a source, and sensitive in nature. I can send the IP address, though."

"Send it now."

"Done. Can I get this back tomorrow?"

"No," he said. She huffed. "Hold your horses," he said and put her on hold. He returned, and said, "Staples Store at Sixty-Sixth Street and Second Avenue."

"OK, thanks," she replied and hung up before he asked her for payment. She had the Staples Store telephone number on the screen and got an associate on the line. "Hi, I was there earlier and used the self-service computer stations to send an e-mail and it was never delivered. I need proof that I was there this morning. Do you happen to have recordings?"

"Yes, we do. What time were you here?"

She consulted the e-mail and found the time. "Nine-fifteen," she said, "a.m."

"Hold a second," the man replied and placed her on hold. He returned, and said, "This must be you, Sinia Ferguson-Love. Black hair, tall, used your American Express at nine-fifteen to pay for seventeen minutes of Internet usage."

"Yes, that's me," Brandy said with her suspicions confirmed. "Could you print, scan and e-mail what's in front of you, especially a still shot of me from the video to Brandy Scott. She's in human resources at the *Times* and I need to prove that I was there and did forward my resume to her this morning."

"Sure, what's Brandy's e-mail address?"

Brandy hung up and waited for the documents to be sent to her. She had no plans to use them, but they'd go a long way in her decision with Naim going forward. She actually liked him, and it had been some time since a man made her feel special and admired. Her biological clock ticked and her marital clock tocked. She needed to handle both.

Brandy Googled, Naim Butler, and found a few references, mostly dealing with legal cases that he worked on, and there was a piece on his being made partner at Baker and Keefe. Quinn Berkeley's article was there along with her later correction piece. His federal indictment was there, too. Seven counts of access device fraud, and a total loss amount of four-hundred-seventy-four-thousand dollars purloined between the seven compromised corporate American Express credit cards. She was shocked to learn that he had investigated and solved three murders for clients of Baker and Keefe's Pro bono Project. *That must be where he made his name and money*, she thought. There was nothing in his personal life beyond what Quinn had reported.

She checked her e-mail and found one from her new *source* at Staples. She opened it, then the attachment printed it and saved it on her desktop. She then took the paper from the printer and examined it. Sinia was a pretty woman, but a lunatic. She decided to look her up next.

The Google search turned up fairly bland details about Sinia. She was an elitist of the Raleigh/Durham millionaire scene, divorced with one child. She owned a delivery service and received money from a cosmetic surgery accident that caused her to develop breast cancer. It was reported that she was being treated by the infamous UNC physician and professor, Austin Mills.

Brandy turned away from her computer and walked to her office window overlooking Eighth Avenue. She took in a deep view of the sky and looked across the river into New Jersey. She heard someone clear their throat from her office door.

"What'chu working on. Must be good to need an IP address?" Jenny asked.

"Can't tell you, yet. I assure you it'll be good." She didn't want to be put on any crappy assignments while she tried to crack the case before her.

"I see. Well, get to it. There's nothing out there, but..."

"My next story."

"You got it," she said and walked away.

CHAPTER 27

On December 30th, a Hump Day, Naim was catching up on his case load when Ginger buzzed him.

"A Mrs. Daphne Pettiwick, from Davis Hall, on one."

Naim picked up the phone. "Naim Butler. Good morning."

"Good morning, Mr. Butler," the woman said. "I'm Daphne Pettiwick from Davis Hall. I head a little section at the school that works to keep our budget balanced," she said.

"I see." *Oh, really?*

"As you know, a school with this status and prestige needs a huge endowment, because tuitions alone can't keep the school up. We rely on the support of our alumni and the parents of our students to help keep Titanic from sinking."

"Oh?"

"It's been brought to my attention that your son saw some equipment that needed updating and we've noticed that he hasn't committed to starting Davis Hall this coming semester. I've assumed the missing equipment was stopping him."

"We did notice that the pianos were out being repaired. But the holiday overshadowed his school prep. Pardon us."

"No problem. So he is going to join us?"

"Yes, I have your schedule of fees here and will take care of tuition today."

"Perfect. Davis Hall would be very grateful if you could squeeze in a donation of fifty-thousand-dollars, too. That's reasonable to assure that your promising prodigal son would get the best out of our music program."

"Let me run this by his mother, and I'll get back to you."

"Certainly, Mr. Butler. Here's my direct line."

Naim wrote down the number, hung up, and then called Sinia.

"Hey, hey."

"I know that it's early. Are you awake?"

"Just laying here staring at the ceiling."

"OK, you remember that I suggested Davis Hall would hit us up for a donation?"

"Yup. They already have, huh? He hasn't even attended a class."

"Well to guarantee that he does, they've requested fifty big ones. A Mrs. Daphne Pettiwick called and specifically asked for that amount. She mentioned upgrading music equipment."

"Interesting. Marco seems to think it costs nearly a quarter-million to overhaul what they have."

"I'm sure that he knows," Naim said.

"Oh, Naim, just write them a check for the two-fifty using the checkbook that I left with Marco. He knows my signature. I need to have signature cards sent over to you so that you can add yours to it for times like this."

"No problem." Naim had questions, but her nice attitude suppressed them.

"If that is all."

"It is. Thanks."

Naim hung up and smirked at their bland telephone call. He called Daphne Pettiwick back.

"Yes, Mr. Butler."

"We'd like to make a donation of three-hundred-thousand, Mrs. Pettiwick."

Pettiwick's voice perked up. "Well, that's very grand, Mr. Butler."

"We have a small request or two. We'd like every cent used in the music department and we'd like this to be donated anonymously."

"No problemmo. Of course."

"The check will be sent over via courier service in the next hour, or so."

"Perfect, and tell Marco, welcome to Davis Hall."

"Will do," Naim replied and hung up.

He called Sinia back.

"Sorry to bother you again, but we need to discuss money."

"I talked to Max Devers at the firm and he's working with the bank to get you access to the account you made the donation from."

"If that's what you want," he said and paused. After quietly rehearsing his lines, he said, "We have to get this straight."

"And we will."

"Not that," he said dismissively. "I'm not sure how much money you make, and I don't care, but gifts of quarter-million-dollars will be joint efforts. I'm sending the school three-hundred-thousand, which we will split fifty-fifty."

"Oh, Nai, that's fine. Just know that we won't have to argue about money."

"That would be uncomfortable."

"I understand completely," she said. "In the last year since Baker and Keefe have been handling my investments, my net worth has increased nearly forty-percent. I talked to Max about that this morning."

"Did you now?"

"Yes, we discussed my will," she said. "He suggested you'd want no parts of the planning, so we had a new will drawn up without your input."

"He was right."

"Good, the new will has been e-mailed to Ginger for you to put up."

"OK, let me ask you this. Marco seems to think that your cancer may be back. Any confirmation on that?"

"None. I'm fine," she said quickly.

He didn't believe her.

He said, "Know that our problems aside, I'd support you one-hundred-percent to be nursed back to good health."

"Nai," she said with aggression in her voice. "I'm fine."

"OK. I have to run," he said and hung up. He had no desire to argue.

After lunch, Ginger came into Naim's office and informed him that she had printed Sinia's wills. "Here's the original and one copy."

"I don't want to see them. Delete the incoming e-mail and delete it from your computer's trash bin, also."

"Right on top of that, boss."

"Put them in manila envelopes. Seal them both with red wax. Write the date on the envelope. And put them in the safe. I never want to see them."

"No problem. I'll take care of it right away," Ginger said and then walked toward the door. She stopped, and asked, "Boss, is she all right?"

"So she says," he replied, "she doesn't confirm anything to me or Marco."

"Sorry to hear that. You'd be a super support system."

"Thanks, Ginger. You know, after you get those wills put away, you can take off for the day with pay."

"Geesh. Thanks. I need to compliment you more often."

"Don't bet the house on that."

They laughed and she left the office.

CHAPTER 28

Naim was having breakfast in bed on the first Monday of the New Year. Marco appeared wearing a down jacket over a sweater, and a button-up, with jeans. He carried a leather MCM book bag. "Good morning, Pater," he said, "I'm off for my first day."

"Sounds promising," Naim said, "and you're certain you don't want a ride? It's quite cold in New York City in January."

"Dad cut the crap," he replied, laughing. "I cannot get a ride to school. Not on the first day. Maybe in a few weeks when my Butler's smile and charm take over the school, then, I can make getting a ride to school cool."

"Spoken like a true leader. Never follow Marco. Always lead."

"Always," replied Marco. "I have a Metro card, Dad, from Ginger, fully loaded. I'm taking the bus and can walk the other couple of blocks."

"OK, cool. Lunch money?"

"Dad, you gave me a hundred bucks yesterday for a trip to the movies with Stef. I still have most of that."

"No doubt. Well, get going, and shoot me a text when you arrive, too."

"Dad, I can fight. Good. And will. It wasn't easy growing up a smart pretty-boy. I fought a lot. Don't worry about me."

"Oh, Lord," Naim said, laughing. "This is New York and every time you're not near me, I'll worry. Just be safe."

"Cool. I gotta go."

"Peace, Son."

"Back at ya," Marco said and left for school.

———— ————

Brandy Scott and her friend from Baker and Keefe, Arnold Ishkhanian, arrived at Hector's at three-thirty and were seated at a table in the back of the place. They were out of sight from the patrons that walked in; just the way that Brandy wanted it.

"Perfect seats," she said.

"Of course, we got the deal done for Hector to get this place. It's marked as a historic landmark," Arnold replied.

They ordered libations, and Brandy watched the cooks doing their thing behind the glass, preparing for the lunch crowd. She also kept her eye on the tables up front. "He's getting late," she said.

"Why are you so antsy to see him?"

"I can't tell you that. It's personal and private."

"Brandy, don't start. I'm not some source that you can use to track down my colleagues, but not tell me why."

"I am not treating you that way, either, because I won't tell you my desire to see Naim. It's no big deal, Arnold, trust me. And it won't cost you any trouble. I promise."

"You don't know how he'll take you being here unannounced."

"As far as he'd know, this was a chance meeting."

"Yeah, all right."

Marco and Stefon, a suave, blonde haired kid walked into Hector's and took seats at the bar. They nodded at the wait staff and ordered drinks like the regulars of the place. Marco was getting used to his new lifestyle.

"Excuse me for a sec," Brandy said. She got up and walked over to where the two teens sat, drinking Sprites. "Hey, guys," she said. "My name is Brandy. What's yours?" She was amazed at their manners. They both stood up to address her.

"Well, I'm Stefon," he replied, "and this is—"

"Jason," the other boy said quickly.

"Nice to meet you," she said, and then added, "let me ask you—"

The maitre'd walked up to her and tapped her shoulder. "Don't even think about it," he said. "Don't bother my customers at all. I know you're new around here, but don't push your luck."

"Come on, take it easy," she replied hesitantly, strolling back towards her own table.

"You're lucky Hector didn't catch you," the maître d' said to her back.

She sat down and Arnold said, "You're going to get kicked out and banned. Hell, all media will be banned because of you. That's not the reputation that you want."

"I was doing my job," she said defiantly.

"Don't do your damn job here," Arnold replied with a smile. "You need to just call the brother and stop the games."

———— ————

At the bar, Stefon said, "Why'd you lie and tell her your name was Jason?"

"She's a reporter," Marco said. "I think that she played a part in my mom and dad's flare-up. Don't talk to her at all, bro."

"Damn, I'd like to hit that. Did you see her rack?"

"I did, and she'd probably let you Jon B," Marco said and laughed. "But you may regret it."

"Never."

"My man, you need to be mindful of a reporter's job. They look for the stories that destroy people, not uplift them. You'll see in the future."

"Whatever. You're too serious."

"Am I? Why'd you thought Giancarlo rescued us? They know all of the New York players and they know that your dad is a prosecutor and my dad is also in law enforcement, too. We're targets."

Giancarlo came over. "My apologies. We like to keep this place press free."

"See that," Marco said. "Who is she?"

"Brandy Scott. She's a rising player at the *Times*. What did she want?"

"Our names. I lied from the door," Marco said.

"Good move. Lunch is on the house today."

Stefon shrugged. "I'd still fuck her."

CHAPTER 29

Brandy left Hector's angry with herself and it kept her awake that night. The following morning, she did the unthinkable.

"Good morning, Brandy," Ginger said. "Have a seat. Would you like coffee?"

"Thank you, Ginger, yes," Brandy replied, taking a chair. "I'm sorry to come over unannounced." She sat her briefcase on her lap.

"It's no problem. He seemed delighted that you were here," Ginger said, making the coffee. Naturally, she knew all of the pertinent facts about Brandy.

"That's encouraging," Brandy said when Naim walked into the reception area of his home office.

"Welcome to my home, I mean, office, Brandy," he said, shaking her hand. "Let's chat in the family room. I've had some refreshments prepared. The office is nice, but you're welcome to my home."

"Thanks, Naim," she replied, following him. "I'm sure you know, but this is a nice bachelor pad."

"That's not my choice," he said and smiled. "Perhaps, you can help me change this into a family dwelling." He winked.

"Funny. No matter the situation, you'll be your bewitching self."

"Is that troubling to you, Brandy?" he asked. "Take a seat." He gestured to a long armless sofa. A tray of tea and cookies sat on a serving cart near them.

"Thanks. And, no, it's not."

"I suppose that's why you came here?" He sat next to her. Close, but not close enough.

"This is why I came," Brandy said and handed him some papers from her briefcase. "They were e-mailed to me. I tracked the senders IP address to a Staples a few blocks from this house. And it seems that the document and e-mail were sent by Sinia Love."

If he was surprised, he hid it well. He looked page by page at his criminal history, which was a boring read at this point of his life. It didn't define him; only narrated a part of his past. "Everyone has a history, this you know. Mine just happens to be criminal."

She looked him square in the eyes. "Very true, which is why I am here this morning."

"OK. Explain."

"Nothing to explain. I don't care why she sent this to me. My thing is this," she looked down at the floor coyly and then directly into his eyes, "I like you, Naim. A lot. And that hasn't happened in a long time. It's as if I'm attracted to everything about you. Seeing your home makes me even more into you. Not for your money. But your living space says a lot about you."

"So, it's settled. Let's get married," he said, smiling. She giggled. "On a serious note," he scooted closer to her, "I adore you. You're smart and beautiful inside and out. I am not fond of my criminal history, but it made me into the man that you're attracted to. Every woman that I've ever dated reacted differently to my past. I did tell you the basics, but I just don't feel compelled to get a copy of my police record and tell the women I'm *dating* each and every crime I've ever committed like I'm some rapist or molester."

"I understand that, and I don't expect you to have done that."

"Well, Sinia, the scorned woman that sent you this did," he said and tossed the papers into the fire place.

"How so?"

"She was with me when I was arrested for using stolen credit cards. The actual crime had happened three years before I had met her, and the entire time that I knew her I had not committed any unlawful acts. But at my bail hearing in order to have me denied bail, the prosecutor ran down all of my priors and Sinia heard all of it. Her main reason for not sticking by me was because of my past, and me not telling her every morsel of it."

"Wow. Now that's deep. I think that was an excuse to move on because you probably was a bad boy to her and her family and friends. So rather than be seen as dating a criminal, she bailed."

"Same thing all of my friends said. But I'm just not going to say to people 'hey, I have ten priors' like I'm a serial killer." They laughed at his delivery of the true statement. He had to lighten the mood.

Brandy's sensuous mouth curved into a smile. "You're an excellent man, Naim, and now that we got all of that cleared up, where does that leave us? What's the nature of your relations with her now?"

"She's back in Raleigh and our son lives here with me. We're over and that's been nearly seventeen-years now." He wrapped his arm around her.

Brandy slipped from his grasp, stood up, but didn't get far. He stood in front of her at arm's length. She swallowed nervously. Suddenly what had appeared to be a large family room at first glance now were the proportions of a two-gallon fish bowl. Her pretty brown eyes moved warily over Naim. He was wearing a gray suit with baby-blue pin stripes, the jacket fits snugly over his wide shoulders; with a white dress shirt and navy-blue and baby-blue stripped tie, he looked devastatingly attractive and infinitely menacing.

He made no effort to touch her. His stance was a curious one. But his dark-brown eyes scanned her from head to toe, and then back to her face. "You're a beautiful woman." She stood there. "Are you afraid of me, Brandy?"

"No. I am simply surprised that I am actually into you more than the norm."

"It's OK to be into me more than the norm. I am not a normal kind of guy." He smiled tightly, and his hand reached out towards her, but she took a small step back.

He stepped closer, lifted a brow and a ruthless smile appeared. His eyes were as glued to her as a mouse on a trap.

He moved closer.

"No more pretending, Brandy Scott," he said, lifting a hand and tilting her chin with his fingers; his eyes intent on her face.

Vicious color rushed to her cheeks. She wasn't sure it was because of the warmth of his hand on her face, or her sheer attraction to the whole package of Naim Butler. Tentatively, he slid his hand to her slim waist and pulled her close to him, locking his hands carefully behind her back. She was too astounded to resist, even a little.

"I know I've been foolish in the past. But I have allowed you into my mind and soul. It was not my intention to hurt you with the drama that happened at Hector's or with my past. I want you, Brandy. The past has no bearing on where my life is now, or where a future is with you."

Brandy swallowed nervously, unsure where Naim was leading the conversation. Deep inside a tiny flicker of mutual attraction unfurled. "So, are you asking me a question?"

"From the second I set eyes on you, I wanted you," Naim began in a deceptively seductive tone. An erection had formed in his pants and pressed subtly against her. "Right now, I'm asking to get to know you more deeply and perhaps exclusively." His hands tightened behind her back, pulling her closer, as though he was frightened she would say no and leave.

"Yes, Naim. I think that I want to date you exclusively," she replied, and raised her hands and palmed them on his broad chest because she desired to touch him.

She was powerless.

It was the pin-stripes.

"Good," he said and gave her a wicked smile. "Now that's settled, you may kiss the bride," he said and placed his lips on hers.

Delicately probing with her tongue, she initiated a kiss that was sensitive and passionate, adoring and giving; a kiss like no other they had shared with anyone in the past.

When they parted, he frowned, and said, "I'm all dressed up for a court appearance, but how about dinner tonight?"

"Yes, why not? And not Hector's."

"Definitely not. Text me your address, and I'll pick you up at six."

"How about five, but I'll pick you up," she said and pressed a finger to his lips before he could protest. "Let's not argue about this. This isn't a competition, but I can treat you, as well as, you treat me, Mr. Butler."

He stood there for a moment staring at her. Admiring her zeal. He said, "You know, mutual intimacy and romanticism is what I've missed in this life."

Her only reply was that she would see him at five, as he walked her to the front door.

CHAPTER 30

"Let's take attendance," the Honorable Jeannette Bowers said, settling on the bench. She was a jovial, Bronx native with spunk.

The AUSA stood, and said, "Ralph Jacobs for the Government, Your Honor."

"Trevor Milan, on behalf of Mason Carter, Judge," Milan said and smiled.

"And, I see you have Naim Butler at your side looking his absolute sartorial best, Mr. Milan. Good morning."

"Good morning, Judge," Naim stood and said.

"And, Mr. Carter is present, the person that has us all here. Let's see," she said and shifted in her seat, "for sentencing. So far so good." Both lawyers agreed. "Let's get to it then. I have before me a pre-sentence report, along with letters from Mr. Carter's family and friends, sentencing memorandums from the Government and Mr. Milan, and lastly, a brief that outlines mitigation circumstances by Mr. Butler. Probation has determined that Mr. Carter is deemed a career offender with a starting guideline range of 188-235 months sentence exposure because he has two prior drug convictions. Mr. Jacobs tell me about that."

"Certainly, Your Honor," Jacob said and stood. He was sharply dressed as expected but extraordinarily tall. Jacob's and all of his six-ten frame moved to the well of the courtroom like a giant. "In 2009, the defendant was convicted of possession with the intent to distribute heroin on two different occasions. He was sentenced to serve three years for both offenses, which were to run concurrently. It's those two crimes that evidence the 4B1.1 enhancement according to the United States Sentencing Guidelines." He returned to his seat.

"Before you sit," the judge said, "Tell me the dates of these two convictions."

"May twentieth and May thirty-first in the same year."

"OK, you've responded to Mr. Milan's motion for a departure and you opposed the defense's motion," she consulted the Government's motion, "because you believe that Mr. Carter is indeed a career offender, but it seems that you base that solely on the definition, and not looking squarely at the defendant. I don't see how a twenty-two-year-old with this record could be deemed a career-anything."

"Well, Your Honor," Jacobs said, "Congress and the Sentencing Commission has a wide breadth of information analyzed before they enact the sentencing enhancements. And in this case, I find it clear that Mr. Carter is a career-offender."

"Interesting. That same Commission enacted section 4A1.3, and I am going to use that section to grant the defense's motion because clearly, the defendant's criminal past is over-represented in the guidelines. You can take a seat."

Milan whispered to Carter, a quiet, slim, man that sat stoically. "I think that she's on our side."

"Now that that's settled," the judge said consulting the probation officer's report and sentencing recommendation, "I just can't put this young man away for 188-235 months with such a relatively minor criminal history. Fifteen-years to nineteen-years for a reverse sting operation is not appropriate for this defendant. Quite frankly, there was no robbery, there were no kilos of drugs, no money to be found, and, most notably, no house. I understand that this sting is designed to get guns off the street, and being a convicted felon in possession of a firearm would have earned the defendant a trip to jail for not more than five years, and I am just not going to send him away for three-four times that for a fictional crime. A crime that could not possibly happen. And I hope that I am making it very clear my position on these sort of arrests. With that, before we get to step two of the sentencing process, I need to determine how I plan to depart from the fifteen-nineteen year absurd advisory range. Any suggestions?"

Milan stood first. "Yes, Judge, I'd like to ask that Mr. Carter is sentenced with his guideline range had he not been deemed a career offender. That would be 70-87 months." He sat and smiled. Things were going according to plan.

Jacob was quick to his feet. "That's too lenient, Your Honor. Regardless of ATF's mission, Carter agreed to rob a drug stash house. I suggest that we take Mr. Carter from category six to five in the same level of thirty-one and the range should be 168-210 months."

"OK, but that's not a difference from the 188-235," the judge said. "For the record, the departure motion is granted, but now I am going to entertain the defense's motion for a variance, and I'd like Mr. Butler to get this mitigation evidence on the record. I'll advise you prematurely that I am certainly considering granting a variance downward in time with respect to that motion just based on the paper submission."

"But, Your Honor..."

She held up a stiff hand and gave Jacob a wicked glare. "Don't but Your Honor me," she said sharply. "You'll get your chance to express aggravating factors, but for now I'm just looking to complete the record with why I made my decisions today because I've surmised that your office will undoubtedly appeal, and I do not want to be overturned."

Everyone heard the loud cannon blow the prosecutor out of the courthouse. Not only was the judge going to sentence the defendant the way she wanted, she wasn't going to leave the prosecutor any room to appeal to the Third Circuit Court of Appeals for a re-sentencing.

Naim strolled methodically to the witness stand and swore to tell the truth.

"Mr. Butler," the Judge said, "you've submitted a thoroughly detailed mitigation paper outlining several things leading to Mr. Carter's arrest in this matter. While normally your submission suffices to demonstrate those factors and your appearance isn't necessary, I've asked you here today to orally express what you have in writing."

"Certainly, Your Honor. Where would you like me to start?"

"Just provide for the record a truncated edition of your findings."

"Judge, I had the opportunity to visit with Mr. Carter's family and it appears that he was abandoned and driven to a life in the streets as a teen. He had two drug addicted parents and raised himself to be the man that he is today. When arrested he was a college student, although failing, I found through talking to him that all he needed was a push, a pat on the back, and perhaps he would have had better grades. What's not in the report was a scenario that Mr. Carter told me about him once meeting with classmates for a study group which he felt extremely out of place because he had never interacted with people in such a way. A close inspection of Mr. Carter's school records evidence that his high school classes were completed at a disciplinary school because of his poor adjustment to public school and his harsh home life. This spilled over into his adult life and affected his college adjustment. He seemed extremely hopeful about getting a second opportunity to finish college. He also wants to get therapy and training to maneuver through life as a successful and law abiding man. I suggest that the probation department assist him with getting out of his current living situation and into some programs that can help him rework his thinking. Certainly, what he needs to learn to stop peddling drugs to feed himself won't be obtained in a prison."

After Naim's testimony, he took a seat next to Milan and continued to watch the show. He remembered the mitigation specialist that briefed the court when he was sentenced nearly twenty-years earlier. It was that moment that he had truly decided if a stranger could believe enough in him to give him a chance to turn his life around then he could. He could also help someone else in the same fashion. He came out of his daze, just after Carter's mother had spoken briefly about her son, and Carter said a few apologetic words to the judge.

After careful thought, the judge said, "I'm only going to depart one criminal history level downward from six to five. And then I am going to vary pursuant to section 5K2.0 for the various reasons that I heard today; chiefly, the defendant's lack of guidance, upbringing, and his potential to be a law abiding citizen in the future. Had Mr. Carter not been deemed a career offender his guideline range with the drugs and robbery would have been 121-151 months. But, I find that because no drugs were involved in this case and were in fact wholly a fiction, I am determining that the drug quantity is zero. There was also no robbery, so the punishment for it should be zero. However, guns were recovered and simple possession of a gun by a convicted felon would have been a sentence very low, so I am going to vary to level twenty in criminal history category three for a range of 41-51 months, and sentence you Mr. Carter to fifty-one-months imprisonment to be followed by eight years of supervised release. And I admonish the Government that it shouldn't continue to invade poor communities targeting people for reverse sting operations with an expectation that judges will put people like Mr. Carter away for fifteen or more years. This sting should be reserved for gun traffickers and people with a perverse history of robberies."

"Thank you, Your Honor," Carter said, as the US Marshal stood behind him with his handcuffs out.

"Before you go," the judge said, "I want you to know that I was actually thinking of 120-months for an even ten years. You have eight years of probation after serving the fifty-one-months to pull your life together as Mr. Butler testified. Make it count, because I assure you, if you violate this probation with a new case, you'll face five years in jail and I promise to give you all of it to run consecutively to whatever time you receive for the new case. Keep that in mind on your journey, Mr. Carter. That is all. We're adjourned."

"You got off very easy," the prosecutor said to Carter as the marshal escorted him out of the courtroom. "Thanks to that criminal."

"Ex-criminal, sweetheart," Naim said and blew Jacob a kiss. "I win and you lose."

"Be nice, you two," Milan said, smiling. "Let's go, Naim, we have a celebratory lunch to get to."

CHAPTER 31

When Naim arrived at his desk, Ginger tossed a slip of paper onto his keyboard and smiled. "Henry Winthrop would like you to have a late lunch with him and a friend at Grand Central Oyster Bar and Restaurant at three-thirty," she said.

Naim looked at the paper. "His friend?" He furrowed a puzzling brow at her. It was already three, he had already had lunch, and the paper had urgent written on it.

"He didn't mention who, even after I inquired, but your calendar was empty so I accepted for you."

"No problem," Naim said.

"Also, Milan called and faxed over a Notice of Appeal with regards to the Carter case. The Government isn't happy about the fifty-one-month sentence." She handed him a document. "Here's a copy of it."

"Jacob works fast, I see," said Naim.

"Well, yes, there's scuttlebutt that he didn't like your input and finds your appearance on federal dockets offensive."

"What's he going to do when the US President fully expunges my past making way for me to join the BAR? I'll be looking for cases assigned to him, just to kick his ass."

"Get 'em, boss."

"Get Milan on the line for me, please."

Seconds later the phone chimed, and Naim picked up. "Good afternoon, Milan."

"Hey, Naim, what's up?"

"I won't keep you, I read the appeal notice. There is an organization kicking up steam in DC called, Reverse-Sting Awareness. I'm going to get their fee to write an amicus brief in the Carter matter addressing how the stings racially target the poor, Black and Latino communities."

"OK, perfect. Keep me posted."

"Will do." Naim hung up.

———— ————

At three-thirty, Naim walked through the busy Grand Central train station passing an Apple Store, before he walked up the stairs to the station's namesake oyster bar. It was a place frequented by New Yorkers that liked how the train station's noise masked their conversations. He spotted Henry Winthrop at a table with a strongly built gentleman in a weird suit. The man had ear length gold wet hair like a Canadian. He didn't recognize him.

Henry and his guest stood as Naim approached the table and proffered his hand. "Naim Butler, I'd like you to meet Kevin Curry."

The men shook hands and had seats.

"Drink?"

"Voss for me," Naim said.

Winthrop ordered waters around and menus were handed out before he went on. "Naim, Kevin is a bit of a quandary and asked me to meet him here at once. As you can see his hair is a bit wet."

"I thought that it was recently styled," Naim said, and then smiled.

"It was," Kevin said, "by the New York Harbor after I took a swim in it."

"It's January and that's illegal." Naim's eyes widened.

"It is, and two thugs had me at gun point on a tour cruising to Ellis Island, so I sought refuge in the water and swam like my life depended on it, because it did."

"Who saved you from the water?" Naim was holding back laughter.

"No one. I swam like a fish to Lady Liberty and saw a dock with a ladder. I found a bathroom and used the hand-dryer to get this far. I got warm and dried my clothes a little and then mingled with the tourists right onboard the ferry for the return trip."

"OK, why am I here, Bud?" Naim said. "Let's get to it."

"Why did the men hold you at gun point?" Winthrop asked.

"Well, it wasn't a holdup, you know?"

Naim chuckled. "I didn't, but go on."

"I'm set to testify against some corrupt bankers and I'm thinking, they're some soft knaves, but they're being backed by the mob. I should have known when the dead fish was left on my car two months back. I've been hiding real good until today. I'm leaving the prosecutor's office and two guys follow me."

"You're in deep shit," Naim said. He looked around for goons, preparing to take cover.

"It's complicated, Naim," Winthrop said. "See, he was supposed to lie on the stand to get the bankers off, but the mob has decided they don't want him to lie anymore because they want to replace the bankers with new people. And because he knows this, they want Kevin dead."

"They're shitten me. I'm not ready to die."

Naim laughed.

"And that's where you come in, Naim."

"How so? I'm not a hit man," Naim replied and chuckled. This was comical to him.

"But, certainly, you know people." Kevin looked deadly serious.

"Hold on. Let me check my contacts," Naim said, scrolling through his phone jokingly. "Nope, no gunmen here."

"Come on, Naim," Kevin said. "I need your help."

"You need help that I don't provide."

"Kevin," Winthrop said, "he's not a hit man and I didn't invite him here for that."

"Why then?"

"Yes, why?" Naim was on the verge of terminating his friendship with Henry Winthrop and returning the multi-million dollar check that he had written for the rights to Marco's album.

"The assistant US attorney on the banker's case is Derrick Adams. I need you to help Kevin work this out so that he's not thrown under the jail for obstruction of justice or killed by mobsters."

Naim thought about it. "I have to say that this is a very tall order."

"Name your price," Kevin said.

Is this a Progressive commercial? "I don't want any stolen Wall Street or mob money," Naim replied and smiled. "You're asking me, a devout defense strategist to work with a prosecutor, albeit my best friend, he's a cop. That just doesn't sit well with me," Naim said, just in case he was being recorded.

"Ah, I see," Winthrop said.

"Do you?" Naim replied.

"Perhaps Kevin, we need to get you an attorney and have them do this, but Naim I'd want you apart of this the entire step of the way."

"Fine, I know just the attorney," Naim said and called up Trevor Milan. Into his phone, he said, "Hey, Milan, sorry to bother you again, but remember that favor that I owed you. I have a huge payment for you."

———— ————

Naim walked out of Grand Central Station and headed a few feet away to the front of the Grand Hyatt Hotel. He had the bellman whistle down a cab for him to get away quickly. He wanted no parts of Kevin's mob worries and was glad that he was able to offer the job of negotiating with a prosecutor to Milan. His phone buzzed as he hopped into the cab.

"Max, how are ya?" Naim said, greeting his pal.

"Great, Nai, thanks for asking. Just a heads up that I finalized Sinia's will and I'm happy that you steered her to Baker and Keefe to handle it."

"Of course."

"Have you read the will?"

"No. No plans to either. I had it sealed and placed in a safe."

"As you wish," Max said. "We've arranged things nicely for her. You'll be impressed."

"Thanks." He didn't care.

"How's Marco over at Davis Hall?"

"He's eating it up. It's all that he talks about."

"Great. Sounds like you have life under control."

"So it seems," Naim replied, paying the taxi driver and hopping out. "Thanks for the call, Max."

"You got it."

Naim hung up the phone and walked slowly up the stairs to his home, with thoughts confirming that he had a good day. He couldn't wait to see what Brandy had in store. He was used to picking the place and time for his dates and didn't even know how to wait for one. She had already changed his life.

CHAPTER 32

Marco knocked on Naim's bedroom door, crunching on carrot slices pulled from a Ziploc bag. "Your reporter date is here. She's looking good, Dad. You sure know how to pick 'em."

"No doubt," Naim said and smiled. "I hope that you pick as carefully. Don't bring any chicken-heads around here."

"Oh, you're kidding right. You have to be, as you know I want to produce pretty kids with brains, so that's out." They both laughed, and then, Marco said, "Now, I want you in by midnight, ya heard. And no fornication, either. We don't want any more little Naim's running around quite yet." He laughed. "I'm the sole heir to this throne."

"Roger that," Naim said, clicked off his TV and then looked into the mirror. He popped in a mint, and said, "School is tomorrow, so you should be in bed by the curfew that you just gave me."

"And I will be; but, you remember that this lovely home's surveillance will record the time that you get in," Marco replied, laughing and walked to the guest room.

Naim Butler bounded down the stairs with a smile showing under his neatly trimmed mustache. He was in jeans, a Ralph Lauren Polo shirt that exposed his biceps, and loafers. He carried a blazer. "Aren't you beautiful?" he told Brandy who stood in the foyer admiring a painting.

"Well, thank you. You're looking good yourself. And so is this painting. Is it an original Van Gogh?"

He gave her a hug, and said, "If I have it you can bet that it's real. This was a gift from a client."

"Ah, yes, the perks of wealthy clients. I need to rethink my career," she said and laughed. "Let's go, though. I have a great evening planned."

"Where're we headed?" he asked, putting on his blazer.

"Wait and see," she said, walking out of the door.

"A mystery. I like mysteries that are laced with romance and good endings."

She smiled.

Naim anticipated flagging down a taxi as that was the customary New York City thing to do in an effort to avoid the parking fees and gridlocked traffic; but, they climbed into her two-door Lexus. They were barely off Seventy-Fourth Street when Naim realized that he was in for a treat. Something special. Brandy wore her seat belt and driving gloves; something about the way that she maneuvered the car was sexy to him.

"Music?"

"Sure."

"What do you like? Your choice since you're a guest."

"I like it all," he said, as she turned from Seventy-Fourth onto Fifth Avenue. She was headed downtown.

"OK," she said and played a track by The Weeknd.

After a brief moment of silence, he said, "Interesting night. I don't think I've ever been picked up by a woman and taken out on a date."

She had assumed that. "It's a first time for everything," she said and swerved around a taxi that stopped abruptly to pick up a fare. "I also assumed that you work a lot and often have to be in control of things, so I decided to take a load off you tonight."

"Thanks," was his automatic reply. "You're quite right, though. I always plan every detail for my outings and vacations."

"What's wrong? Problems trusting people?" she asked at a light. Her eyes were staring at him.

"You have bright eyes," he said.

"Thank you," she said, smiling. "But let's not dodge my question. Do you have problems trusting people?"

"I have to say no. I'm not the jealous type at all, either. I expect women to be able to keep any man from disrespecting me if she loves me. So trusting isn't a problem for me."

"OK," she said and rode through the light. "But outside of that are you a trusting person?"

"Yes, I'm just not used to having people to do things forcing me to rely exclusively on them."

"I can see that. I have the same problem when it comes to feeling like I always have to do the planning of anything. Even simple vacations with my girlfriends I have to decide what to do."

"That's me," he said and smiled. "So thanks for tonight. This is a first."

"Our first date night. Tuesday's could be our official day for date nights," she said, pulling over in front of a hotel.

A doorman opened her door, and said, "Welcome to the Pierre Hotel, madam. Checking in?"

"No," she said, getting out of the car. "Reservations at Cafe Pierre." She pressed a twenty into his hand.

"Perfect. There's a fine group of Julliard students playing modern renditions of Beethoven concertos on piano and violin tonight. I'll take care of your car, and you enjoy," he said and handed her a ticket.

Naim joined her on the curb, grabbed her hand, and they walked under the awning over the red carpet into the luxuriant hotel. Their soles crushed against marble flooring as they walked through the lobby, passing the front desk en route to the restaurant.

They approached the head hostess and, Brandy said, "Reservations for two, Butler."

Naim smiled. She had already used his surname and it had its intended effect.

"Certainly. Right, this way." They followed a well-dressed woman to their table in a cozy corner and took seats. "Will San Pellegrino do until, Jon, your waiter assists you this evening."

"Yes," Naim said, and the greeter left them. "Thanks," he said to Brandy.

"You're very welcome."

Forty-minutes later, they were three glasses into wine flutes and finishing osso buco, which they both nibbled on while basking in the Cafe Pierre's stellar ambiance and their stimulating conversations.

"Tell you something that you don't know about me," he said, repeating her question, as he broods the most solid reply. "I enjoy making people laugh and cheer people up. It makes me feel good when I make other people feel good."

"A little deeper," she said and sipped her wine. "I get that already."

"I may seem a little detached or unemotional at times, but beneath all of that exterior strength, I'm hurting. That'll drive me to go out of my way to fix something once, but I won't try if the other person isn't. I'm unconventional and always full of excitement."

"Wow, and you're not afraid to open up, either." She smiled.

He raised his glass, and said, "My third glass of wine."

"Oh, please, that's nothing," she said, giggling. "I'm sure you're not a light weight."

"Hey, what do you mean? I'm not a lush. I just like an occasional nightly liquor fix." He was laughing.

"You're crazy, and I like it," she said. "Dessert?"

"Nope."

"Watching your figure?" she asked, touching his shoulders and chest playfully. She made a gesture for the waiter to bring them the bill.

"Not at all, but I'm paying very close attention to yours," he said and his eyes glanced all over her body.

The bill arrived and she pressed her credit card into the waiter's hand without even looking at it. He liked that, but Naim reached into his wallet, and pulled out his American Express and handed it to the waiter also.

"We can go Dutch tonight, only because I don't want to deprive you of your moment to pamper me. But rules are rules."

The waiter smiled and pivoted before Brandy could protest.

"That's fine," she said, "because I have these." She fanned two Broadway tickets in the air. "Front row for *All the Way* at seven-thirty, so we have to go."

"I'm excited about seeing that. My secretary and I just put this on my to-do list." He didn't reveal that he had just seen it with Marco and Sinia.

"Well, now it's done. Come. Let's get a cab to the theater and leave the car with the valet.

"That's smart," he said and smiled. "You're full of tricks."

"Not tricks. I just know how to cut corners."

———— ————

After the play, Naim and Brandy took a brief stroll from the theater and through Times Square, before they hailed a taxi back to the Pierre Hotel. They retrieved her car from the valet and drove back to his home. Brandy didn't pull up front and drop him off, but she rounded the block twice and found an empty parking space.

Lowering the radio, she said, "It's a nice, clear, night out."

"I can't complain," Naim replied. "It's a full moon, too. I would invite you in for a night cap, but there's no telling where that'll lead." He was looking at her with his body shifted so that his back rested on the car's door.

"You know, Naim," she said, looking at him. "No one will ever know where it'll lead, but I wouldn't tempt you in such a straight forward way."

"Oh, you'll do it clandestinely?"

"Perhaps. I just want to sit here and round out our night with a brief conversation."

"OK, start by telling me something about you that I don't know."

"Really. Could you be any more original?"

He laughed. "I can, but I'd like to keep this light and simple. That is if you don't mind."

"Sure. Tell me anything," she said. "I am independent and the ultimate friend. I don't hold grudges and can be very forgiving."

She paused and, he said, "More."

"I bounce back from unfortunate events relatively easily. I can be a tad self-centered but my heart keeps it under control." She paused again.

"All done?" he asked, and she nodded. "But, I knew all of those things. That's why we're on a date now. All of that summed up what made you deal with the e-mail that Sinia sent you."

"That wasn't purposeful. It's just me. Whatever happened to you and her regarding that?"

"Not a thing," he replied. "I have you, while she's lonely and miserable. It made no sense to even confront her about it. When we're married with children, she'll see that she wasted her time and money on the fees associated with sending the e-mail."

"Oh. Married *and* children? You have a lot of work to get there."

"That's fine. But you have a lot of work to get me there," he said and smiled. "For the record, I am a hard worker, though. Known to shock and deviate from the norm," he said and put his hand on her ear to turn her head to face him. "Don't be surprised when what I say happens."

"You're too much, and we better call it a night." She squirmed in her seat.

He leaned in and they shared a passionate good night kiss. There were no other ways to respond to her ending the night. As bad as he wanted to grope and feel her up, he controlled himself and held it to a salacious kiss.

"Good night," he said, sitting in his seat and straightening his clothing. "Be sure to let me know that you arrived home safely, too. In fact," he said, opening the door, "how far do you live?"

"Brooklyn," she said and started the car.

"OK, where about?"

"Park Slope, and no you can't have my address," she said and laughed.

"Maybe not today, but in time," he said and offered her a good night again. *Of course, she lives in the most expensive area of Brooklyn.*

"Good night, Naim. I'll be sure to call when I get in."

CHAPTER 33

The following afternoon, Naim attended a meeting at Baker & Keefe headed by Max Devers. The meeting involved the criminal division department heads, and Naim was one. He devoured a double espresso after lunch in an effort to stay awake, and to prevent his head from slamming into the conference table at an unseasonable moment. Too many facts that weren't gathered by him bored him, and he had other things on his mind. Well, one other thing: Brandy Scott. Once or twice, he was called upon to provide input on a prosecutorial motion or a particular investigative technique. He was able to speak sagely and eloquently, but he did more nodding than talking. At the end of the meeting when everyone stood to leave, he shook hands and then retreated to his well-appointed HQ office. They had spared nothing to convince him that he was wanted and appreciated at the firm.

Before his office door closed, Devers entered and had a seat. "Well, that went well. It's a murder case and you showed very little interest. What's on your mind, Nai?"

"I met a woman that I'm scared of. Petrified that the fright of rejection that I live with may make me run if she continues to melt me."

"Oh, boy, Naim Butler, masterful bachelor, is in love."

"I've known her three weeks. That's impossible."

"Love at first sight. We all experience it at least once in life," Devers said and smiled. "Glad you had the espresso because she really consumed you, man."

"Cocaine may have worked better, since you noticed," Naim replied and laughed.

"You have a point, but that's not a real option."

"Right. I forgot that I've never done drugs."

"Well, not that. Had you had a line of coke, you may have giggled at crime scene photos." He laughed.

"Man, I woulda broke out in song." Naim chuckled, and then said, "This is insane."

"I tell you what, let's do dinner at Hector's later and talk about it."

"Can't."

"Let me guess. A date?"

"You got it."

"Liking this. You're the only bachelor that I know. It'll be nice for you to come over to the happy-wife-happy-life side of the world. Great career, health, and marriage."

"New son, new love affair. I'm on a roll."

———— ————

Naim got back to the house in time to be there when Marco returned from school. He saw Naim walking through the hallway and danced into the door. *Classic Man* by Jidenna was blaring through his ear phones.

"Someone's happy," Naim said.

"Yup," Marco said and turned his music off. "Me. Your son. I aced the admissions test. Got every question right."

"Damn. Wow." Naim was speechless. "Congrats, Son."

Marco hung his coat while smiling. "That was what the school execs said to the person that proctored the test. And the word spread quickly that I'm smart and handsome, and wealthy," Marco said, singing the hook to the Migos song, and laughing.

"I like that," Naim said. He didn't know how to reply. He had missed out on so much of the boy's life and his anger at Sinia resurfaced all over again.

"Dad, how many seats does the theater hold?"

"Twelve."

"OK, perfect. Can I have eight people over from school to watch a film and hang out a bit on Friday? Well, ten people, because Stefon should be home on Friday, and I'd invite him and a date."

"You can. All classmates, right?"

"Yes," Marco said, heading into the family room. He had a seat on an ottoman in front of a lit fireplace. "I was wondering two things, Dad."

"Shoot," Naim said, pouring himself a goblet of whiskey.

"Do you think that we can squeeze money in for me to take a few classes at the Brooklyn Conservatory?"

"Squeeze money," Naim replied and took a seat on the carpeted floor. Certainly, there was plenty of money for classes that advanced his prodigious music skills. But there was an even greater reason for his son to gain an education in Brooklyn. Brooklyn was home for Brandy Scott, and his classes created the perfect reason for Naim to spend more time there. "I think that we can find money for the conservatory. You look into which classes and let me know the benefit to you and the costs. What else?"

"I have an interview this weekend."

"Like, a job interview?" Naim was perplexed.

"What other kind is there?" Marco was chuckling, but Naim gave him a stern glare, and he straightened up.

"Maybe college. I don't know."

"OK, I have an interview for a sales rep position at Bloomingdale's at Fifty-Ninth Street and Lexington Avenue. It's a part time job and not that far from home."

"I see," Naim said, and then sipped his cocktail. "I'm not sure that I want you adding a job into your already busy schedule."

"I am busy, Dad, but three nights a week tops won't hurt. Well, two nights and sometime on the weekends. That shouldn't interfere. I won't let it."

"And if it begins to?"

"I'm sure you'd notice and make me quit."

"You got that right," Naim said and smiled. *Because I am all knowing, buddy*, Naim thought assuringly. "So what movie do you want for your little shindig. And, nothing Rated-R."

"Really. I am not a kid, Pater."

"No, you're not, but I don't know whose coming, or their ages. The last thing that we need is for someone telling their parents that they have seen questionable content at Marco Butler's theater."

Marco laughed. "You're kidding, right?"

"I'm not." Deadly serious.

Marco had never seen his father so humorless. "OK, so what do you have in mind, oh-sage-one."

"How many boys and girls?"

"Five boys. Five girls." Marco smirked.

"A romantic comedy," Naim said and laughed. "Sounds like you need a chaperone."

"Naim Butler." Marco smiled in spite of himself. "I'll get back to you on the movie choice."

"Did someone say movie?" Ginger said, walking into the room.

"Yes, Marco here plans to have guests over to watch a movie on Friday. I've suggested nothing Rated-R."

"He's too overprotective and cautious, Ms. Ginger," Marco said, heading for the entry way into the room. "I'll leave you two to your business."

"Too much, that kid," Naim said. "What brings you to this area?"

"There's a woman in the office reception area that needs your representation. Well, not for her, but her son. Are you available, or not?"

"I am and will see her. Let me change, get rid of the whiskey breath, and then I'll see her in my office. Thanks, Gin."

"No problemmo."

CHAPTER 34

Ten minutes later, Naim emerged into the small waiting area of his home office and smiled at a Black woman dressed in a dark business suit and flats.

He held out his hand, and said, "Nice to meet you, Ms. Moore."

"Likewise, Mr. Butler," she replied and pinched her lips together. "Thanks for seeing me without an appointment."

"No problem. Let's convene in my office," Naim said and offered her tea and crackers. She declined, and he offered a seat. Seated, Naim asked how may he help her.

"I need a private investigator. I'd like you."

Naim had been known for his discrete inquiries, but he had to carefully consider what jobs he committed to now that he had a son. He couldn't risk his life so much anymore. Besides, he prepared to have the senator's strength to take the BAR and become an attorney. He had to be careful not to jeopardize that good fortune. And then, there was Brandy.

"OK," he said, "I've been known to do a little of that, but usually at the direction of an attorney at the firm, not privately."

"You see," she said seemingly ignoring his comment. "My son's friend is setting him up. In fact, he's out running the streets freely, while my son sits in jail. I'd like you to prove that he's lying on my son. Have a chat with him. Perhaps see what's going on. My son is an honor college student and I can't imagine him murdering anyone. He had no reason. He's told me as much." She wiped a lone tear from her face, and Naim handed her a Kleenex.

"This is tough, ma'am. I'm not sure that I can interfere with the prosecution of your son, although, I feel sorry for what his friend has done to him. I'm not fond of trials being won solely using co-defendant testimony."

"Good, but my son is no one's co-defendant. He is innocent," she said and scanned the office. "My son read an article you've written on the subject, published in the Criminal Law Reporter. He asked me to look you up. When I did, I learned of your past and wanted to ask for your help to protect my son from this tragedy."

"Why would he just lie on your son?"

"Well, maybe you should ask my son. But from what he's told me, his friend is a career-offender facing fifteen years in federal prison, and he's looking to get a reduced sentence if he points the finger at my son during the trial." Naim's eyes widened. "And on my spare time I have been researching some criminal law and sentencing stuff, and know that this is not only possible but happens all of the time."

Naim inhaled deeply. He was all too familiar with stone-cold killers turning into cheese-eating rats for reduced sentences. He couldn't see how he could help this women, because anyone looking to get a reduced sentence is not likely to recant their lies. They have no morals and will have their mother indicted for a reduction in sentencing. And with that, he wanted out like an investor on the hit TV series, *Shark Tank*.

"Please." Her plea was sincere. She pulled a checkbook from her purse.

"Ms. Moore, money isn't the issue," he said and sighed. She looked lifeless, so he brainlessly sought to revive her. "Give me your son's name. I'll visit with him and get more details, OK?"

"Should I make the check out to you or your firm?"

"Neither. I'm not formally having the firm take on this case. I will talk to your son and look at some of the papers filed on the docket sheet of the case and help with guidance from there. Fair enough?"

"Yes, and thank you."

Naim stood, and said, "Don't thank me, yet. I'll be in touch." He walked her to his office door and asked Ginger to get some information from her, and then see her out.

CHAPTER 35

Early Friday afternoon, Naim was cleaning the kitchen, singing along with Brian McKnight whose song *Never Felt This Way* blared from an iPad on the kitchen island. June stood in the kitchen doorway carrying two grocery store shopping bags filled with goods for Marco's gathering. She watched her boss spray and wipe down the stove, swaying to the piano notes of the song and singing like a true balladeer. She didn't disturb his groove. She actually liked listening to his smooth tenor voice sing around the house.

Naim turned around and gave her a toothy smile.

"Someone's in love, I see," June said, entering the kitchen and setting the bags on the counter.

"I am not, ma'am," he said and raised his eyebrows.

She rested a sassy hand on her hip and shook her head. Her soft, snow-white curls whipped side to side. "You're a dark, young man, but you're blushing, Hun. I can see the rouge on your cheeks blossoming." She laughed and then quickly gave him a stern stare. "It's OK. It's time to fall in love. You're at that point in your life where any woman that genuinely wants you will pursue that without reliance on your past."

"True," he said and sat on a stool at the island.

"I'm serious, sir," she said and rested her hand on his shoulder. "This Brandy woman is in the picture before you become a professor or an attorney. At least we know she's not about money and status, per se."

"No, she's not," he said and tossed his hand to his face to cover up his blushing for the second time. "She's a phenomenal woman, June. I've never met a woman like her."

"And, you've met a lot." She smirked.

"June," he exclaimed and laughed.

"Well, you've had your share of them. I've approved none. Apparently, Brandy is in the picture because neither have you. So here we are."

"We, huh..."

"Yes, I am not taking care of a woman that I dislike," she said. "Would you fire me if you were married?"

"What, June?" He was struck by her question. "Of course not. This is a lifetime appointment."

"Good. So we have a get together to prepare for. Let's get to it."

"Brandy will be joining us for this evening's festivities."

"Oh, my," June replied, "the surprises with this woman never stop."

CHAPTER 36

June had fed Marco's guest's truffle fries with chicken wings simmered slowly with garlic, shallots and herbs then finished in five styles: Buffalo, barbecue, Parmesan-parsley, lemon-pepper, and honey-lime. They enjoyed dinner, followed by apple crumb pie dessert topped with whipped cream, and were now enjoying the movie.

Furious 7.

Naim was able to score an advanced screening copy; a perk accompanying a home theater, reciprocated with a review. Brandy and Naim were seated in the theater with the teens, who all seemed to welcome them. *What a mature bunch*, Naim thought, watching the movie and wondering who Marco's date was. His son hadn't introduced Amber as such, but a father knew, and his arm draped around her confirmed it.

Glass jars of popcorn sat between everyone, as opposed to the typical popcorn buckets. Under the cover of darkness when Naim's and Brandy's hand attempted to dip into the jar, Naim made a move to hold her hand. Instinctively, she slithered her hand to lock with his. She looked at him. She smiled. He smirked, raised his eyebrows, and then refocused on the movie. *If only the kids weren't here*, he thought.

After everyone started to file out of the house, Amber stood in the doorway and looked back at Marco who chatted with his father.

"I have to take her home, Pater."

Naim checked his watch. "And where's home?"

"I know that it's late, and I am not certain, but New Jersey."

"New who? I don't think so. How'd she get here?"

Marco smiled. He giggled. "You're kidding, right?"

Naim looked past Marco into the mirror behind him. No one ever told him that fatherhood would be so difficult. When he was seventeen, he had no one to give him a curfew or guidance. Certainly, he was not going to allow Marco to swim through the muddy waters of life without a parental life jacket.

"I'm not, but I don't want to create a conflict here either. Obviously, she has to get home. You cannot by law drive on your permit alone this late."

"Dad, it's nine. I'll be right back."

"That's not the point," Naim said louder than he wanted through clenched teeth. Amber looked at them, and Naim said, "Um, Amber, come here a moment."

Amber had the kind of young woman beauty that forced men's worlds to go round and round. Marco had a nice catch, but not nice enough to force Naim to stop being a parent for the sake of seeming loose.

"Yes, sir," she replied.

And she has manners, Naim thought and smiled. "Where do you live?"

Her eyebrows raised. The blunt force of his question shocked her. "I live in Alpine, New Jersey, sir."

Now it was Naim's turn to raise his brows. Alpine, New Jersey was home to Sean "P. Diddy" Combs, Stevie Wonder, Eddie Murphy, Britney Spears, Reverend Run, Lil Kim, and the like. Naim knew that Forbes Magazine ranked Alpine as America's most expensive zip code.

He had contemplated moving there to avoid the busy Manhattan atmosphere. Now, his son had to take a friend there; potentially, a girlfriend that he'd later marry. How much more complicated was life going to become? *You need to make a quick decision,* Naim thought.

"OK," he said, estimating it would take Marco a half-hour to forty-five minutes to get there on a Friday night of traffic congestion. "Thank you." He then looked at Marco, and said, "Come with me a sec."

They retreated to the kitchen and Naim grabbed his keys from the kitchen counter. He removed a car key and held it in Marco's face. "Let me ask you a question. Is Amber your girlfriend?"

"Dad, no. Geesh. I've known her a week." He was laughing.

"Safe to say that you'd like her to be, though?"

"Was that a question or statement?" Marco had a sarcastic smirk on his face.

"Don't play with me." Naim was laughing.

"Yes, I like her."

"Tell me about her parents. No. What're their professions?"

"Dad, an obstetrician. Mom, she's a Wall Street broker. What's with the car key?"

"Take her home in the Benz, Marco. Do not make any stops. None. When you're on her property, put the car in park and you open her car door before walking her right up to her front door. You got that?"

"I do. Now can I go, please?"

"Yup," Naim said and started to make a pot of coffee. "Text me on your way back. Before you actually pull off. No texting and driving, it's against the law here, and I don't want you stopped for driving while black and end up like our brother, Eric Gardner."

"Got it, Mom," Marco replied, laughing. "I mean, Dad."

Brandy walked into the kitchen as Marco walked out. She walked up to Naim and snuggled up to him. He wrapped his arms around her.

She said, "I heard the tail end of that conversation."

"Did you now?" he asked and looked at her lovingly. "I hope you approve."

"Yes, very fine advice and fathering. Young boys need more men like you in their lives to mold them into fine gentlemen with respect, polish, and mannerliness. I like that about you."

There are no words to express how lucky you make me feel, Naim thought, but couldn't say it. His handsome, aristocratic features were assaulted by blissfulness. The face of a man who had leap into the abyss of romance.

He nodded his head towards the coffee pot, and then said, "How about that night cap?" Anything to avoid being mushy at such a vulnerable time of the night.

"I'd like that," she replied and kissed his lips. The subtle peck from a woman confident that she had a man's undivided attention.

———— ————

After walking Brandy to her car, Naim enjoyed a talk with his son, before he found himself in a deep hot bath.

He thought about her.

Brandy Scott.

He remembered small details of their conversation in the kitchen. They shared experiences from the past that were of inflated value, simply because they were used to get to know each other more deeply.

Toweling himself, he inspected his image in the steamed mirror with a critical eye. He was chiseled and hard and burned dark as a well-done steak. He watched the play of his muscles under the skin as he moved, and he knew that he was as fit and as mentally prepared for three things. His forties. Raising a son. Carefully, driving a relationship to marriage. And he had to do them all simultaneously. He shook his head thinking of life's pressures and winked at himself before walking into his bedroom with his towel wrapped around his waist. He stretched out on his bed to wait for the sun to come up to give him another opportunity to say good morning to his son and Brandy Scott.

CHAPTER 37

Naim awoke to the delightful sound of Marco playing the piano. After clearing the morning fog, he tossed the comforter from over his body, threw on his robe, and then opened his bedroom door.

Marco noticed the light illuminate the salon area and turned towards his father's bedroom while never missing a note of the song that he played. He nodded a good morning pleasantry to his father and continued to play.

"What're you playing?" Naim asked and then covered his mouth to yawn.

"I just made it up, so I haven't named it, yet."

"Oh," Naim said blankly. *What else would the music genius be playing*, he thought.

"The piano records my keys, so whatever isn't committed to memory I can replay." Switching gears, Marco said, "Mom told me that you could sing. Well, a little..." Naim's eyebrows raised and he held his mouth open. Marco chuckled, and then said, "You're hilarious, Dad. She said you could sing well enough to win a bar full of people over back on the South Side of Chicago."

"Is that what she told you?" Naim asked. "I cannot sing."

"That's funny because Ms. June told me the same thing over breakfast two days ago. She's a very wise woman, and I doubt that she lies."

"She's wise and I doubt that she lies, too."

"So can you sing or not?" Marco asked and played a piano chord that sounded a lot like a modern rendition of the Alfred Hitchcock's *Psycho* score.

"That sounds scary," Naim said and smiled. "But I can sing a little. Enough to get a chair to turn around on the Voice."

"I'm done," Marco said, laughing and getting up from the piano. He backed towards the guest room. "I have that interview today at Bloomies in two hours, I'm going to get ready. I will be looking at some things for the suite upstairs, too, so that I can get ready to move out of the guest room."

"Sounds like a plan. What are you wearing to the interview?"

"A suit," Marco said, shaking his head. "What else?"

"What color?"

"Blue."

"Pin stripes?"

"Yup."

"And what color tie?"

"Not sure."

"Red. And a white shirt."

"Now, you're a fashionista?"

"Nope, but the all-American red, white, and blue always exude confidence at an interview."

"You act like you've been on an interview in ages." He chuckled. "But I get your point."

"Let me know when you're ready and I'll drop you..." Naim saw the angst in Marco's face and paused. "I know. I know you don't need a ride. You'll be eighteen next week. I get it. But for your info, I'm headed downtown to visit a federal inmate and I can drop you off along the way."

"Oh, OK," Marco said, and then added, "Cool."

"Afterwards, I'm going to surprise Brandy at her job with some lunch."

"Is that right? You're really laying it on her."

"Come on. Woman love lunch dates. You want a woman to melt, surprise her with a lunch date. It's easy, but the gesture goes a very long way."

Marco simply smiled. He learned something new every day from the man before him.

"Smile on young grasshopper. One day you're going to bloom into a praying mantis."

CHAPTER 38

The attorney's check-in booth at the Metropolitan Detention Center allowed Naim to bypass the line of screaming toddlers and family members of inmates residing at the federal palace. He had special permission from the warden to enter the facility to conduct interviews for attorneys like anyone else who didn't have a BAR card.

He waited and watched the mostly brown and black faces pile into the prison trying to gauge how this particular inquiry would go. After twenty minutes of strategic mental planning, he was escorted by a USCO to a small attorney's interview room to wait for his potential client.

After quick introductions, Naim set out to get the gist of why he was there without small talk. He had read the indictment and some other documents filed on the docket and had Paris Moore fill in the blanks of the Government's allegation that he committed murder at the direction of the leader of a drug trafficking organization to aid said organization.

"So, if you didn't commit the murder, why'd he blame you?"

"I don't know why, but perhaps because I met his girl at a bar and fucked her the same night. She had thrown that in his face and we had a fight, but I thought that was the end of it. Why he would pin a murder on me is crazy. I think that he's been paid to get me off the streets by his boss, and then offered a deal from the prosecutor to testify against me," Paris said angrily. He was under the impression that Naim was just another legal person out to make a quick buck, but he was laying it all out to give him the benefit of the doubt.

"And this is a guy that you grew up with that sells drugs with a rap sheet as long as the block this jail sits on?" Naim asked the man. He wasn't confused by the story, but couldn't figure out what the man slated to testify against his potential client stood to gain besides a reduced sentence for his involvement in the conspiracy. Naim needed to get to the bottom of that to understand why his client was being falsely accused.

"Mr. Butler, I'm sure you're aware, but prosecutors use serious criminals to put people away every day. Prosecutors have a lot of nerve. They don't really want to protect the public from criminals. They give lying ass killers and robbers reduced or no sentences all of the time in exchange for trumped up lies against other people. But I'm innocent, dammit." Paris slammed his fist on the table between him and Naim. "I've never killed anyone. Never even touched a gun, much less pulled the trigger of one. Check Jackson Brown's record. He has committed all sorts of crimes and has gotten off for snitching."

Naim was aware of what Paris had offered and understood his frustration. "Sadly, the public has no idea how screwed they are because of the false belief that the criminal justice system protects them. Killers testify against their accomplices, get reduced sentences, and kill again upon their quick release. Poor people get arrested. Are later released poor. And eventually, raise poor children that think poorly. Two million people in jail. Twenty million just not caught, but should be in jail. I get all of that, Paris, trust me on that."

"At least you don't pretend not to."

"Based on the rat's proposed testimony in your case, if he takes the stand against you, you'll spend your life in a federal jail. The only way that I can help you is if he doesn't. Did you bring a picture of him like I asked?" For some reason, he could not find a mug shot of Jackson Brown.

"No. You think I'd have pics of him in jail with me?"

"OK. What's his Instagram and Facebook names? You give me them and I'll see what I can do to prevent him from taking the stand." Naim mischievously raised his eyebrows.

———— ————

Across town, Marco walked into the Apple store on Fifty-Ninth Street and Fifth Avenue. The place was packed with hordes of customers and staff, but only one of them was of interest to him.

Amber King.

She was showing a couple an iMac and he tapped her shoulder. Startled, she turned around ready to give the person that touched her a piece of her mind.

"Oh," she said, smiling.

"When you're done with them could you help me, please?" Marco asked like an ordinary customer.

"Can't," she said and tapped his shoulder. "I'll be going to lunch after I finish with them. Sorry." She smiled.

He replied with a smile, and then said, "Even better. Meet me in the lobby of the Plaza Hotel when you're done with them. Lunch on me."

"You see that, Carl?" the woman that Amber was helping said to her male companion. "When's the last time you took me to lunch."

"Farrah, please," the man replied.

Marco chuckled, and said to Amber, "Good luck and I'll see you in a bit."

———— ————

The Plaza Hotel was direct across the street from the Apple Store. True to his word, by the time Amber found Marco in the lobby of the luxuriant hotel, he had a silver tray with two covered plates on a table between two chairs.

He stood, gave her a hug, and then said, "I hope you like chicken Caesar salad. It was the fastest dish on the menu to have prepared. I had them bring a side of shrimp, also."

They had seats in huge, velvet covered chairs and he took the top off of their plates.

"This is a beautiful salad, Marco. I don't even want to touch the plate," she said and took a picture of the entire food presentation.

He smiled. "How long is lunch?"

"Thirty minutes."

"We better eat," he said and stabbed Romaine lettuce and chicken onto his fork, "I'm starving."

"Me too," she said and placed a napkin on her lap before digging into her plate.

After a few bites and breaking their silence, he said, "How's it going in there today?"

"It's always hectic. That store is open twenty-four hours and it's packed like that at two a.m."

"New York is so much different than Raleigh."

"I suppose so. I've never been."

"Perhaps, your parents will let you visit there with me in the coming weeks. I want to get some of my things to get more comfortable here."

"Marco," she said and dramatically dropped her fork onto her plate. "I'm nineteen. I can travel without a permission slip from my parents. They want to meet you, by the way."

"Meet who?" Marco said, chuckled, and looked around the room. "Your dad. I'm scared of dads." He was laughing. "You told him about me?"

"No. You did."

He gave her a blank stare, and his eyebrows nearly touched at the top of his nose.

"A black kid dropped me off in an S-600, opened my door, and walked me to the porch without even trying to get a kiss."

"He saw me?"

"He saw a drug dealer and was ready to kill me with a lecture," she said, laughing. "But when I told him that you go to my school and what your parents did, he was pleasantly surprised. He figured that was why you had the semblance of manners."

Marco glowed with delight. He sighed, adopting what was supposed to be an innocent expression.

"Let me talk this over with my dad," he said, and then sipped his Sprite.

Amber leaned in with her face close to his. She gave him a hard stare, and then asked, "Do you ask your dad everything?"

He kissed her lips. It was soft and exchanged romantic energy.

"I didn't ask him to do that," he said and then leaned back in his chair to adore her with his eyes. "Look at that," he said, looking at his watch. "Time to walk you back to work."

She could not stop smiling and blushing. The mixed emotions were palatable. "Yes, we should go. I can't be late and right now, I don't want to go back. We can just sit here all day."

"Is that right?" Marco said, stuffing cash into a waiter's hand.

"This is my best lunch break," Amber said, and then added, "My first lunch date actually."

Thanks, dad, Marco thought, watching the excitement spread across Amber's face. He had made her day thanks to advice from his dad. Of course, he planned to run things by him.

"Maybe we can do this again?"

"Boy, don't be trying to spoil me," she replied and playfully punch his arm.

"Trust me, I'm not trying to spoil you. When, and if, I do, you'll know."

"Well, what do you call it when you come to my job and treat me to lunch? None of the fools I met before you ever came to my job to take me to lunch. Hell, I could barely get them on a date unless I asked them."

The exterior of the Plaza Hotel was blanketed with red carpet and snow. Marco stopped on it and turned to face her. He gently placed his hands on her shoulders, looked into her eyes, and then to the ground. Her eyes followed his.

"Let's call this the red carpet treatment," he said, causing an awkward smile to creep onto her face. "And try not to compare me to the other fools. They'll never measure up."

"OK," was all that she could reply.

Marco removed his hands from her shoulders and, he held out a hand for her to grab. Hand and hand they walked back to her job under a cloud of puppy love.

CHAPTER 39

Later that evening, Naim was at his kitchen table enjoying soup and in a heated verbal confrontation with Sinia.

"You know at this age, I tend to ignore what people say and pay very close attention to what they do," Naim said to Sinia. He was having Facetime with her using his iPad.

"Look, I didn't call you to get lectured. I'm just looking to ensure that my son doesn't end up like his...father."

"What, a successful millionaire with more class than what's offered by Harvard and Steve Harvey combined."

"You're an arrogant ass. You know that?"

Naim laughed, flashing a lot of teeth.

"I really hate you," she said with venom and frowned.

"You must have sent Sinia a copy of my criminal record in an effort to destroy my relationship with her. But, you see, it didn't work. That's the kind of evil, spiteful, and hateful behavior I'd actually hate for my son to learn."

"I did no such thing."

"And you're a liar. A bad one. Another thing I'd hate for my son to learn."

"This ain't about me. It's about allowing my child to drive at night without adult supervision. He coulda been killed."

"Which you saw on an IG post when he was home alive." He chuckled. "And opposed to asking me why you call disrespecting me." He took a spoonful of his chicken and rice soup. "This is good."

"You know what," she said angrily. He watched her face twisted with rage.

"No, I don't, but what I do know is, you and I are fully aware of my upbringing, lack of guidance..."

"Ain't that the truth."

"And I'm determined to be sure that my son has a great father-son experience. One that grooms him into an eloquent, wise, intellectual, and charming man, just like dear ol' dad. He's here with me and will be eighteen next week, so him being here is a decision he's capable of making. Like I'm deciding to be a near perfect father, so he has everything that I missed out on. What more do you want?"

She didn't reply. She rolled her eyes, and said, "All that sounds good, but I don't trust you to do the things that you say."

"Guess what. I'm not your father, so you don't have to."

"Your mouth really irks me. You're so damn nasty."

"Me. I'm going to terminate this call because you're not looking to be an adult here. Is this high school? Just know that I'm being a good father to Marco, not you."

She sucked her teeth and then pressed the end button on her iPad to end the call.

CHAPTER 40

Mid-morning, Marco found Naim at the kitchen table and June putting final touches on brunch. Naim had the *New York Times* Sunday edition spread on the table while scrolling through his iPad.

"How nice of you to join us this fine Sunday morning," June said and smiled. She placed a glass of orange juice in front of him, and then said, "You're rather late."

"Anytime," Marco said and laughed a little. "I had a long night."

That line forced Naim to pull himself from the iPad. "You went out last night?"

"No. Not at all," Marco said and snatched a piece of bacon from a tray in the middle of the table. "I was up talking to Amber until five and it's all your fault."

"My fault?" Naim replied and grinned. "I didn't did nothing."

They laughed.

"You know," Marco said and scrolled through his phone calling up his Instagram app. He found Amber's page and then passed the phone to Naim.

Naim read the caption of the picture below two salad plates. "Lunch date for two," he said and sat the phone down. "Why'd she tag you?"

"Because she's on the date with me," Marco said, as June slid pancakes in front of him. "Look at the comments, and please don't say that I told you so, either." He smothered his pancakes with syrup and took a bite. "These are nice, June."

"Thanks, Hun," she said, and then looked over Naim's shoulder at the photo's comments. "Someone seemed to have passed along his charm gene to his son."

"Stop, Mama June. I didn't mean for this to happen. Everyone thinks that we're a couple now."

"Is that so bad?" Naim asked, and handed him back his phone.

"No, but the attention is overwhelming. It's cool, but it's like they've never seen her taken out to lunch before. I don't want all of this attention," Marco said, looking at his plate. He looked up, gave a sinister smile, and then said, "Maybe a tiny-bit," and then laughed.

"Shaking-my-damn-head," Naim said and sipped his mimosa. He went back to his iPad.

"What'chu reading?" Marco asked.

"A book on reclaiming fatherhood: *Time To Man Up* by Leonard Anderson. A friend recommended it."

"Any good?"

"Yup, it's a quick read, but it's about a father of six that was absent from their lives until he got his own life on track. His six children wrote letters included in the back. Very impactful, and they taught me a lot."

"Sounds interesting," June said. "Just like you to go above and beyond to understand things and to put things into perspective."

"Must be where I get it from, because I research everything," Marco said.

"As you should," Naim said, and then added, "Which brings me to this. I'd like you to join me in the Bronx today for a bit of research later this evening."

"If he's not busy with Amber," June said and laughed.

Naim and Marco laughed, too.

"I'm not. She's working today."

"Oh, maybe another lunch date," Naim said and continued to laugh.

"Oh, you two really have jokes this morning."

CHAPTER 41

Slutpoint.

There was a flavorful assortment of goods. Chocolate, vanilla, strawberry—a tasteful bowl of hookers. Many were young, but some were over forty. All of them tip-toeing on cheap high heels and wrapped in faux mink. Most wore garish make up to cover their worn faces. Nothing could hide their pencil thin frames or the track marks covering their arms, though.

Naim had parked a half block away from the Hunt Point's hoe stroll and had Marco along for the Bronx experience. The Yankees Stadium and Bronx Zoo were not on the agenda. He wanted his son to understand that he wouldn't miss anything if he skipped out on soliciting a prostitute. He also wanted his son to see firsthand how he investigated for a client. Who knew how the exposure would affect Marco's career decisions or his life decisions for that matter.

Naim plucked a photo that he had printed and flashed it to Marco. "There's our guy," Naim said. "PimpatthePoint."

"Really, Dad. Unbelievable the things that you come up with."

"What?" Naim laughed. "His name is Jackson Brown, but PimpatthePoint is what he prefers to use on IG. Take that up with him."

Brown looked like an NBA player. Tall, a tad wide, some bulging muscles. He wore a fitting sweater forcing his arms to look like tree trunks wrapped in cheap cotton. No coat. He had on skinny jeans, and Naim wondered how he walked. He actually wobbled.

"Never let me see you in pants that tight," Naim said.

Marco chuckled. "Not a warning that I need," he replied, and then asked, "woman actually pay him their hard earned money?"

It was eight at night and Brown wore sunglasses and enough jewelry to make a rapper blush. Notwithstanding prostitutes talking to potential buyers about their contaminated goods for sale, the area was quiet. How else could they keep police out of the area? Brown was actually making a drug sale. He had previously vacationed on Riker's Island and had two short stints at Clinton State Penitentiary. Mostly for petty drug offenses. Strong armed robbery, once. Statutory rape, once. Assault and battery, twice. Thirty-two-years-old and a combined career offender and menace to society. A plus was that he had served time, but the ball was dropped because he spent his time lifting weights. A violent man's dream was doing time building his physical strength to be released with a stronger ability to administer fear and maim with relative ease. Brown had taken full advantage of the great New York prison system.

Naim used his cell phone to snap dozens of photos of his target selling drugs. He immediately forwarded those photos to his e-mail to preserve them just in case his phone was lost or taken by whatever agent allowed this criminal cretin to stay on the streets. He didn't put it past some rogue cop to watch Brown's back. Hell, they watched him testifying before a grand jury.

Brown completed his drug deal and stuffed cash into his pants pockets. It was a magic trick. How tight his pants were, Naim wondered where the cash went. The customer was surely under eighteen, too; a scrawny young lady that stumbled when Brown slapped her ass as she walked away. With his prior sex offense, Naim figured he was a registered offender and shouldn't have any contact with minors; definitely, not touch them sexually. They headed in different directions. Brown walked towards Naim and Marco.

"That girl kept wiping her nose. So young and hooked on nose candy," Marco said.

"What the hell you know about that?" Naim asked. "Hold that thought. Stay in the car," he said and stepped out just as Brown was about to walk pass. "Jackson Brown?"

Brown gave him a contemptuous stare down. "Who the fucks asking?"

"Nice," Naim said. "You sound smarter than I expected."

"What the..." Brown said, and then peeked into the car and saw Marco. "I'll fuck y'all up. Who the hell do you think you are stepping to me?"

Naim passed him a business card. "I'd like to talk to you."

"What the hell about?" Brown said quickly. He stepped into Naim's face. "Matter-of-fact get the hell out of here before I kick ya ass. Both your asses," he said, and noted Marco standing beside Naim.

"Marco get in the car," Naim said without taking his eyes off Brown.

"Best advice you've heard all day, pretty boy."

"Back up outta my pop's face," Marco said plainly. "Not going to ask you twice."

Brown charged towards Marco trying to mow him down like a car striking a deer. Marco spun to the side and delivered a heavy-handed punch to Brown's chest cavity. Brown's wind was knocked out of him and he bowled over, wincing in pain.

Marco grabbed Brown's chin and caused him to stand straight up. "Put your hands on your head and breathe," Marco said and then added, "and do something about that IG name. That's even better advice."

Naim blinked uncontrollably in a state of awe at the blend of confusion, rage, and most important surprise across Brown's face. Naim looked around to be sure no one watched this thug get checked by his son. "I just have a few questions, man."

"Fuck you..."

Marco shook his head. "You have parents, I'm sure," Marco said. "Please do not disrespect mine. This can't end well if you do."

"In the car, Marco, now," Naim said. "Now."

"Not a chance." Disobedience.

Brown was enraged. His eyes said it all. He wasn't going to be disrespected on his turf. The pain remained twisted on his face, and that didn't compare to him not having any idea what the men wanted. Brown acted as if he was in more pain than he really was and stumbled closer to Marco. He wanted revenge. When he was in position he tried again.

He must not have been paying Marco any attention, or really stupid. Marco had no problem handing out lessons on top of lessons.

Marco dipped and came up with a solid punch to Brown's stomach. Despite his six-pack, it sounded like Marco punched a wet sponge. Brown barked and fell to the ground. Marco raised his leg for a kick to the midsection, but Naim held up a hand to stop him.

"Look at that," Marco said. "Despite your disrespect, dear ol' dad saved you."

"I'm spitting up f...." He stopped and grabbed his stomach. "You did something to my insides. I'm spitting up blood."

"You've been to jail enough times. You should be used to people doing things to your insides," Marco said calmly.

"Who in the hell are you?"

Naim said, "I've got a few questions. You should really answer them."

"My stomach, son. I need a doctor."

"Just as soon as we're done."

"Look, I don't have much to say about anything."

"Sure you do. Tell me about," Naim paused as a car drove past, "Agent Warner."

A surprised face replaced Brown's angry one.

"You've been put up to lying on a childhood friend, Paris Moore. Why is that?"

Panic now. "Who are you?"

"I gave you my card."

Silence.

"Why're you setting up Paris? Besides the obvious sentence reduction?"

"A favor. I was paid."

"By?"

"Can't say."

Marco said, "There's a lot of organs in that midsection of yours."

"OK, man. What the fuck..."

"Language." That was Marco.

"Marvin Davis paid me to do it."

"Do what?"

Brown shrugged and sighed. His stomach was swelling badly, but he feared that he had to keep going. "You don't understand." He grinned as his memory returned. He told the father and son what he wanted them to know.

Brown's stomach was stirring violently. Marco looked at his work without interest.

"Is that all?" Naim asked.

Brown smirked.

"You leave, Dad," Marco said and raised his leg in the air.

Naim hesitated.

"Come on, man. You've already set me up to be killed by the Bloods or a federal agent." His voice shook.

"Leave," Marco said.

Naim smiled and shook his head. "I'd rather not."

Marco intently searched his father's face. He then stood over Brown who was trying to crawl away but had no strength to do so.

"Don't murder the man," Naim said, and couldn't believe that his son had made such a great sidekick.

Marco ignored him and continued to step with Brown's crawls.

After moving six feet, Marco stopped and stared venomously at Brown. "Pussy," he said before hopping in the car.

"Let's not, OK?" Naim said, and then pulled off.

"What? I told you that I could box."

"Not that. The language. Practice what you preach."

Naim looked over at Marco and they both chuckled.

"Where to now?"

"The police station."

"Why?" Naive.

"To report your self-defense. It's called offense."

"Oh," Marco said. "What about him selling drugs to that little girl? You going to report that, too?"

"Nope. That's called defense. Leverage. Watch and learn, Son."

They rode in silence for a few blocks before Marco said, "I'm definitely going to law school."

"Good, but no more assaults or I doubt you'll get in," Naim said and they both laughed.

CHAPTER 42

Monday morning.

Naim Butler and Max Devers were meeting with Keith Cassick, Paris Moore's court-appointed attorney, and eighties throwback. He was a big lummox-esque man dress in a brown suit and gold dress shirt. Both were ugly. It was the height of winter, yet he wore penny loafers with quarters in them and was sock-less. He had a slick comb-over *a la* Donald Trump and his hair color suspiciously matched the color of his shirt. For some odd reason, he had on designer sunglasses and a cologne that absurdly smelled like orange over musk. Keith was the definition of time warp, and sadly juries undoubtedly picked up on how out of touch he was with the twenty-first century.

They were in a Keefe & Baker boardroom, and Naim was laying out the details of the night before with respect to his encounter with Jackson Brown. "I mean, certainly, a part of his plea agreement involves him refraining from committing any new offenses, and selling to a minor would get his plea pulled," Naim said.

"Especially, because it involved a minor," Max added.

Keith ran a small comb through his hair and then clapped. "Wonderful tale. I smiled, I was in awe, it was really alive."

Max Devers looked up and smiled awkwardly. He wasn't used to such stupidity, but he was clearly amazed that a federal judge appointed this clown to defend a man accused of murder. "Get the hell off the case if what Naim has told you doesn't impress you. Your investigator should have found these details."

"If this guy has an investigator," Naim said.

"What do either of you expect me to do?"

"Start with confronting the AUSA to have the plea pulled," Naim said. "I can't believe we have to spell this out."

"Don't be an ass. I know that. But pulling the plea means that Brown won't testify, so that's not in the interest of the government," Keith said, and then smiled condescendingly. "But since you have this fancy operation, you knew that."

"We did," Naim said. "But your client is the chief concern and not the interest of the opposing party."

"Oh, you speak for Devers, too? Nice."

"Now who is an ass?" Naim said. "If the plea isn't pulled you'll use the recording to impeach Brown on the witness stand, but I am sure that you have to disclose this material pursuant to *Brady*. You can even call me to testify to its authenticity. I'm more than willing to take the witness stand to help your client."

"That's great, but in case you haven't noticed juries find people guilty after hearing sworn lies all of the time. I'll impeach him. You help. And he still gets found guilty. A wonderful justice system that we have."

Naim stood up. "So that means you don't want to present this angle?"

"This is my case," he said and stared at his nails. The pinky was long.

Nose candy, perhaps, Naim thought.

"Do you know a guy named, Marvin Davis?"

"Who doesn't with this case? He's the biggest dealer in the Bronx."

"And apparently, he paid Brown to lie on Paris about killing rival gang leader, Sammy Block, and shooting two others."

"Let me guess, you have proof of that?"

"In fact, I do," Naim said and played the tape of Brown's confession.

"Sounds like a confession was beaten or coerced out of him. That'll never fly in court."

"Very optimistic," Max said.

"How about tracking the money? Look to prove it wasn't a lie." Naim was the optimistic one.

"This is a waste of time," Keith said plainly.

"Get out," Max said. "And submit a motion to withdraw from the case."

"Let me guess," Keith said, and then stood, "Naim's going to take over? Oh, I forgot, he's not an attorney."

"Out." That was Naim.

"We should hit the town together one day. Maybe see *Cats* or something on Broadway," Keith said, smiling.

Naim smiled back. "Another morning. Another asshole." He shook his head, and then said, "Before you go, withdraw by Friday. That's best."

"Who's going to make me?" Defiant.

"Perhaps, the recording of this meeting leaked to the media if you lose this case will make you," Max said and pointed to a small camera mounted on the room's wall.

CHAPTER 43

Amber shot again and the basketball slipped into the rim with a whoosh. All net. She was a star high school player, but not tall enough for the WNBA so abandoning the pursuit of that destiny was an easy decision. Shoot a-rounds and suicides remained a constant in her life for cardio purposes, but today she was showing off for one, Marco Butler, in the Davis Hall gymnasium.

"Look at that shot," Marco said to her. He was scanning her body: her breasts squeezed in a sports bra, voluptuous ass prominently shown in yoga pants.

"You need to make it, or game over," she said and twirled girlishly in his face.

He threw the ball up and it was an air ball.

"Sad," she said.

"No fair," he said and hugged her. "You distracted me," he said, leaned back, admired her, and then added, "with all of this."

Amber giggled and then had a seat on a bench on the sideline. She fished in her gym bag for a water and protein bar. Marco sat next to her and pulled off his sweat-soaked tank top.

"Look at you. Show off," she said and punched his bicep.

"I was born like this," he said and laughed.

"You're crazy," she said.

"About you maybe."

"I know you let me win, too."

"Come on, I wouldn't do that." He smirked.

"Liar."

"This is a nice gym," he said and smiled. He opened a bottle of Gatorade.

"Nice segue," she said and laughed. "Much better than what I grew up using."

"Is that right?" Marco looked at her and tried to picture the space she learned to play basketball.

"Yes, very. Newark courts were littered with guys peddling drugs or stolen goods. There were the occasional gun shots nearby for half-time entertainment." She laughed. "It wasn't always Alpine, you know."

"Now I do."

"You probably had a basketball court in a suburban driveway that you and your friends played until your mom called you all in for lunch," she said as two men wearing suits walked into the gym.

"Not exactly," he said and then chuckled as the two upbringings collided in his mind leaving him speechless.

"Marco Butler?" one of the suits asked, flashing a badge.

The first reply that came to Marco was the one that Jackson Brown offered his father when he accosted him the day before: "Who are the fucks asking?"

Marco said, "Yes. May I help you?" He was calm.

"I'm DEA Agent Warner, and we need to chat."

Marco had his phone in his hand dialing when he said, "About?" He looked at Amber and couldn't believe that she had to witness this confrontation. Into the phone, he said, "Dad..."

Agent Warner snatched the phone and hit the END button. He tossed the phone to his partner, and then said to Marco, "Turn around and put your hands behind your back."

"What?" Marco stood, and then stepped back out of the agent's reach.

"Marco, just do as they say," Amber said. "I'll call your dad."

"I don't know his number," Marco said as the agent handcuffed him.

"Don't worry. I'll Google the firm and they will find him," Amber said. She then asked, "Where are you taking him?"

"Our HQ. Google the address," Agent Warner said sarcastically.

CHAPTER 44

Ready or not, you coward, here the hell I come...

Naim burst into the DEA Manhattan offices, approached the receptionist protected by bullet proof glass, and demanded to see Agent Warner. There was a thin line between love and hate, and Naim was flustered with respect to which emotion supported his attitude towards the agent. He hated him for arresting his son; but, loved how the agent had taught him a lesson. Naim vowed to never jeopardize his son's freedom again. The agent also had him consumed by another emotional desire.

Revenge.

He was exhausted with thoughts of paying someone back for causing his son this perverted injustice. This was hell for Naim, and someone was going to pay.

Agent Warner came into the lobby with an outstretched hand. Naim ignored it.

"I was expecting you," the agent said.

"Where's my son?"

"He needs a lawyer..."

Naim had gone crazy and stepped into the agent's face. Crazy and looking at a death wish.

"I suggest you back up, before you need one, too," the agent said and then smiled.

Naim didn't move backward. He inched closer. "Where's my damn son?"

The agent pushed him sparking a wicked smile to spread across Naim's face. He cracked his neck and then blinked uncontrollably. "This is where I prove to be smarter than a fifth grader," Naim said and imagined his arrest for assaulting a federal agent. A move that would block all of his upcoming blessings.

"I can hear your heart beating from three feet away," the agent said.

Naim swallowed hard and remained silent. *Anything I say can and will be used against me,* even bogus threatening agent charges if *anything I say is deemed as such.* This was a losing battle. He stole a lot of nerve to remain calm and silent to avoid further escalating the problem.

"In ten minutes your son will be let out of that very door that I walked out. I gotta hand it to you, he's a smart boy. Didn't say a word to me, but he requested a lawyer. You've taught him well. I mean, that son of a bitch, and I mean that literally, didn't say a word."

"We will see who's the bitch."

"I had no idea that he was a minor, although that's changing on Friday. A fact that'll change his life if you insist on sticking your nose in my investigation. Take this as your only warning. Stand down, Mr. Butler or both of you will need attorneys."

CHAPTER 45

Like a missile, Marco shot out of the DEA's offices, his hands outstretched. He hugged his father, and Naim felt the imaginary punch that Agent Warner had given him. It almost brought him to his knees. *What kind of animal locks up a man's child to prove a point?* Naim released his boy and looked around the waiting area. His eyes landed on the receptionist, whom no doubt, knew what was transpiring. She averted her eyes like a jury that rendered a verdict calling for another human being to be put to death. As luck would have it, Naim felt dead. The question was, how was his child?

"How are you?" Naim asked, looking squarely into his son's eyes for any emotional signs indicating distress.

"I'm good, Pops. Prepared my whole life for a bogus arrest," Marco said, and then smiled. "They just sat me at a desk, although, I was handcuffed for the ride over here."

"Sad. And they did it at your school in an effort to embarrass us," Naim said, walking towards the exit. "Amber was shocked but remarkably calm."

Marco looked at his watch. "She grew up in Newark and seen it all before so I am not shocked that she wasn't hysterical. She's at work now, so I can't even call her."

"You sure you're fine?" Naim had to ask again because Marco didn't appear affected by the arrest. Once again, he seemed numb to the seriousness of a situation.

"Dad, that was nothing. They know I didn't do anything to that creep. Brown tried to attack me, and I defended myself. I'm fine, but I hear that he spent the night in a hospital. I just want to go home and shower. They arrested me while I sat on a gym bench after playing basketball. After that, I want to do my homework and pretend this never happened."

"I see, but we have to deal with your school, I'm sure. This is terrible," Naim said and shook his head. "And your mom."

"No," Marco said tersely. "You cannot tell her this. No way," he said, and then asked, "where are we walking to?"

"I'm so damn confused, I don't even know."

Marco stopped walking and faced his father. He slapped his hands on his shoulders, shook Naim, and said, "Dad, snap out of it. This never happened. I'm OK, man...I mean, Dad." Naim hung his head low in shame. "Now how do we get from near all of these police agencies and home?"

Naim was silent. He had been used to living in his own world. He never thought that he would have to think for two people. Apparently, Marco's adroitness proved that he didn't have to do much. Sadly, he had missed out on the boy's upbringing or he'd know Marco was *fine* as he claimed.

"Yeah, let's head home. I have to meet Max, and then Brandy." Then it hit him. The first person that he had called after talking to Amber was Brandy.

He was in love.

CHAPTER 46

"How's it going?" Brandy asked.

Hours later, Naim was slouched in the passenger seat of Brandy's Lexus. His face was illuminated by a street light, and he looked drained.

"Isn't going at all. I've been in a mental coma for the past few hour."

"I certainly understand that," she replied and placed a hand on his thigh. She patted, and asked, "And, Marco?"

"The boy is on the phone with his girlfriend like nothing happened. It was the same thing yesterday when he flat-lined Brown. He didn't have a care in the world."

"Hence, you need to lighten up on yourself," she said and pulled from in front of his home. "He's a smart boy. He's going to be OK. You will, too. I'm going to just ride a bit."

"OK. I don't know why it seems like I failed, though. I took my seventeen-year-old to a hoe stroll, and watched with glee as he assaulted..."

"Self-defended."

"Yeah, that," Naim said, catching himself. "He hit the guy like it was another day at the park. Then he's arrested at school and questioned by a rogue DEA agent." He huffed and stared out of the window watching the treasures of Central Park along Fifth Avenue whiz by.

Brandy laughed lightheartedly. "He's a superhero...like his dad."

His eyes widened. "Oh..."

"Yup," she said and smiled. "You over think. And not about the right things."

He sat up and looked at her. "What's that supposed to mean?"

"The thing you should be focused on is how to put a stop to that moron, Agent Warner."

He smiled. "Precisely. See that's what I like about you. Always putting things into perspective."

"It's the reporter in me." She smiled back.

"Yeah, Max Devers from the firm and I are working on a plan to take care of the agent. No one threatens me and gets away with it."

"There you go," she said and hit his shoulder.

"Stop with the love taps," he said and winked.

"That wasn't a love tap for crying out loud."

He planted a kiss on her cheek. "Was that?"

"That was," she said, before adding, "don't kiss me while I'm driving." She looked at him sternly.

"Pull over then," he said and looked around. "This would be the perfect place to pull over," he said looking at the hotel on the corner.

She complied.

After a hearty kiss, they were inside of the kingly Peninsula Hotel and found the front desk.

Naim checked them into a sweet suite for the night. Brandy was at his side. The front-end clerk focused his attention on the computer to Brandy, recklessly eyeballing her with lust and Naim with envy. A post-Christmas party had livened up the normally quiet lobby. Men in cover of GQ worthy suits; beautiful woman in Valentino and Givenchy gowns. Despite the party guests having dates, men stared agog at Brandy, who was dressed for a Brooklyn Nets game.

Naim noticed every double take and figured he had to learn to deal with that. The attention was pleasurable, and he wore a grandiose you-can-look-but-she's-all-mine sneer on his face. His supreme confidence forced him to smile at every man admiring his lady.

For Brandy, Naim was the only man in the lobby. She was practiced at artfully being unbothered by lewd stares.

Their suite was on the twenty-third floor with a desirable view of New York City. They had no opportunity to enjoy it; the hotel room's door was barely closed before they kissed. Brandy's hands darted all over his body, making him dither helplessly. He lifted her button-up over her head; no time to undo every button. His eyes widened at the sight of her. One of his hands unfastened her pants and the other caressed her breasts. Both made him heady; her body a glass of wine. She released lustful emotion in his ear intensifying the moment.

Onto the bed, they landed with soft precision.

Their lovemaking was intense, attentive, but that only seemed to mask the animalistic encounter as tender.

Time passed. A lot of time passed before they pulled apart and sat up. He leaned over and kissed her on the cheek. "We're not driving, so I think that was legal."

"That was," she said, "but what happened shortly before was a crime in all fifty states."

"What can I say. I still have my criminal side. You weren't bad." He winked.

"Oh, really? I was spectacular."

"You were."

She rolled off the bed and stood in front of it; all of her glory exposed. "It's been a while. That was incredible."

"You sure sounded like it." He tilted his head to the side and smiled.

"I wasn't that noisy," she said, pulling her hair back.

"Lauryn Hill in an MTV Unplugged special isn't noisy. You were...um...loud. The neighbors know my name."

"You're too much, and I don't recall hearing a complaint, Hun. I distinctly remember hearing you ask 'what's my name' as if you forgot."

"Really, how could you hear me over the screams?" He jumped up and hugged her. "The lambs, Brandy. Silence the lambs."

CHAPTER 47

At six-thirty a.m., Naim walked into his home and bumped into Marco who was pulling on his coat. He looked at his watch and then shook his head while looking at his father.

"You're dressed in yesterday's duds, so it's safe to say you weren't out for a morning run," Marco said, smiling.

"Great guess. Don't ask. Don't tell," Naim said, heading for the stairs leading to the second floor. "I just need ten minutes and then I'll be down to escort you to school."

"Why? They haven't asked for that, and I don't want to make this a big deal. If they ask for you then you can come over, but please don't worry about this."

Who's the father here? Naim thought. "Why are you leaving so early then?"

"Well," Marco said, and grinned. "I am going to pick up Amber. We're going to breakfast before school."

"Excuse me," Naim said and headed back down the stairs. "You're not going to New Jersey this morning, Marco. Out of the question."

Marco chuckled. "I know. She's getting the NJ Transit train to the city and I'm picking her up at Penn Station. There's student parking at a garage near the school."

"Oh." Speechless.

"Can I go now?" Marco asked and then pat his dad on the back. "I don't want to be late."

"For school or picking up your girl?" Naim was laughing.

"Get out of here. School. Both," Marco said, laughing too. "I'll call you if anything gets out of control at school."

"Take her to Junior's," Naim yelled out.

"What was that?"

"It's in Brooklyn. GPS the directions. Go there for breakfast."

"Got it."

Two hours later, Naim was at his office desk researching the Paris Moore criminal action. He had reviewed the indictment and all of the documents filed in the matter using PACER. The defense had put up a very little fight against the prosecutor's allegations. There were no defense motions filed. In a murder case that was odd; an oddity that Naim was determined to get to the bottom of. He had pulled Jackson Brown's and Marvin Davis's rap sheets, as well as, searched for any criminal proceedings that named them as defendants. He couldn't believe what he had read.

Next, who was the murder, victim? That was the pressing question. Why had Sammy Block been killed? Why had Marvin Davis paid Brown to frame Paris Moore? Naim pushed back from his desk, grabbed his jacket, and was headed to talk to Paris Moore. He wanted to get to the root of the case. After he did, he planned to drop back in Agent Warner's world and shift its axis.

Naim pulled his office door open and Ginger barged in. She was frantic and breathless.

"What on earth?" Naim said, "Are you OK?" He reached inside his desk for a gun.

"No, I'm not," she said. "You have an urgent meeting which I just accepted and set up travel."

"I can't, Gin," he said. "Cancel, I am on to something."

"Naim Butler," she said and handed him a sheet of paper. "You've been summoned to the Oval Office. You need to be there at one, so I've booked you on the next flight out of JFK and your driver will be here any second. The Secret Service will be picking you up from the airport with a sign posing as ordinary drivers." She threw her hand on her hips, and then said, "Now should I cancel or not?"

"Not," he said without thought.

"Good. Change and be ready in fifteen minutes."

CHAPTER 48

At 10:45 a.m., Marco Butler put on his patchwork Moschino blazer, exited his Calculus class, and headed to meet Nancy Slomsky in the executive alley of Davis Hall. The bright sun lit up the hallway and promised another cold wintry afternoon. Marco was saturated with perspiration that mirrored a late morning shower. It was the perfect time to call his father to handle this situation, but he had poked his chest out and committed to handling this problem on his own. He would.

He reached the headmaster's office, masking his anxiety with smiles. As if she had seen him enter the main office door, her office door opened, she invited him in and offered him a seat.

"Let's get to it," she said and sat behind her desk. "You're in our music program, but you've thrown some pre-law electives in your coursework to eventually become an entertainment lawyer. Right so far?"

He nodded. *Where is this going?*

"So, I don't need to tell you that when an attorney asks questions, they typically know the answers."

"No, ma'am, you don't," he said and rubbed his sweaty palms on his pant leg.

"You were arrested in *my* gymnasium. Explain why?"

He raised his eyebrows at her blunt query.

"Well," she said, and then added, "remember I told you at my home that I am all knowing."

"I do."

"So, let's get to your version, as I have a federal agent already."

And with that line, he panicked even more. "OK," he said, and looked at the floor. "I was accused of assaulting someone. But it was a misunderstanding and all cleared up."

"Is that right?"

"Yes, ma'am."

"Let me be frank, Marco. This just isn't the time or place for misunderstandings with the police. You have an extremely bright future ahead of you and one false move on your part would blacken it. Remember that the next time you decide to do anything that leads federal agents to *my* school. You got that?'

"Yes, ma'am, I do," he said, and then added, "I'm sorry."

"No need to be. Let's get you graduated and on to greatness. Not many young, black boys achieve greatness without sports and rap professions. Remember that, Mr. Butler." She clasped her hands together, and then said, "That is all."

CHAPTER 49

The oval-shaped rug featured the Presidential Seal dead center in the room. Around the rug's border was five historical quotations of meaning by Martin Luther King, Jr. and four former presidents: Lincoln, Kennedy, and both Roosevelt's. Two paintings flanked the south windows behind the famous Resolute Desk. *Avenue in the Rain* by Childe Hassam, depicted Fifth Avenue adorned with flags and banners in support of the Allied war effort during World War I was of particular interest to Naim Butler; after all, he had jogged through the scene many times. The only glimpse Naim ever imagined getting of the Oval Office, though—or the White House—was during a CNN broadcast or a collection of photos published by the president.

"Josh, how about you join Butler and me on the sofa this afternoon," the president ordered, and then said, "Naim scoot over a bit."

"Certainly, Mr. President," Naim said. He had always wanted to say that, 'Mr. President.'

Radcliffe was making it clear that this was his office and his assigned seating.

Josh Meacham, the White House press secretary was usually perched in a seat on the side of the desk next to the president's flag. He was usually seen, not heard; and, ready to report—or spin—what he'd seen and heard at a moment's notice to the White House press core. But today, the president wanted him at one of the best seats in the house.

"Tea?" the president asked his guest.

"Yes, sir," Naim said. He didn't have a desire for tea but wondered what brand of tea was offered to White House guests. Not just any guests on a tour, but those finding themselves in the West Wing inside the Oval Office.

A butler placed a tea tray with Japanese-inspired hand painted, porcelain tea cups on it between them. The cups were a gift from Japan's leader. The butler poured the president and Naim a cup and then disappeared into thin air.

"Now, then," the president said, and then coolly sat back crossing his legs. "Let me start by telling you what I know and why you're here. You're born in Chicago, undergrad education at Tulane, law school at Penn, and a doctoral candidate at Yale which will be granted in May. Congrats, by the way. You're currently a single dad with a son attending a prestigious prep school and you're a partner at Baker and Keefe specializing in federal sentencing mitigation techniques that pose as sentencing reform that rival some of the senator's bills that can't seem to get tabled, voted on, and put on my desk."

Naim's eyes widened, and then he smiled. Sipped some tea: Earl Grey.

Radcliffe smiled back; a handsome and gregarious grin. He had more applause for the ex-convict. The president opened a folder and right on top was a color mug shot of Naim.

"The only evidence of your prior arrests is this mug shot taken at your probation officer's office when you completed your three-year federal sentence. If not for this proof, I'd have no idea that a man with your resume committed a crime. You remind me of myself and what my life could have become had I not had the kinds of support structures, the second chances, and the resources that would allow a young man to survive mistakes. You've survived and I salute you because unlike myself you didn't have the benefit of a comfortable upbringing and attending a prep school like I did; and like you're offering your son, Marco. Job well done."

"Thank you, Mr. President." Naim smiled and a lone tear fell from his watery eyes.

"That's why I've brought you here today," the president said and handed Naim a box of Kleenex. "Tears of joy. You've earned them, and this," the president said and Poof! out came a framed pardon. "The presidential pardon."

For Naim, it had as much significance as the United States Constitution. Life had progressed for him, and he had stopped taking things for granted nearly twenty years ago. Today it paid off, and he said, "Thank you, sir. I assure you that I won't disappoint or upset your legacy."

"I'm sure," the president said and nodded at Josh. "Has Senator MacDonald arrived? We have to get this sentencing reform bill signed while we have Mr. Butler here. It's this man's hard work that promises our nation that long prison sentences aren't the only answer to arresting crime. I want him here for the signing of this profound legislation, and in the official signing photo."

Naim smiled again. "How could I repay you, sir? I mean, I know that I can't, but this is unreal."

"Ah ha! Good ol' *quid pro quo*, Mr. Butler. Just give back. That's essential. The democratic way. Senator MacDonald could possibly use your help in New York," the president said and winked.

———— ————

Outside of the White House, Naim sent a text to his son, Brandy, and Derrick. It was a picture of him with the president and senator, along with the message that he was taking an Amtrak train back to New York to let the events of the day sink in. He asked all of them to meet him at Hector's for a celebratory dinner.

CHAPTER 50

Agent Warner paced methodically around Assistant United States Attorney Clarke Duncan's office hopelessly trying to explain his little problem: Naim Butler. The mitigation specialist was on track to put his decision-making ability on the front page of the *Post* or *Times*. The agent had worked years to take Bronx drug dealers off of the streets and he refused to allow an ex-con posing as a law-abiding citizen to ruin all of his hard work.

"Enough is enough," Duncan said and clasped his hands together. Duncan was a small man, with an equally smaller complex. He was such a New York Giants fan that whenever he had the opportunity to dress down, he donned tops with the Giants team logo. He was a walking cheerleader for the team. But what he did better than root for his home team was prosecute scoundrels.

"I thought that this would be a slam dunk," the agent said, playing off his colleague's surname. He sighed and seemed defeated. "It's like I've jumped in traffic and this SOB could potentially run me off the road and destroy years of investigative work."

"You still haven't told me what you've done," Duncan said and then grabbed his cell phone.

"And I plan to keep it that way, too. Some things qualified immunity can't rescue you from, Dunk."

"I see," the veteran prosecutor said and smirked. He totally understood his point. "My hands are tied then with respect to helping you."

"Maybe. Maybe not. I still have an ace in the hole," the agent said and watched the prosecutor's eyes bulge while looking at his cell phone.

"I hope that you have four aces because things have just gotten really real," he replied and then showed the agent the photo of a smiling Naim Butler in the Oval Office flanked by the President and New York Senator.

"Who sent you this?"

"My colleague, Derrick Adams. He's Butler's best friend."

CHAPTER 51

Naim Butler came back alert, but slowly from the darkness, conscious first of his ability to only take short breaths from the extensive bandages that wrapped his chest.

His eyes roamed about the hospital room, and next, he became aware of Brandy Scott. He assumed that she was there the entire time that he was in the darkness. Their eyes met and she sat her lap top aside; joy bloomed in her face, signaling her relief that he was awake and prayerfully going to make a speedy recovery.

Approaching his bed, she smiled and an incandescent glow filled the room. She ran her hand along his waves, kissed him softly on the lips—despite them being dry—and then pressed the panic button. "Everything is going to be all right," she whispered and then held his hand that wasn't laced with an IV. A rueful smile spread across his face, and he nodded affirming her position.

A nurse entered the room and began to address Brandy. "Is everything..." She paused, and said, "Glad to have you back, Mr. Butler. I'll inform the doctor of your status. He removed the endotracheal tube an hour ago and will be pleased that you're alert."

Naim coughed. "How long have I been...um...gone?" he whispered with his eyes examining the monitors, which helped him breathe and provided him vitamins and nutrients.

"Dr. O'Brien will be in a better position to answer that," she said and headed for the door.

Naim's eyes locked onto Brandy. "Well..." His throat was dry and he spoke in a raspy drawl.

"Two days," she replied before consulting her watch. "Forty-nine hours to be exact. It's Thursday, January 14th. Seven-twelve p.m."

He tried to sit up.

Gloom surfaced on his face. He groaned and immediately pressed his back to the bed again.

"You have to lie down," Dr. O'Brien said, entering the room. He slipped glasses over his eyes and collected a clip board from the bin at the foot of his patient's bed.

Naim's hand roamed the side of the bed and found the button to slowly lift the back of the bed to sit up a little. "My son, Marco," he said to Brandy. "Where's my son?"

"Naim." Her eyes looked at a duffel bag in the room's corner. "While you've been in an induced coma, he's been right here. He showered here this morning and was driven to school escorted by armed sentry provided by your firm out of an abundance of caution. He just left a moment ago to take Amber to the train. She came here after school with him."

Naim blinked uncontrollably, working with some effort to clear the fog from clouding his memory to recall the events leading to his hospitalization. He squeezed her hand.

"Trust me," she said, "he's fine, albeit fearful of losing his father. He really loves you."

"Thanks, Brandy," he said, and then turned to the doctor, "what you got?"

Dr. O'Brien chuckled and tapped an expensive pen on the clipboard. "Well, there was a bullet lodged in your right vertebrae. Missed any major parts, and didn't leave life threatening damage. Loss of blood forced you into shock and we induced a coma to rest your brain, but we've taken care of that. There will be a scar less than an inch on your chest, barely visible to the eye unless someone is very close. I'm sure your wife will be the only one taking a look, despite you being all over the news. Congrats on the pardon, by the way."

"That's right, Doctor," Brandy said and smiled. She looked at Naim and shrugged.

"Police want to talk to you. I can keep them away if you need me to. Other than that, you need to be observed a few days, but you should make a great recovery," the doctor said, checking Naim's vitals.

Naim raised his eyebrows. "Thanks, doctor. How many days is a few?" he whispered.

"Can't say right now. We will run tests and at least be sure your wound heals properly," he said and slipped the clip board back into the bin. "I'll have some water sent up for you to sip, and will be back soon. Do not eat any food or drink any liquids."

When the doctor left the room, Naim asked Brandy, "Well, pretty lady, how long have we been married? I need to know just in case someone asks."

She laughed. "Two days, but we're getting a quickie divorce the moment you're discharged. I had to lie because hospital reception wouldn't let me up here. It was Marco's idea."

"I'mma kill him," he replied and tried to laugh. "Geesh, I hope you signed a prenup." He grinned because laughing hurt, and he tried to avoid it. "I am impressed and thankful for your ruse to be by my side. Thanks, Brandy, you continue to amaze me."

"What'd you expect me to do? You've been featured on the news the last two days and someone had to protect you from the media and detectives. Marco is not an adult, and you have no immediate family here, so here I am. Derrick, Hector, Max, and Ginger have all been here, and yup, they've backed up my wife story, too. Thanks to the news, everyone knows that an ex-con with a special license to carry killed a would-be robber in a gun fight outside of the highly populated Madison Square Garden." Naim furrowed his brows and shook his head. "Detectives have been here around the clock. Marco has been furious about it. They have gone on the record and want to know how you managed to get a license to carry a concealed weapon? They're calling it suspicious and intend to fully investigate."

Naim pressed his index finger to his temple, channeling his inner Malcolm X. He winced in pain from the sudden movement and put his arm back to his side. "I killed someone?" The rhetorical query forced her to slowly nod an affirmation. "I do remember shooting one of the *two* men, but...Brandy they knew my name, where I lived, and that I was set to receive a doctorate from Yale. And with that, the police have the nerve to be worried about my properly licensed gun."

"Marco and I assumed that someone randomly tried to rob you..."

He cut her off by shaking his head. "No, babe, someone tried to have me killed."

CHAPTER 52

Four days later, Naim's dark and quiet hospital room brightened and Naim heard Marco's voice emanating from the doorway. It was a metallic and cold voice, laced with unmistakable arrogance and solid sarcasm.

"I am an NYPD detective, young man." Naim heard another voice; it was scruffy but calm.

"And..." Marco replied. "I've seen you on TV talking disrespectfully, very, very, very, very disrespectfully about my dad. He's been shot by thugs and I'm not going to allow you to badger him. You should be looking for his attackers. They're on video for crying out loud."

Naim felt his muscles tighten, the shreds of happiness from being protected by his son was profound. For a moment, he felt the familiar feeling of having a family and that collision of thrill and privilege derived from that kind of love. Then, the fear that overzealous NYPD placing his son in a banned choke hold kicked in.

"Brandy please let the detective in and calm down the tiger." He smiled. "Take him to the cafeteria or something. But before you go set your lap top up behind the curtain leaving a view of the room and record this interrogation. Please and thanks."

She smiled. "I got it," she replied and followed his order. She adored his terse acuity. At the door, she noticed two detectives. She said, "Detectives, Mr. Butler will see you now," and when they walked past her to Marco, she said, "Come with me for a minute, darling."

Naim lay motionless and gazed up at the two detectives. The eerie details are given to him by Brandy regarding their potential desire to question his license to carry had him prepared to call for a mouthpiece to cut them down with a scythe the moment things went haywire.

"Good evening, Mr. Butler. I'm Detective Douglas."

Wrestler build. Red hair. Freckles. Pork-chop beard.

"And I'm Detective Moss. We're from the Midtown Manhattan precinct."

Pencil thin. Six-feet-four inches. Salt and pepper cropped afro.

"Detectives," Naim said and nodded. He was glad that his voice had returned to ninety-percent normal. "You've found my attackers?" He wanted to nail down the purpose of him allowing them into his room right out of the gate. Naim was fluent in English, Spanish and Bullshit. He had no discretion when it came to his charming sarcasm; apparently, his son was born with it.

"We haven't. That is why we're here," Detective Moss said with an air of politeness.

Ah, the Black, nice cop, Naim thought. "Well, I'm fresh out of a coma, and I have no clue about who the men were and why'd they want to harm me. Very vague memory with regard to descriptions."

The bad cop pulled out a mug shot from his back pocket and handed it to Naim. "You killed him. Know him at all?"

"What's his name?"

"Why do you need to know his name? You either know him or you don't." That was Detective Douglas.

OK, that's how you want to play it, Naim thought. "Has ballistics confirmed that I killed anyone?" Naim shot at the officer. His lawyerly instincts had kicked in. *I am not a lawyer, my ass.*

"Come on, Butler. Save the smart-ass act."

"I assure you that it's not an act."

"We have a robbery, a murder, and an ex-con with a questionable granted license to carry."

Naim chuckled. "There's nothing dubious about it," he said and pressed a button to sit up a little. "Let me help you two fine detectives come up with a viable plan to do your job."

"Aren't you quite the pretentious prick?" Detective Douglas said.

Naim ignored his name calling. "When I exited the Amtrak New York Penn Station, I was accosted by two thugs who called out to me, 'Hey, Mr. Butler.' When I turned around one of them said, 'Should be getting that doctorate soon. Must be nice.' I backed up and one of them discreetly pulled a gun and asked for my wallet and cash, which I denied having. He then offered to take me to Lenox Hill to get some. In case you didn't know, I live in the Lenox Hill section of the Upper East Side."

"Fascinating tale; suspense writers should emulate your ability to craft a story. We have a dead man. Get to that part of the plot," Detective Douglas said, moving closer to Naim's bed.

Ignoring bad cop again, Naim went on. "So now I'm panicking because there's a massive crowd outside of the station, and these hoodlums knew or claimed to know, where I lived. One of them, the one with the gun, grabbed me and pressed the gun into my side. The other hailed a taxi. When the taxi stopped, I pushed the gunman into it and ran. A bullet rang out, so I took up position behind a car and pulled out my properly licensed gun and returned fire. I'm assuming based on what you've said, one of them took a bullet, but the other man took off in the cab, I assume with the taxi driver held at gun point. He was probably robbed. I would check that out." He curled his lips and nodded.

"So you drew a weapon at Forty-first Street and Eighth Avenue? Sounds irresponsible. I mean the corner of MSG, Amtrak, and hordes of the passerby. What were you thinking?" That was the bad cop again.

Naim grinned. "So that I'm clear, Officer Doug-Ass. Out of all that I explained, you've managed to focus on the passerby and me protecting myself."

Detective Moss interrupted his partner's response. "Where can we find the license, Mr. Butler?"

"Up your partner's ass. How about you get the hell out and retrieve it from the state I got it from. And while you're at it, dig deep and find some common damn sense. You come into a man's hospital room, never pull out pads to take notes, because you never even intended on taking any. You never even asked the most basic question about the crime that landed me here."

"And what might that be?" Detective Douglas asked and then glanced at his partner.

"The race of the damn other perp. Please, see yourselves out, unless you plan on foolishly charging me with a crime," Naim said and furrowed his brows. One of them began to speak, and he said, "No...no. Nothing else to say unless it's on a witness stand to send the clowns that shot me up the river."

"Well tell us something..."

Naim cut Detective Moss off mid-sentence as the hospital door opened. "I want a lawyer, and I am done talking to either of you without one. There's something."

"OK, detectives," Marco said, entering the room. He sat his attache on the windowsill and smirked at Detective Douglas. "I think that my dad means that you're trespassing. You two should leave and I'll have his lawyer contact you for further questioning, if necessary, that is."

"What he said," Naim said and smiled.

CHAPTER 53

The next morning, Naim was having his dressing changed when the hospital room's telephone rang. He looked at the outdated rotary phone and asked the nurse to answer it. She did.

The nurse said, "Mr. Butler, it's your mother."

Shock and angst spread across his face. He blinked uncontrollably in an attempt to figure out what to say. He was lost for words.

"Tell her that I'm being tended to and will call her back."

She did.

Then, the nurse said, "You don't have her number, so how are you planning to do that? Her question, not mine."

"Please take down her number, and then let her know that you have to go. Thanks."

She did, and upon returning to tending to his wounds she had a look of concern. "Is everything all right?" she asked him.

"Well...I haven't talked to my mother in nearly twenty-years," he said matter-of-factly. Nothing else needed to be said. The deep wound that divided him and his mother were deeper than the one being cleaned by the nurse. Addressing the matter would need to be cared for as gingerly and under his current state of mind, he wasn't prepared to do that.

"I'm sorry to..."

"Don't be," he said, interrupting her. "It was best," he said as she affixed the last piece of tape to the bandage.

"All done," she said. "Breakfast should be up shortly."

"OK, thanks," he said and watched her leave the room. His eyes immediately darted to the phone number, and his memories of his mother intensified a fact that he had always lived with. Despite the problems with his mother, he knew that if he was in this sort of predicament, she would be right by his side. And she didn't even know that he had given her a grandson. The facts forced water to well up in his eyes. He missed his mother and her call proved why.

Before a tear could fall, the nurse returned to the room. She approached the side of his bed, and said, "I have some excellent news."

"I can use a bit of that."

"Good, because Doc says that you should be good to go home this afternoon or evening."

"I reckon you were right. Excellent news."

——————— ———————

Naim looked at the clock on the hospital room wall: fifteen after four. Brandy had walked into the room a moment ago and it was time to face the music. She looked at him and then averted his eyes.

"What's wrong?" She smiled. "You're looking away from me like a jury about to deliver the bad news." She chuckled.

Naim didn't.

He twirled his fingers together and tried to think of something to say to her. Words were scrambled in his head. He was gripped with confusion. Then the confusion gave way to anger. Anger at his mother for complicating his life and recovery by calling. She had mentally taken him back to Chicago, a place that haunted him. He never wanted to return, not even to visit; but, dear old mom had him there. She had reached out, he presumed to bridge the gap between them.

"My mother tried to make contact with me. She called the room's number, and I had the nurse blow her off. We haven't talked in years, but I feel terrible. In my time of need, she found it in her heart to console me and I didn't let her."

Brandy sighed. She was going to cry because she felt his pain. Pain dominated her face, and she knew that she couldn't take it away from him.

She said, "We haven't talked much about your parents. Or, mine, really."

"I'm not surprised that you're confused about that. I try to stay away from the subject of parents."

"Perhaps," she said and grabbed his hand. "Your parenting skills are a reflection of your dealing with your parents. That's quite apparent."

"It is. I'd never treat my son badly as I was. The funny thing is that I've grown up and forgiven my parents for their neglect and un-supportive natures."

"So you're saying that you're ready to take a call from mom?"

"Maybe," he said and smiled. "I don't even know how to talk to my mom anymore."

"Of course, you do," Brandy said, and kissed him. She pulled back and looked at him intently. "It's like kissing or riding a bike. You never forget how to talk to mom."

CHAPTER 54

Naim was at his home office sipping a latte and nibbling on a coffee cake when Ginger peeked in.

Over the last three weeks, his world was fairly quiet save for his investigations. He devoured discovery from the Paris Moore case and had two investigators working a case that he hadn't officially been assigned to defend. Naim had two different investigators looking into the backgrounds of the men who assaulted him. What he wanted was a connection to Agent Warner to surface and prove the agent attempted to take him out to assure that he didn't get in the way of a successful Paris Moore bogus conviction.

Ginger handed him a written report from one of his investigators, and the college of the dead man that tried to kill him was highlighted. Naim smiled wickedly.

"I know that grin, Mr. Butler," Ginger said and smiled.

"Then you know that someone is going down for disturbing my life."

"And that someone is?"

"Can't tell you that this second. But it's going to send shock waves through my adversaries across the country," he said and snatched up the phone. He called his confidant, Max Devers.

Max picked up the other end, the men exchanged pleasantries and Naim updated Max on the status of his health before he got down to business.

Naim said, "I potentially have proof of who had me shot. With that out of the way, I'd like to take the BAR exam immediately and then go on the record as counsel for Paris Moore."

"Very well, let me know if you run into any problems. Senator MacDonald is looking to work with you on his prison reform bill, so I am sure he'd help you if the courts give you any problems. Just get the test done as early as possible to make magic. And what are you going to do about Agent Warner?"

"I'm going to bring that son of a bitch to full froth."

————— —————

That night, Naim and Marco went on a double date to the Knicks game with Amber and Brandy. As planned the players wore the FAMM T-shirts and the web site was trending on Twitter. Carmelo Anthony offered a heartfelt expression of his feelings toward the ballooning incarceration rates live on ESPN. The foursome was on the second row and watched Carmelo deliver the FAMM message to the country.

After the first quarter, Jacqueline Beard called Naim and informed him that the FAMM site had crashed.

"Are you crying?" Naim asked over the roar of Knicks fans.

"Tears of joy, my friend," she replied, and Naim imagined her waving a cigar in the air.

"Well deserved tears," Naim said. "This is just the beginning. Wait until the concert. Me and the team were thinking of making it a tour. The FAMMily tour."

"Now, that sounds exciting."

"It is very exciting, ma'am. Now let's get that site back up with the capability to handle the mass volume."

"You got it, Naim," she said, "and thanks for everything."

—————— ——————

Two hours later, Naim had dropped Brandy off at her Park Slope home and was headed back to Manhattan. He passed a twenty-four-hour diner and decided to stop and grab a late night bite. He circled Daisy's Diner in the South Slope section of Brooklyn before he found parking a few blocks away. It was a quiet neighborhood, and Naim felt safe about stopping. He texts his son to see if he wanted him to bring him anything home, and then slipped his cell phone into his coat pocket.

Naim excited his Benz and walked a few steps to a stop sign when he experienced *deja vu*.

"Hey, Mr. Butler..."

CHAPTER 55

Marco had parted ways with his father and was driving Amber home after the game. For convenience, Sinia and Naim and rented a Jaguar XJR for Marco's use. It was supposed to keep him disguised and out of his Audi, but a Jaguar hardly made him incognito. There were many things Marco could do as opposed to dropping Amber off because he wanted to spend more time with her.

"That was a good game," Marco said. The top was down on the racing charcoal-gray Jaguar, for them to enjoy the rare fifties February weather. The car's heat was blasting and mixing with the cool night air. It made Amber comfortable with the top being down, something that she didn't really like. A bug slamming into her face like they do the wind shield was her biggest fear.

"Yeah, it was," she said. "Where are you going?" she asked, having noticed him heading away from the Holland Tunnel.

"It's nice out," he replied, "so I thought we'd take a ride and enjoy it." He wiggled his fingers, re-wrapped his hands around the wheel, and then sped off. "I want to be with you as long as I can."

The car was going faster than he knew. The West Side Highway wasn't ready for his speeds—a four-lane highway with traffic lights. Between the lights and the never ending construction, he had no business reaching sixty miles per hour on the twenty-yard spaces between lights.

"So..." Amber said, before being interrupted by Marco's cell phone ringing. "Valentine's Day is Sunday..."

He snatched his phone from the console. "What's up?"

"Where are you?"

It was his dad.

"Midtown Manhattan."

"Where?" Angry.

"Passing the Fashion Institute. What's wrong?"

"Meet me at Daisy's Diner in Brooklyn. It's in the South Slope area."

"What's going on?"

"GPS it and meet me there. Now, Marco," he said and hung up.

Marco looked over at Amber, and said, "Change of plans."

CHAPTER 56

Naim was in the twenty-four-hour diner frozen. The six blocks that he walked to get there were a daze. He was on autopilot, unknowingly throwing one foot in front of the other. The sounds of the blast continued to ring in his ear. Killing for the second time was the only idea that made him snap out of it when the waiter asked if he'd like something to drink.

"Yes, water, please," he said and folded his hands together. *Do I look like a killer?* he thought. He got up, retreated to the bathroom and splashed his face with water. He pats it dry, looked into the mirror, and said, "Pull it together," before walking back out to his booth.

Marco was walking in and he spotted his dad. Naim embraced his son who was thrust into the familial role that was an amalgam of protector and crisis manager. Marco wore tight driving gloves that seemed most appropriate to choke someone out if need be; like those Isotoners that O.J. Simpson pretended didn't fit. In his peevish mood, Naim looked out the window and saw a cop car pull up outside of the diner. A part of him suddenly felt like running. Instead, he turned back to Marco. They both sat silent for a while and watched the two officers from the police cruiser come into the diner, buy coffee and danish, before leaving. Only then did Naim whisper to his son that they had to go.

When they reached the Jaguar, Marco walked toward the driver's side, but Naim stopped him.

"Let me drive," Naim said. It was a command.

"What's going on?" If Marco panicked, he didn't show it.

"Patience, my friend," Naim said, pulling into traffic. "I'm trying to pull myself together to explain this as effectively as possible."

"Best way is to simply let it out. This isn't court so it needn't be rehearsed and perfect."

Despite the situation, Naim let out a bland chuckle. "Put that way doesn't really make it easier," Naim said and drove some more. Police cruisers were zipping past him, no doubt headed to a crime scene.

His crime scene.

"Put on your seat belt," Naim said. "Cops are everywhere, and surely they'd use any excuse to pull over two Black men in a Jag."

"Um...OK, Dad. You're awfully..." Marco let that linger because he was lost for words.

"Scared," he said and banged the wheel twice, "Fuck my life."

"Dad, what's going on, man. This mystery is killing me."

"OK, dammit," Naim said. "Dammit, Marco, I just killed another human-damn-being."

"What?" Marco threw his head back. "Pull over."

"Hell no. I need to get as far away from here as possible."

"Dad, pull over."

"No, I can't," Naim said and seemed to drive even faster.

"Why not?"

"I have to get out of New York first."

"Are you..." He wanted to say crazy, but Marco stopped talking. "You're not thinking. Pull over."

"Why?" Pissed off.

"Because any bridge or tunnel you go through has cameras. That's just for starters. Second, you need to sit and figure this out."

Naim slammed the wheel again. "It wasn't my fault, man. I dropped Brandy at her home up in Brooklyn, and then someone approached me with a gun pointed at me after I got out of my car to go to the diner. We wrestled for the gun, which was tossed some feet away. I broke free from the man and then tried to run to my car. I darted out into the street. The man was behind me but was hit by a car speeding down the street. I kept running, but as fast as the car was going, I am sure the man is dead."

CHAPTER 57

Naim awoke the next morning with the memory of Max Devers bringing his car to his home. His conversation with the fine lawyer and professor remained vivid. They had run through many hypotheses before mustering a plan to help the police answer questions about the death of the man that held him and gun point.

Just after seven thirty, Naim sent his son off to school with an armed driver and then took a swim and shower. Freshened up and relaxed despite his complicated livelihood, he threw on a jacket and headed for the police station. He arrived, approached the duty officer, and requested to see the detective assigned to acquire justice for the man who died the night before.

As luck would have it, the detective and prosecutor were standing behind the duty officer with grandiose sneers on their faces.

"What an astounding moment in my career," Detective Hyatt said and smiled. "Never before has a suspect just walked into the police station looking for me. I usually have to track them."

"I'm sure my timing is impeccable. But I'm not a suspect of yours." Naim was stunned, but he put on his most impressive poker face. "My lawyer," he shook his head and smiled, "my lawyer should be here any second now, and we can get this show on the road." He thought he'd never need a criminal lawyer again. So much for that.

———— ————

"Your yellow-brick-road leads directly to Rikers if you lie to us," the prosecutor, Paige Trenton, said and then tucked hair behind her ear. They had agreed to talk after the state had outlined their case against Naim.

Naim may not have liked how Max Devers—his attorney—had phrased it, but if the polices' theory wasn't "killing" him...Despite not arguing in a courtroom in eons, Max remained arguably one of the finest barristers in New York City.

"So, to summarize," Detective Hyatt said and smiled. "It's your story that an esteemed professor, which you threatened in December, who happened to be sleeping with your ex-girlfriend, tried to kill you?"

"You make it sound like a Dateline story," Naim said.

"Yes, who are you, Lester Holt?" Max said and raised a cryptic eyebrow.

"Save the sarcasm," ADA Trenton said.

"For?" Max asked. "Certainly, not a court. Mr. Butler isn't a murderer."

"You know, you're right," she replied and retrieved a CD from a file before her.

"Look," Naim said and stared at the one-way glass. Just in case they were recording his interview he wanted to look right into the camera in the event they decided to play it for a jury of his peers. "I did not kill, Professor Austin Mills. I have a recording of my advice, not threat, that he terminate his harassment of my client who happens to be the mother of my son. I am here with an attorney whom I called right after this unfortunate tragedy and he advised me to come to the station now. My ex was going to file a restraining order against this professor..."

"By the looks of things," Max had cut in, "you needed a restraining order from this crazed lunatic. Who tries to kill someone at the busiest train station in New York City?"

Naim continued. "I gave you the gun that I wrestled from this so-called esteemed professor that held me at gun point and confessed to being the getaway driver for the two men that shot me. If need be I'll submit to a polygraph and any other forensic tests to help you close this case in, what is it, forty-eight hours."

"And with that, we're done here unless you plan on arresting Mr. Butler," Max said and stood. Naim stood, too, and threw on his jacket. "Good day, Detective Hyatt."

"Sit down," the prosecutor said.

"Yeah, not so fast," the detective added. "We, well, you have a problem."

"That is?" That was defense counsel.

"We have a video of the encounter so we do believe you," ADA Trenton said.

"We do, and, my partner and I, confronted the professor with the video," Detective Hyatt said.

Naim and Max both looked puzzled; confusion enveloped them.

"He's not dead." That was a baffled Naim Butler.

"Certainly, he was hit by a car and knocked out. However, at the hospital, he awakened and was under observation when he elected to talk to us. We confronted him with the contents of the CD and he feigned pain and asked to postpone the chat until he hired a lawyer. Through the night, he slipped out of the hospital. He is on the loose."

CHAPTER 58

Indebted to his smart lawyer who cautioned him to hire a security team to escort his son to and from school, Naim was at his kitchen table just after noon, following an in depth brainstorming session with Max Devers and Ginger Robertson. He was armed and prepared for the good doctor. He wouldn't run or hide.

Since his hospitalization, Naim had avoided Sinia. It was time to face her, and while Marco was in school it was perfect timing. He cued up his iPad and got Sinia on the screen.

"Oh, what a pleasant surprise," she said, and then pouted. "Now you want to chat? My little boyfriend is in a coma, but I bet you have your editor-bimbo right by your side."

What on Earth have I just walked into, he thought. "Well, that clears up my thoughts of if you were OK. By the sound of things you're perfect."

"I am," she said, and then asked, "So, you tried to kill him. The video of the incident has gone viral."

Naim chuckled. "He tried to kill himself. He had too many degrees not to know to look both ways before crossing the street."

"Here you have a man nearly dead and you're still your arrogant self."

"What do you expect? Your *little boyfriend* tried to kill me." He smiled.

"I hate you."

"You must too have sent that e-mail to my editor-bimbo."

"Oh, pah-lease." She looked shocked.

"So you deny sending Brandy my rap sheet?"

"I do."

"You're such a pathetic liar."

"I'm not. And I resent that."

"Sinia, I once had a tracker on your cell phone. I know all about your ability to blatantly lie." She looked dumbfounded. "Yes, I once installed a spy app on your phone and I saw all of your cheating and filthy text messages. The only reason that I never said a word to you is that you never physically cheated or met anyone and despite that, you were still the best thing to happen to me. Considering my family, I now know that it was easy for you to be the best thing that I ever had." He paused and looked pitifully at her. "Why do you think you're not standing by me when I was arrested hurt so badly. I had put up with all of your bullshit and you didn't stand by me. Do you know how hard it was to smile in your face after reading all of your text through the day for months?"

The silence between them screamed obscenities.

"I didn't cheat on you. Ever."

He shook his head. "I know all about you and Mr. Love's flirty messages, Sinia. I am not shocked that you ended up marrying him. It never struck you as odd that I showed up at the skating rink the one time that you drove him there. I knew you had picked him up. When we left the rink and I hopped into the front seat, I was so glad that he didn't even ask to get in the front, because I was surely going to beat his pretty little ass."

Silence.

More silence.

"You hacked my phone? That is some real creep shit."

"Maybe, but it's just like you to focus on the most irrelevant thing. This is why I would never re-date you."

"You're an ass. I'll be up there this weekend to check on my son," she said and sipped champagne from a goblet. "You hacked my phone." She laughed.

"Um, it's Valentine's Day this weekend, and he has plans. As you know, it's also my birthday, so, I will also be busy. It's not a good weekend to visit, but you know that."

"Must be nice to have been born on such a romantic day. But I'll be there, so this year should be a mess for you."

"I doubt it. You're not welcome here this weekend. Let the boy enjoy his woman for the day."

Wide eyed, she said, "Let me be clear about something. I will always be his number one woman."

"I hope so. You're his mother. And you have Mother's Day."

She poured champagne into her glass and held it up to the screen. "See you this weekend. Tootles." She ended the call.

———— ————

Thirty-eight minutes later, Marco walked into the kitchen. He dropped his book bag on the floor before walking to the cupboard and grabbing a large glass. At the refrigerator, he said, "So, Dad, what's the emergency. Bad enough, you have armed men chaperone me to class. To have them waltz into the band room and pull me out is a bit much." He poured himself a glass of orange juice.

"Well, my son, it seems that the good doctor isn't dead. In fact, he's on the loose after police confronted him about holding me at gun point."

Marco massaged his temples. "Deep."

"Very," Naim said and sat his iPad to the side. "Max has learned that Professor Mills has withdrawn a substantial amount of cash from his bank account and has taken a leave of absence from UNC."

"Oh." He sipped his drink. Suddenly, he understood and agreed with the extra security. "This new life of mine is a bit much, but I am riding the wave."

Naim laughed. "Thanks," he said and shook his head. "Who knows if he's coming for me again, so we're going to have to be very cautious here."

"OK, I understand."

"Very good." Naim looked puzzled.

"I am OK," Marco said. "I can see the confusion on your face."

"You seem un-phased."

"Emphasis on seems. I just have a cool way of showing when I'm stressed or under pressure. Don't be fooled."

"Duly noted," Naim said and stood.

Marco's cell phone rang. It was Amber.

After answering the call, Marco said, "It's for you."

Naim furrowed his brow and squinted his eyes. He snatched up his son's phone and greeted the caller.

"Good day, Mr. Butler," Amber said. Her politeness was remarkable. "My father would like to speak with you."

"Sure, put him on." Unbothered.

Parker King was a man proud of his urban upbringing and eventual escape from the Newark ghetto that he grew up in. It was heard in his soothing voice. He sounded very professional with a street flair.

Parker said, "I just wanted to thank you for assuring that your son takes very good care of my daughter. He's quite respectable and I admire that. Considering I have always had reservations about every guy my little girl has dated, I just thought I'd commend you for rearing one that I didn't want to shoot." He chortled.

"Why, thank you. I am quite fond of Amber, also. Remember this conversation if they ever have a conflict," Naim said and chuckled.

"I'll try," Parker said, and then added, "we have to do lunch."

"Absolutely."

They ended the call and Naim smiled. He handed Marco his phone, and then said, "He's quite a guy to call me with a compliment as opposed to calling me to express he was going to kill my son."

Marco burst into laughter. "I'm not looking to die."

"Very well," Naim said. "I'm going to rest a bit. It's been a long day."

"Catch you later."

"Indeed," Naim said and threw the peace sign at his son before retiring to his bedroom.

——— ———

Later that evening, Naim made waffles and turkey bacon for himself and Marco, and then they went to bed early.

CHAPTER 59

By six-thirty a.m. they met with an interior decorator to draw up plans for Marco's third-floor living area. Afterward, Marco was escorted to school and Naim went into his office to get some last minute studying done for the Bar exam. He was scheduled to take it at ten and wanted to ace it.

Ginger arrived at the office at eight and walked right into Naim's office. She still had her coat on and carried a *New York Post*.

"For your reviewing pleasure," she said and dropped the paper on his desk; it had as much effect as a Russian bomb landing on an ISIS camp in Syria.

Naim smiled at the sensational headline: NAIM BUTLER ESCAPES DEATH. Two photos of him were on the front page, one twenty-year-old mug shot and his photo from the Baker & Keefe web site. There was also a picture of his home with the estimated value of three-point-six million.

"At least it's partly right." He smirked while opening the paper to the article. "I did escape death, but this lavish home is worth five-point-six million. I'm just saying." He shrugged. After speed reading the article, which recounted the facts and indicated his potential killer was on the run, he handed the paper back to Ginger.

"At least they have the facts right this time. They're usually all wrong," Ginger said.

"That's exactly what I was thinking," he replied and smiled.

———— ————

That evening Naim and Marco got ready to go to Hector's to meet friends to celebrate Naim taking the BAR exam. He was confident that he had passed with flying colors.

In the garage, Marco told his father, "I'm going to pick up Amber. I'll meet you at Hector's."

"How're you planning to do that? There's no security for that." He opened his blazer and flashed his holster carrying a Smith and Wesson. "I'm the flash light cop tonight." He laughed.

"Glad this is funny, Dad, but I have it all figured out. I'll drive the bullet proof Cadillac."

"And what do I drive?"

Marco looked around the garage, and said, "Take your pick. You have the gun remember?" He winked.

———— ————

En route to Amber's house, Marco wondered why she needed him to pick her up from New Jersey and not Penn Station like he normally did. When he got to her home she stood at the fountain in the driveway and her father stood in the front door. Marco beeped at Parker, and he waved.

"We need to talk," she said as soon as she got into the truck. She was on edge.

"OK. About?" Puzzled.

"My parents. They like you, but, of course, my nosy dad saw the article about your dad so now he's concerned about me being around you until this professor is caught."

Marco looked flustered. His mood shifted immediately; his mind reeling.

"He asked me to stay in tonight and I refused. I wouldn't miss helping your dad celebrate his big day."

"That's cool of you, but your dad may be right. This professor has really messed up our lives. My dad's walking around with a gun. Former cops escorting me to school and work. I'm driving around in a bullet-proof truck. Shit is real, so your dad doesn't mean any harm by not wanting you in a position for something to happen to you."

"And I get that, but I am not going to live in fear. He taught me that after the nine-eleven attack."

"No, don't live in fear. I'm not, but I am being cautious."

Marco looked out at the famed New York City skyline searching for the right words to comfort her. He wasn't about to suggest she defy her parents.

"Will he try to punish you? I can take you back to avoid any conflict in your home," Marco said because he thought that her father could start to dislike him for contributing to his daughter rebelling against him.

"I don't want to go back. And if he even tried to punish me, I'd move out."

"Come on, Amber. How will you support that?"

"Marco, I have a trust fund from my grandparents. I have an allowance and a job. Trust me, I could live on my own quite fine." Amber pulled out her cell phone and called up her Internet browser. "In fact, I'm not going home tonight. Let's go to a hotel."

He didn't know how to play this. With all of his own father's paranoia, he was not going to even try to stay out. "Naim is not having that. He's petrified that something may happen to me. He barely wanted to let me out of his sight to pick you up."

"If you're scared..."

"Stop." He laughed. "I'm far from scared, but I'm not stupid either. He's not having it."

"Then, I'll stay by myself."

"Absolutely not." He looked at her and frowned.

"Now you're going to tell me what to do? Pull over."

"We're in a tunnel. Stop it," he said and laughed. *What the hell*, he thought, but had to laugh to mask his true feelings.

"I can't believe this."

"Come on, being a brat. I'm not letting you stay at a hotel alone."

"What then?"

"Just stay with me tonight."

"Your dad is not having that either."

"I'm not going to tell him."

"No, Marco. If he catches me spending the night, he'll have a fit."

"He won't know. The top floor is all mine and it has a private entrance. He won't even know that you're there."

She thought for a moment, as they exited the Holland Tunnel.

"How many other girls have you had up there?"

"What? None. You're kidding, right?"

She punched his arm. "It better be none."

"It's none, Amber," he said and smiled. "Don't worry, I got you. Things will work out."

CHAPTER 60

The whole kit and caboodle met at Hector's. After popping bottles of bubbly, they sat down for dinner. Naim noticed that Marco and Amber weren't their ordinary selves. Even Stefon was more talkative than them. They were uncomfortably quiet, so he decided to engage them directly.

"Since the three of you have committed to Columbia..." Naim began.

"Boooooo," Derrick said, interrupting him. "You all should be headed to Tulane."

"Or, U Conn," Brandy said.

They all laughed.

"Would you two quit it," Naim said. "They could go anywhere and that is applaudable. But since you chose Columbia, have you all narrowed down your majors?"

Marco spoke up. "Pre-law for me."

"And me," said Stefon.

"Same here." Amber agreed

"The law offices of Adams, Butler, and King," Marco said.

"Coming to a corporate complex near you," said Amber.

"That's nice that you have it all figured out," Derrick said. "We need to tour the campus."

"Why?" Stefon asked.

"To look for housing. It's time for you to go."

Everyone laughed.

This was all that Naim ever wanted. Family and friends. Suddenly, he had an epiphany: *I want my mom.*

———— ————

Outside of Hector's, Naim gave Marco the explicit direction to take Amber home and to return home without stopping.

"Right," he replied.

Ten minutes later, Marco and Amber were at the back of his home.

He pointed at the stairs that led to the back entrance. "That's the steps to the top floor. Just wait right here for me, I'm going to park the truck in the garage, run up to the suite to let you in, and then go back down to the guest suite where I sleep now. I have to be sure the alarm is off and the cameras aren't rolling. He records everything because of his paranoia masked as safety."

"OK." They kissed, and she said, "Thanks for taking care of me, Marco."

"You're welcome, but this is just the beginning."

———— ————

Naim bumped into Marco coming down the stairs from the suite.

"Decided to sleep up there tonight, since I'll be moving up there. I can look down into Central Park from the balcony up there." He sat at the piano bench in the salon.

Naim joined him, and said, "That's cool. How're you holding up?"

"I'm OK, Dad. Really, I am."

"A lot has happened in the month and change that you've been here with me."

"And I wouldn't have wanted to miss any of this. I'm your son. I'm supposed to experience your drama."

"You certainly are."

"I can't believe this professor tried to kill you. You think he's been caught by now?"

"I doubt it. He has a lot of money and friends, I'm sure. But have no fear, I'm sure they'll catch him. They better before I do."

Marco grinned. "I wish they catch him and he goes to trial and we can really get on with our lives."

"Maybe there won't be a trial. He's on camera holding me at gun point. He took large sums of cash from his bank account and e-mailed the school's president a lie about why he couldn't finish teaching the semester."

"Sounds like direct and circumstantial evidence."

"It is indeed," Naim said and stood. "I have to head to bed. Long day ahead of me tomorrow."

"OK. I'm going to grab a few things from the guest room and then take it down myself." He couldn't believe that he was lying to his father.

———— ————

Just after midnight, Brandy Scott walked into the Park Slope West Bar and Grill just a few steps from her apartment building. She found her best friend Caroline Dexter in a booth nursing a vodka double. Brandy threw her purse into the booth and then had a seat herself. She flagged down a bartender and ordered a screw driver.

"Girl, I so needed a night out," Caroline said and sipped her drink. "Jason and the baby are getting on my damn nerves. Well, not exactly the baby, but Jason's up for a promotion, so he's stressing all of the time about work. No one wants to hear complaints about a job that you got a degree to perform. He didn't even want to stay home with the baby so that I could meet you tonight. Some nerve, right?"

Brandy simply nodded and thanked God that her life was complex but manageable.

"Enough about me; how's your life with Superman. I mean, he's been shot and was about to be shot another time. Sounds sexy. I have to meet him."

Brandy laughed. "Bitch, you're crazy," was all that she could say.

———— ————

Despite the quietness of Coram, New York, Aleah Mills was startled awake by the vibration of her cell phone. She rolled from on top of her husband and peeked at her bedside alarm clock. It was four-seventeen in the morning. The vibration stopped, and then her home phone rang.

"Who the hell is that?" her husband asked.

"I don't know," she said, and then snatched the phone from the receiver. Then it hit her, "It has to be my brother." Into the phone, she asked, "Are you OK?"

"No, Aleah, I'm not." His voice was weak and needy. "I really can't explain what I've gotten myself into, but I really need your help."

"With?" Her voice was laced with apprehension.

"I know that voice, sis. Come on. Please don't abandon me here."

"Austin, allegedly you tried to kill a man twice. I just don't even know what to say to that accusation."

"Don't believe what you hear?"

She sat up. "I've seen the video, Austin. I've been looking at you for over fifty-years now, I think I know what my little brother looks like. It's only a matter of time before detectives come knocking on my door looking for you or asking questions. What am I to tell your niece and nephew, Austin? Their uncle, a doctor, and professor, that they admired woke and decided to be a killer. And in of all cities, New York. You choose freakin' New York to ruin your life."

"I'm at a hotel in New Jersey."

"And what the hell is that supposed to mean." She couldn't believe his audacity.

Silence.

He asked, "So me coming to hide out at your house is out of the question?"

"Absolutely, Austin. I cannot and will not attempt to help you stay on the run and potentially get you killed by these trigger happy police. You better turn yourself in put this behind you. I know plenty of top of the line attorneys. I am not exposing my kids to this. You can forget it."

"Sounds like you have already thought this out. Like your mind is made up."

"It is."

"And so is mine. I love you big sis, and good bye."

CHAPTER 61

Friday morning, Marco awoke no longer a virgin.

At seven, he was in bed next to Amber smiling. It was official; she had helped him become a man. A fact he'd never forget. She was wrapped tightly in his arms with her head rested on his chest. To wake her, he kissed her forehead. She moved, confirmed that she was awake, and he whispered, "Good morning," with his lips brushing her ear.

She shivered, grabbed him tightly, and said, "What are you doing to me?"

"I didn't even did nothin'," he said and gave her a comical smile.

"You're so silly," she replied and rolled onto her back, pulling the sheet over her breasts.

There he was, the morning after, and couldn't stop smiling. He was admiring the large room and imagined them spending countless nights there exploring each other mentally and physically.

"Are we going to school, or not? I don't care either way, but I need to know to figure out how to spin my Dad."

"We're going to school. I have an exam. I want to get a shower here, and then we can drive somewhere for me to get clothes."

"OK, cool. Under one condition, though."

"What?" she said facing him.

"You have to shower with me."

———— ————

"All rise," said the judge's criminal clerk, and officially set things into motion like a movie director yelling, 'And Action!' The courtroom well was the set and on the prosecutions' side sat a stone-faced AUSA Duncan and his untrustworthy sidekick, Agent Warner. Opposite them sat Naim Butler and his first client, Paris Moore. They were in Honorable Juan D. Sanchez's courtroom for a ruling on the defense's Notice of Appearance, which the prosecution objected to on the basis that Naim hadn't taken the BAR. Hence, he wasn't an attorney and the judge had no reason to entertain his appearance notice. Naim had other plans, though.

Juan Sanchez, a thin, tall man, emerged from his chambers with a smile on his face. He'd been wearing his black and white costume and matching salt and pepper hair for twenty-four years. This whole routine was a perfunctory part of his life, and he was about to give it up.

Getting the show on the road, the judge said, "We'll go on the record counsel. We're here in the matter of United States vs. Moore, 15A-22761. I'll ask counsel, please, to identify themselves for the record."

AUSA Duncan spoke first, and Naim didn't like that he had that privilege. "Clarke Duncan for the Government. Good morning, Your Honor."

"Good morning," replied the judge.

"Good morning, Your Honor. Naim Butler on behalf of Mr. Moore from Baker and Keefe." If there was any law firm to be from in New York City, this was one of the most recognizable on the court dockets.

Judge Sanchez said, "Good morning, Mr. Butler. And good morning, Mr. Moore."

"Good morning, Your Honor," Paris said as politely as he could despite his growing hatred for the veteran judge.

"You understand, sir, we're at somewhat of a crossroads today in your life. Are you prepared to proceed?"

"I am," Paris replied flatly. Of course, he was, and with Naim Butler as counsel of record.

"All right. For purposes of the record, I have reviewed the Government's opposition to Mr. Butler's Notice of Appearance and a submission from Mr. Moore requesting Mr. Butler to be his attorney. I've asked you here for an oral argument, and I'll hear from Mr. Duncan first."

Of course, Naim thought.

"As we've indicated in our response," AUSA Duncan said, "this Court need not consider Mr. Moore's submission, as Mr. Moore is not a pro se defendant in this court. I would also note that even if the merits were appropriately before this Court, the defendant's positions are simply his compendium of why he personally would like Mr. Butler as counsel. His position is not supported by case law, and furthermore, it's nothing more than a specious document outlining his dislike of his current and prior counsel. So we would ask the Court to disregard it. But also, Mr. Butler is not a licensed attorney in the State of New York or any state; ergo, he cannot represent this defendant or any other." He sat and folded his hands together. Perhaps, gave himself an imaginary pat on the back.

"Counsel, I'll note for the record that this is a non-jury proceeding, so I will consider the pro se motion for what it's worth. All right?"

"Understood," AUSA Duncan replied.

"Mr. Butler, you say what?"

Naim stood. Flashed the pearly-whites. Showtime.

"Going to the substance of my Notice of Appearance, I'd like to present Defense Exhibit 1, which is a copy of my fully expunged record. Defense Exhibit 2, is also the transcript of my criminal record being sealed. And lastly, Defense Exhibit 3, a letter from the President of Yale University confirming I'll receive my doctorate degree from him in three months to add to my Penn law degree. I have taken the

BAR exam days ago and sure that I've passed to become licensed in this fine state. Trial is scheduled on this matter in June and by then I will have the fore mentioned license. Mr. Max Devers from Baker and Keefe is in the gallery today, and he will oversee my activity with the case. For what it's worth, I've read every document disclosed by the Government to current counsel pursuant to *Brady* in this case and every PACER filing. I am more than prepared to defend Mr. Moore in a trial in this matter." He smiled again and sat after patting Paris's shoulder; a trick that Max had taught him.

"Any rebuttal counsel?"

AUSA Duncan said, "No, Your Honor, except it's clear that Mr. Butler isn't an attorney based on his own admissions, so he needn't be assigned to the case."

"Very well. Mr. Moore, obviously you're in an unfortunate situation, as counsel of your choice is a fundamental Sixth Amendment right. I am going to take this matter under advisement and withhold ruling on this until June tenth. In the meantime, Max Devers is appointed counsel, but I'll forewarn counsel that if Mr. Butler is licensed on June tenth, I'll be abeyance to grant the defense's motion for him to proceed as lead counsel. Counsel, is there anything else that requires attention?"

AUSA Duncan, once again replied first, "No, sir," pissing Naim off. He would have to get used to that.

"No, Your Honor," Naim said. He had his first case and planned to knock it out of the park. He felt sorry for Duncan and needed to drink to that. *Hector's here I come,* he thought.

CHAPTER 62

By eleven a.m., Professor Doctor Austin Mills electronically checked out of the Downtown Newark Marriot Courtyard. He didn't risk going to the front desk, despite his little effort to disguise himself. The professor carried two duffel bags, which he tossed onto a cart outside his room and rolled to the curb before collecting them. He had a four block walk to the Newark Penn Station to take the NJ Transit train into Manhattan. He was headed to a sleazy motel in the Times Square neighborhood, where he had made a reservation under an alias.

He scanned his surroundings for suspicious police activity, but they were all focused on monitoring the hordes of African-American, Newark denizen who were buying phony Gucci and Louis Vuitton products on Broad Street. When he reached the train station he bought a transit card from the machine with cash and looked at himself in the reflection from the window of a pizza store behind the machine.

"I thought that you were a doctor," he said to himself.

He was.

To himself, he replied, "I upgraded to a pathological killer."

His graying hair was receding, and his cul-de-sac hairline evidenced his age. His warm professor eyes simmered in the late morning sun coming through the open roof of the train station. Thoughts of Naim Butler forced him to start to boil. He had ten minutes before the train arrived to meet his fate and to send Naim to meet his. One of his bags were filled with clothing and all sorts of paraphernalia to alter his appearance. There was also gloves to protect his hands from gun residue powder of the 12-gauge Remington police riot gun that he'd bought at a gun show in his other duffel bag. Alcohol pads were in the bag, too, to wipe any stray prints from the gun before he dumped it in the Hudson River.

If the gun was ever recovered, he wanted no parts of the police tracing it to being used by him. After he offed Mr. Butler and rid the world of his snobbish jackassiness, Austin planned to escape to a remote town in Brazil with a 1990s-era IKEA living room, and resort to implanting woman with all of the body parts they ever wanted for a nominal fee.

———— ————

Hours later, under a flurry of snow, Professor Mills squatted on the steps of an unoccupied brownstone across the street, and a few doors away from Naim Butler's home. Donning a recently bought Burberry bomber with matching fedora and scarf, he blended into the neighborhood.

A man from the house next door to where Professor Mills watched Naim's place emerged and asked, "Are you waiting for the agent? He's always late. Just a heads up."

"OK, thanks," the professor replied.

"Good luck," the man said, and slid into the driver's seat of a BMW.

The professor watched the man's rear lights fade away and then he boldly crossed the street, went down a few feet, and glanced into the small slit of a curtain of a floor-to-ceiling window. He saw a desk and filing cabinets. *The secretary's office*, he thought.

He backed up as a Lincoln Navigator pulled in front of Naim's house. A male and female hopped out and raced to the opened front door of Naim's place. *Perfect. The good son and his girlfriend are home. A triple homicide. How delightful.* They didn't use the garage and that confused the professor. The driver pulled off, the kids disappeared inside, and the professor shifted a gun hidden in his waistband.

The Butler Estate, as he had dubbed it, he knew, had a few entrances and was two houses combined into one. All of the possible entry points excited him. It was a home conveniently on Seventy-Forth Street and Fifth Avenue.

The professor walked away from the home as a police car rode by. He assumed the local police precinct was making more than normal rounds on this street to protect the ex-con. Turning the corner, Austin figured that he could murder everyone in the home, slip out, and then have lunch at a cafe right on Park Avenue as police investigated the crime. The visual was palatable. He circled the block and walked by the house again. He was going to murder, Naim Butler, before the six o'clock news aired and not a soul was going to stop him.

Deciding that the timing wasn't perfect, he gave up and then went to the nearby Ralph Lauren mansion to buy his getaway costume: an expertly tailored suit to blend in with all of the other first class passengers headed to South America.

CHAPTER 63

Aleah Mills had left North Carolina to pursue her dream profession as a respected female Wall Street broker and had been successful. She brokered several nine-figure deals, and that was easy. The hardest thing that she ever had to do in her life was turning in her younger brother.

She picked up her desk phone and dialed nine-one-one and requested the number for Detective Hyatt.

"Nice to hear from you, Mrs. Mills? Are you married to Austin Mills?" Detective Hyatt asked as soon as she identified herself.

"No, sir, I'm his sister."

"OK. Can you tell me where he is for his protection? We really need to get him off the streets."

"No, I can't tell you where he is because I don't know. I can tell you some other things."

"I'm all ears." He grabbed a pencil and pressed the button on his desk phone to record the call.

"My brother and I collect guns. It runs in our family. We're hunters."

"Right. So he's not only on the run but armed and dangerous?" He wrote A/D on his pad.

"Maybe. He called me last night and asked to hide out at my home and I told him no."

"And what's your address?"

She told him.

"Coram's on Long Island, so that wouldn't be an ideal place to hide. Certainly, he's smart enough to know that. Would you contact him to lure him to your house for us to try to take him in quietly?"

"I'm sorry detective, I won't do that, but you're welcome to the neighborhood to stake out."

"Can I have his number?"

She gave him a number. "That's his cell phone number, but he called me from a hotel in New Jersey. He didn't say which one."

"Where do you think he is now?"

"No idea. I have never prepared for thinking where my brother on the run would hide."

He chuckled. "I can imagine. Do you know if he has any other properties other than his home? You mentioned you two are hunters, so maybe you all have a cabin."

"He does, but I don't know the address. It's in Bangor, Maine, though."

"OK, about how many guns would you say he owns or has access to?"

"Owns over one hundred with access to an unlimited supply because of all of his memberships to gun organizations. He can borrow guns from anywhere and anyone."

"Holy shit. I have to get this info out and look for these properties. If you think of anything else call me."

"Absolutely," she replied, hung up, and so did Detective Hyatt.

——— ———

The father, the son, and their paramours were in the family room lit by the flames shooting out of the fireplace. They enjoyed a game a Scrabble and finger foods while discussing their upcoming trip to Washington, DC for Valentine's Day.

"That is not a word," Marco told his father.

"Challenge it then. I'm telling you that I know all of the two letter words that have a Z in them," Naim replied, adding up his points. He was a tad tipsy after his lunch libations at Hector's.

Amber said, "Let him have it. It's only twenty points."

Everyone laughed over the sound of Naim's cell phone ringing. He answered and after a brief conversation, he said, "Pardon me, I have to take this."

They all offered him approving nods, despite the anguish smeared on his face.

In the hallway, Naim said, "Detective Hyatt, how may I help you?"

"Start by staying safe and keep your son close."

"The demand was quite candid," Naim replied. "I've been doing just that, though."

"Very good. I got a tip that Professor Mills may be in New Jersey at a hotel with an arsenal. Apparently, he's a gun collector with access to hundreds of guns."

Naim sat on a velvet chair in the hallway. "Is that right?"

"Yes. We're working diligently to track him down."

"My tax dollars at work."

"Exactly. I'm going to suggest you stay armed until we catch this guy. Capeesh?"

"Say no more." They both hung up, and Naim rejoined his instant family in the family room. Without preamble, he said, "This Austin Mills is in the area with a shit load of guns. That was Detective Hyatt. He's assigned to this case."

"Wow," Brandy said. "I thought he'd be across the country or out of it by now."

"You and me both," Naim replied, scrolling through his cell phone.

Marco and Amber were speechless.

"What now?" Brandy asked.

"Well, I'm going to get Polar Security Services on the line to sit outside the house, and I'm thinking we should leave for DC early. Like tonight."

"I haven't even packed." Amber finally had something to say.

So did Marco, "I'll buy you everything you need. No worries." He pulled her close to him.

"I'm game," Brandy said.

"Then it's settled. We're out. Let me make the plans now. Marco, you go up and get packed. I'll be up shortly."

"What about me?" Brandy said, pretending to pout. She smiled.

"I guess, I have to buy you everything that you need, too," Naim replied.

"Yeah, Dad," Marco said, "Can't have your son show you up."

Despite the circumstances, everyone managed to laugh.

CHAPTER 64

Austin Mills was perched outside of the Butler Estate and watched two muscular men who sat in a truck obviously protecting the home's occupants. *How nice of Butler to give me two more victims,* he thought and unbuttoned his coat to access a silenced .357 Magnum. A couple of seconds later, he slid right up on the men and tapped the driver's window with his gun. Before the man could completely turn his head to see who was there, he had a bullet between his eyes.

The other man dropped his Starbucks cup between his legs and reached for his gun.

"Don't even think about it," Austin said through the shattered window, pointing the gun in the man's face. "Slowly place the gun on the floor. That'll be your last spilled macchiato, Jared if you make one false move," Austin said reading the man's name on the side of the coffee cup. Jared complied, and then the professor said, "Step out of the truck."

———— ————

Inside, the ring of the doorbell had caught everyone off guard. Naim walked out of his bedroom into the second-floor salon, as did Marco. Through the frosted glass of the front door, they saw the silhouette of Jared Marlow, one of the security men standing there. Brandy had come out of the family room and was near the front door. Naim asked her to open it.

She did.

When the door opened Jared stepped in with a pained look on his face. "There seems to be a problem," he said.

"What's that?" Naim asked midway down the stairs.

"Me," the professor said, stepping out of the shadows and putting a bullet in the back of Jared's head.

Naim froze. Brandy backed up. Marco fell to the ground and crawled into his father's room.

Before Jared hit the floor, the professor pointed the gun at Brandy, and said, "Join your lover on the stairs."

She complied, and Naim said, "Good evening, Austin," as calmly as he could.

"I told you over the phone, it's Doctor Mills to you."

"Oh, right. How much time do you want?"

The professor had never been more confused. "Come again."

"It's lawyer talk. How much time you want to spend in jail totally depends on what you do from this point on. There are cameras recording your every move and the feed is sent to a security firm, so you can't kill us and take the tapes like they do on TV."

"That's nice. I'm already at the death penalty phase with the two dead men, probably from the same security firm. I wouldn't hire them again." He inched closer to the bottom of the second staircase, and at that time he was sure the homeowner wished he didn't have a dual staircase. "Where's your son?"

"That sounds like none of your business?"

"But you're wrong. I'm going to kill him, and let you and Sinia live very miserable lives, mostly, her though. Can you imagine the pain after leaving her son in New York and him being killed because of her actions? And you." He chuckled menacingly. "Seventeen years not knowing you had a son to have him killed because of your big, fat mouth."

"Why are you doing this?" Amber asked from the doorway of the family room.

He pointed the gun at her. "Sweetheart, you say another word and you die. It's really that simple."

From the salon, there was the roar of a gunshot. "No, she won't," Marco said as the professor lurched forward and fell down the few steps that he had climbed, splashing blood and gore over a painting; the same Van Gogh painting, Brandy had admired the first time that she had visited Naim's home.

Naim grabbed Brandy, held her tightly, and said, "Marco, put the gun down right there." He then reached into his pocket and pulled out his cell phone. He called his best friend. "Derrick, I really made a mess this time. Send the police and an ambulance to my home. And tell them bastards not to block up the street disturbing my neighbors."

CHAPTER 65

Naim sat in his office with Brandy, Marco, and Amber. Ginger was there, having been summoned by her boss to be by his side. NYPD and the bodies had exited stage left and a cleaning squad had scrubbed up the blood stains. Naim pushed a large vodka into Brandy's hand and offered one to Ginger.

"I'm fine, but you drink up. Anything to get over and around this episode," Ginger said to Naim, and then pat his back. To Marco, she asked, "How are you?"

"Believe it or not, I'm OK." He hung his head low. "I'm glad that I didn't second guess."

"Hell, I'm glad my gun was on the dresser," Naim said and gulped down more vodka.

"Yeah, Marco. You saved us all," Brandy said. "Especially, Amber, he may have shot her for no reason."

"Oh, Lord," Ginger said. "The media is pulling up, I can see the headline now: Like Father like Son."

They laughed.

Marco beamed. "I can't believe that I killed someone."

"You didn't kill anyone," Amber said. "You protected your family and friends."

"Wait until Sinia gets wind of this," Marco said and smirked. "She's going to blow up."

"As long as she does it in North Carolina, I'm fine," Naim said and smiled sarcastically.

———— ————

The next day, the foursome drove, without security, down to Washington D.C. to engage in the romance of the capital city. Naim had promised his mother that he'd visit her but thought that he'd make a trip to Chicago to visit her every three months.

That night, Valentine's Day, Marco presented his father with a surprise birthday cake—compliments of the Georgetown Four Seasons' bakery chef—to also celebrate his birthday. They then enjoyed separate romantic dinners before retiring to their own couple's suites. Over the weekend, they visited and took pictures at the White House, Martin Luther King Monument, and the Abraham Lincoln Monument. Bonds were tied. Friendships were solidified. Sinia's calls were ignored by Naim.

———— ————

One month later, Naim took a meeting with Agent Warner to bury the hatchet. The agent apologized for arresting his son. Naim apologized for accusing the agent of having him shot. They agreed to disagree about Paris Moore's involvement in a drug conspiracy and promised to play nice during the upcoming trial.

They were about to part ways, when the agent said, "Congrats on passing the BAR."

"Thanks. I promise to use my license wisely," Naim replied and laughed.

A BUTLER CHRISTMAS

That afternoon, Naim took Marco to BMG's headquarters and they met with Henry Winthrop and his team. They praised Marco's compositions and he blushed. They assured him that they had an artist to perform every song, and planned to list him as a songwriter. He could potentially earn a Grammy for his work. They presented him with a contract, and held a signing ceremony, as they wanted him to write exclusively for them. Marco endorsed a five million dollar check.

"Dad, what am I going to do with all of this money?"

"Well, Son, first, you're going to pay Uncle Sam, or you're going to federal prison. It's the American way."

Everyone in the room laughed. A bottle of Bartenura Moscato was passed around, and even Marco had a glass to toast his success.

PRODIGY GOLD BOOKS
1500 John F. Kennedy Boulevard, Suite 1900
Philadelphia, PA 19102
(267)-844-2805
https://www.prodigygoldbooks.com

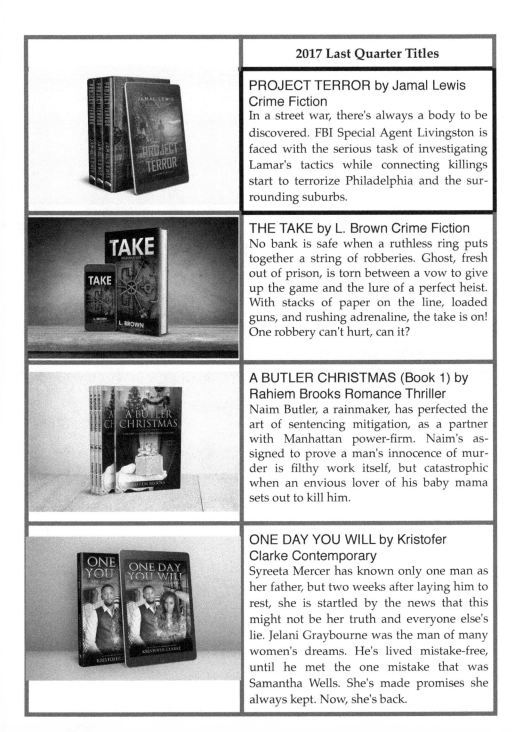

	2017 Last Quarter Titles
	PROJECT TERROR by Jamal Lewis Crime Fiction In a street war, there's always a body to be discovered. FBI Special Agent Livingston is faced with the serious task of investigating Lamar's tactics while connecting killings start to terrorize Philadelphia and the surrounding suburbs.
	THE TAKE by L. Brown Crime Fiction No bank is safe when a ruthless ring puts together a string of robberies. Ghost, fresh out of prison, is torn between a vow to give up the game and the lure of a perfect heist. With stacks of paper on the line, loaded guns, and rushing adrenaline, the take is on! One robbery can't hurt, can it?
	A BUTLER CHRISTMAS (Book 1) by Rahiem Brooks Romance Thriller Naim Butler, a rainmaker, has perfected the art of sentencing mitigation, as a partner with Manhattan power-firm. Naim's assigned to prove a man's innocence of murder is filthy work itself, but catastrophic when an envious lover of his baby mama sets out to kill him.
	ONE DAY YOU WILL by Kristofer Clarke Contemporary Syreeta Mercer has known only one man as her father, but two weeks after laying him to rest, she is startled by the news that this might not be her truth and everyone else's lie. Jelani Graybourne was the man of many women's dreams. He's lived mistake-free, until he met the one mistake that was Samantha Wells. She's made promises she always kept. Now, she's back.

HOW TO BUY

1) All books are $9.99 each for inmates, and $14.99 otherwise.

2) Send a prison check to the address above made out to Prodigy Gold Books. You can add first name: Prodigy. Last name: Gold-Books. Please add $1 per book for shipping.

3) Have a family member E-mail your order to: jhenry@prodigygoldbooks.com (with "Inmate Order" in the subject line) and we will send them a Paypal request to pay for your order, or call them to accept a debit card/credit card via telephone. We accept Visa, MC, and American Express

4) Order all four books for $35, and we will ship them with two books per package. This order requires $4 shipping. Order three books for $25. This order requires $3 shipping.

All books will be sent within three-days of receiving orders. We ship the least expensive way to keep your costs low, so expect books within seven days. If you E-mail us, we will let you know when we receive your order.

CPSIA information can be obtained
at www.ICGtesting.com
Printed in the USA
LVHW02s1530201117
557024LV00002B/613/P

9 781939 665225